SALTINE

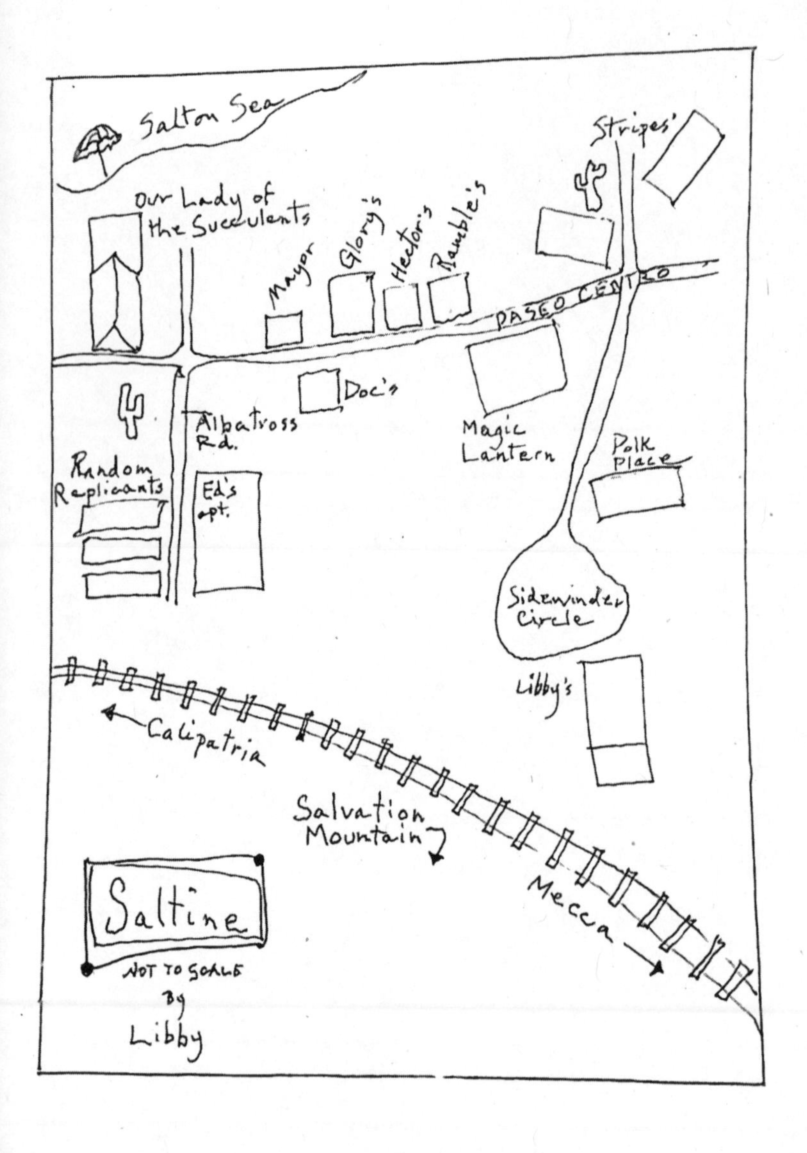
Salton Sea
Our Lady of the Succulents
Mayor
Glory's
Hector's
Ramble's
Stripes'
PASEO CENTRO
Doc's
Albatross Rd.
Magic Lantern
Polk Place
Random Replicants
Ed's apt.
Sidewinder Circle
Libby's
Calipatria
Salvation Mountain
Mecca
Saltine
NOT TO SCALE
By
Libby

SALTINE

Rachel Hoffman

*

OTIS BOOKS
MFA WRITING PROGRAM
Otis College of Art and Design
LOS ANGELES 2021

Book design and typesetting: Julia Zellie

ISBN-13: 978-9980-2-4308-9

OTIS BOOKS
MFA WRITING PROGRAM
Otis College of Art and Design
9045 Lincoln Boulevard
Los Angeles, CA 90045

https://www.otis.edu/mfa-writing/otis-books
otisbooks@otis.edu

This is a work of fiction.
Any resemblance to actual persons,
living or dead, would be fortuitous.

—ROMAIN GARY,
The Roots of Heaven, 1959

1999

Libby woke with the sun and hiked the half mile over sand and scrub to the old rail spur. From dawn until the sun reached two inches above the horizon, the breeze blew from the east, sparing her sinuses the burn of chemicals and dead fish that wafted from the Salton Sea over the town until mid-morning when the wind changed to westerly and she headed home. Most mornings Libby strolled one side of the track north and walked back south on the other, picking up what might have gusted-in or been flung from the hand-pump trolley. She always found something. Christmas ribbon. Corelle-ware shards. Even twist-ties went into her daisy-print pillowcase.

One morning, Libby stumbled on a two-year old package of Ding Dongs, freshness dated 1997, then onto a man lying face-down on the ground with a goat tied to his wrist. She stopped and stood straight.

The goat opened its mouth to bleat, but no sound came out.

"Mister?" She looked around and took a step closer. She said louder, "Mister?"

Mister wasn't talking but he was breathing, panting even, his rib cage rising and falling in shallow bellows. A solitary man. His left hand twitched.

"And he's alive, too," Libby said to nobody. She dropped the Ding Dongs into her pillowcase and nudged his leg with the toe of her work boot.

The man's arms splayed outward. Libby leaned her body in, then stepped over him, feet straddling his butt. She pulled her skirt up around her thighs and knelt, left knee at the man's back, holding him prone should he wake and take a notion to run.

Libby smiled skyward at the hazy blue and said aloud, "Thank You, Lord."

She brushed the fingertips of her right hand over the man's wavy hair, grayed with caked dust, then bent forward, sniffed at his neck, and whispered in his ear, "Hello husband."

Libby keeled to her right so they lay side-by-side, horizontal on the pebbles, cozied-up and sun-roasted. "He'll do." At age 28, she was going to be a bride.

The man lifted his head two inches off the wood tie. He rasped, "Nu-uuuurth...."

"Nuurth?" said Libby.

"Peyton," he mumbled, then bonked his forehead back down.

She poked at his shoulders but he didn't respond. "Peyton? Peyton Neworth?"

Libby slipped her palm over Peyton's butt into his back pocket. Her fingertips felt something solid and cylindrical. She lifted her head and peered around, then wormed her fingers farther and rolled the cylinder out of Peyton's pocket into her palm. "Damn!" The man was carrying a roll of greenbacks. She riffled through twenty-dollar bills and got to her feet. She brushed herself free of dust and tucked the roll into her daisy pillow case.

Libby was not the kind to leave a stranger to die, especially a man with no wedding ring. She gazed down and said, "Don't you go running off."

A hundred years earlier the region east of the Salton Sea was a thriving borax site. Saltine rose as one town among many housing miners and their families. The population exploded into the thousands, but that was all gone now. Libby remembered from adolescence sitting barefoot on a patch of grass near her daddy's single wide, watching families pack up and move away. The mines had been dormant for decades, some of them collapsed with dynamite, some boarded over, some home to squatters. The train no longer ran, but the spur had never been pulled up and the ties were still spiked down so twice a day, young men made a life by hand-pumping a trolley that towed a flatbed from Mecca, north of the Salton Sea, to several miles south of Saltine and back, carrying mail and groceries, dry goods and people who paid money or barter for passage. Riders chucked jetsam overboard, the trash later to disappear with afternoon gusts of wind. The same wind had knocked down most everything that stood higher than a person and erosion gravelized the rest.

Libby had observed it eight trolley-passings ago leaned up against the back wall of Glory's Grocery. Glory would understand. Twenty years earlier she, herself, had walked from Mexico and landed in Saltine with only what she carried. She did what was required.

Libby left Peyton lying face-down and ran west into town to find the wheelbarrow still there. She wondered how metal can rust but rubber not crack in a hot place with no water. She lifted the handles and rolled the bucket on its one tire, the hub grating from corrosion, the wheel skewed and wobbling in its fork. She crossed Paseo Centro and hurried through the open field. Window blinds parted.

"Replicants," she mumbled.

Libby called the citizens of Saltine replicants. Replicants walked human and talked human but weren't. Deep fissures in earthquake-wracked Southern California didn't stop as they reached ground level. The cracks kept going, rising into the air. Just because Libby couldn't see them didn't mean they weren't there. Atmospheric fault lines are why replicants have fractured consciousness. In Saltine, add to this mix non-stop foul winds from the

Salton Sea's Frankenfish tilapia farms, and what could she expect from her humanoid neighbors but a replicant mentality?

"Damn their eyes." Libby took a fortifying breath. She couldn't afford to wait for the cover of night if she wanted to keep her fiancé on this side of the turf, crusty as it was. It wouldn't have made a difference anyway since Saltine's replicants propagated rumors without regard for daylight or the dark. They observed reality equally poorly in both. Libby held her head high and walked east with the wheelbarrow, cud for toothless gums and wagging tongues.

Meanwhile, Mayor Tom Nuckle, Deputy Ed Schotz, and Libby's own father, Maurice D. "Stars 'n' Stripes" Flagler, were enjoying their morning cup of coffee at Ramble's Drugs breakfast counter when Marge Polk popped her head in.

"Hey, Stripes!" she said. "Some daughter you got! Always up to something, eh?" and popped her head back out.

The three men looked at one another.

"That girl...." said Stripes. "You'd think, on a Saturday morning... she'd sleep-in for once."

The three leapt from their stools and ran out the door. They jogged past Glory's Groceries, Hector's Hardware, across Paseo Centro, through the field, and–in a sweat, for at 7:00 AM the temperature had already reached 80°–midway down Euphorbia Road where they caught up with Libby.

"Hey, daughter," yelled Stripes. "What the hell'd you find out here big enough you need a wheelbarrow for?"

"Don't," said Libby. "I mean no disrespect but take your nose hair and clip it somewhere else." She looked straight ahead. "Go. Home."

"You know we won't," said Nuckle. He took off his

Stetson and flicked his fingers along the flannel rim. "Crime may have been committed."

Libby stopped. "Crime?" She cocked her head and eyed the three men.

"Wheelbarrow's been reported stolen," said Nuckle.

"Oh fine. Some replicant file the report? I'm borrowing it, *borrowing* it. Arrest me but where's it written a girl can't go walking?"

Deputy Schotz said, "Walking, sure, but–"

"By herself?" Libby glared at Schotz, whose sweat rings leached down to his belt.

"Now, you listen here, Liberty Belle Flagler. You're my own flesh and blood and–"

"If you've been drinking, Daddy, so help me–"

"Shut your trap," said Stripes. He was grizzled and bow-legged and looked more and more like Yosemite Sam. "Girl, you stole a wheelbarrow."

Libby pinched her lips and flared her nostrils and pulled her sun hat down on her head. She didn't intend to keep her new man a secret. How could she? Nothing stayed quiet in Saltine. But neither was she going to explain to the Old Fart Triplets in their plaid shirts and Carhart jeans what she was doing.

"Besides," said Schotz. "Someone's got to look after you. I mean," Schotz wiped the back of his hand across his neck and looked at Stripes. "You know."

"Right," Libby said. "You know." Libby turned away. She put down the handlebars of the wheelbarrow and thought for a moment. "Alright," she said. "I'll allow you to help. But I found him and he's mine."

*

Stripes and Nuckle turned the man on his back and held his head up while Schotz poured water into his mouth which drained just as quickly out.

"Try again," said Libby. She held the rope to the goat.

"Got to get him into town, to Doc's," said Nuckle. "Out of the sun. Bring that thing over."

Libby maneuvered the front wheel, dust rising from the gravel, with the bucket parallel to Peyton's supine body. She stepped aside.

"One. Two. Three–" Stripes and Nuckle hoisted the man up and in. His legs flopped over the front and his head was thrown back between the handles. Libby bent his neck to the side so it wouldn't break before the nuptials.

"Hey," Schotz said. "Population of Saltine's back up to 294." He lifted the handles. "I'll drive."

That summer had been one for the almanac. For as long as Libby could remember, ice plant grew out of control in Saltine where nothing else would and took over where something else had. But this plague of a plant whose sole redemption was its purple blossoms, hadn't bloomed for two springs, since 1997 in fact, and now, late September, it was drying to dust and turning brown like everything else in the vicinity of the Salton Sea.

Even I'm turning brown, thought Libby. She trotted alongside, rope and goat in one hand, sun hat held, best she could in the other, over Peyton's face against glare and whatever sweat dropped from Schotz's chin. She looked down at the man, a smile on the right side of his face. A sure sign of love requited.

"Doc," hollered Libby. "He moved!"

Doc banged a cast iron pan into the kitchen sink, picked up a glass of Tang, and hurried to his living-waiting room "Did he talk?"

"No," said Libby. "He opened an eye. Closed it again, though."

"Isn't normal. No wallet, no nothing." Doc lifted an eyelid and shined a beam into the man's pupil. "Didn't you find anything with him? Beside the goat?"

"Uh," Libby shook her head. "Well I should probably tell you, Doc."

"Tell me what."

"I know him."

"You know him?"

"His name is Peyton," said Libby. "He is my betrothed."

"He's what?" Doc's eyes widened.

Libby made up the story as she spoke in earnest. "Last year. Remember I took that trip north to Mecca?"

"Yeah," said Doc. He dropped into a waiting-room chair across from the sofa where Peyton slept. "I remember you came back all bright-eyed and tight-lipped."

Peyton opened one eye. Doc jumped up and put the straw in Peyton's mouth. He sucked down the Tang.

"Breathe deep, son. And say something."

Libby scooted a chair across the linoleum floor up against the couch.

With eyes shut and through lips set in a grin that wouldn't go away, Peyton mumbled more breath than sound, "nu-uuurth." Then he passed out again.

"His name," said Libby, "is Peyton Neworth. Peyton

Neworth. It's a fine name, don't you think?" She considered the possibilities. Libby Flagler Neworth. Mrs. Peyton Neworth. Peyton and Liberty Neworth. Wish to invite you to share their joy....

Peyton awoke again 10 hours later. His eyes shifted around the ceiling, then landed on Libby. He stared for a long moment. "Who are you?"

"You don't remember?"

He blinked. "Where's Nanny?"

"What?" Libby had envisioned a love-struck, grateful Peyton, as they'd shared a special moment of discovery and rescue. "I'm Libby," she said. "I don't know any Nanny. I'm your fiancée."

Peyton didn't remember his own name or how he got to be lying on a couch. He couldn't recall anything before opening his eyes to this slight, brown-haired young woman, so he could find no logical grounds to refute what she was telling him.

"My fiancée," he said.

Libby sat up. "Wedding's in two weeks, Peyton." She looked at him straight on. "I thought you were a goner."

"Libby, you say your name is?"

"See?" She blushed. "You do remember."

No. He didn't. But this Libby wasn't so bad looking. "Where am I?"

"Doc's."

"Yes, ma'am," Peyton said. "You're my fiancée?" He raised himself on an elbow to look out a window, but every shade was drawn. "Doc's yes, but, I mean, I'm in Las Vegas?"

Why does he have to ask so many questions? "Las Vegas? Dear," she said. "You're in Saltine. Outside Frink. East side of the Salton Sea. Home. Our home."

Libby had wondered how thin she'd have to stretch the

truth and how deep she'd have to dig the lie and what real life from Peyton she'd have to incorporate to chronicle him thoroughly enough to satisfy everyone. But damn if luck wasn't with her.

"We met in Mecca, last year. You were traveling through, and now you've come to be with me." She spoke with authority.

Peyton opened his mouth as if he should ask a question or make a comment but, bleatless like Nanny, if he said the wrong thing, he might offend the only person who seemed to care for him. It's not like he couldn't remember how to count to ten or flush a toilet. But information–that's what was missing–details that had to do with him personally, his history, were gone. He was conscious of the impairment, and that's what it felt like. Not life-threatening, he simply felt the volume of his consciousness had been turned down, way down.

Libby, on the other hand, brimmed with confident romance. No way could the disagreeable replicants of Saltine trace him to anywhere. She smiled at her own smarts, batted her eyelashes at her groom, commenced inventing a past for him, and envisioning a future for them together.

No family. Never married, and no kids–that he knew of, anyway. He'd told her these things, she said, as far back as their first date more than a year ago. Yes, she would admit theirs had been an unusual engagement. They fell in love at first sight, like in romance novels, Samson-haired Fabio holding Libby's swooning body in the muscled dunes of his bronzed arms. She'd tell him he'd said, "Plan it all," at the end of their week together in Mecca. "I'll be there."

"Shower here, at Doc's," Libby told Peyton. "After, I'll introduce you to Daddy. You'll stay with Daddy while you recuperate."

"From what?"

She smiled and dipped her chin. "Oh you. Always the tease." She added, "About Daddy... you'll probably find him a bit unusual, but be nice to him no matter what, okay?"

"I'll be nice."

"Just until the wedding."

Peyton was up and walking and restless, which suited Libby. She was eager to plunge ahead.

"Thanks, Doc. My fiancé and I are beholden." She took Peyton's hand.

Peyton took his hand back and extended it to Doc. "Thank you, sir. I am in your debt."

Doc took Peyton's hand. "You treat her right." Doc had a soft spot for Libby and had done his Hippocratic best for Peyton, but wanted them gone.

Peyton took Libby's hand. He couldn't remember the last time he felt a woman's skin, though the way her fingers squirmed between his stirred an involuntary physical response he hoped wouldn't show. The familiarity gave him a start but he liked the sensation and responded with a light squeeze.

Libby led Peyton to the sweltering out-of-doors. She would face gossip no matter what, so she gave Peyton's hand a squeeze back, and escorted her Sweetcakes down Paseo Centro to Ramble's Drugs coffee counter.

"I'm starving," said Libby. "You?"

"I should be, yes, I guess I am," said Peyton.

Libby sat on a stool next to Peyton and sipped lemonade. Peyton drained two glasses of ice water, looked around. Libby began to relax. She'd spent an anxious day planning how to make this work, in her head smoothing every angle, and, dang, she was ready to exhale and get on with married life.

"So," said Peyton. "Tell me,"

Libby stiffened.

"How on earth did I get here?"

"Well, what do you actually remember?"

"Waking up on a couch." He shook his head. "Didn't I have a wallet? Or a bag? Anything?"

This wasn't in Libby's plans. "You were tied to a goat."

"A goat? Oh, Nanny."

"Nanny. She was upright but you were face down on the hot gravel." Libby needed to turn this around. "Do you realize how dead you'd be if I hadn't found you?"

"Where is she?"

"Who? Oh. She's in my chicken pen."

Peyton looked at Libby and shook his head. "It's just that I can't remember...." Peyton didn't know where he'd come from or how he got to where he was. He couldn't place this woman whom he'd promised to make his wife. "I'm more than a little confused."

Libby's surging panic turned to tears on her cheeks which she dabbed with a paper napkin then blew her nose. She looked at Peyton.

He couldn't bear the misery in her eyes. "Aw, Doll," said Peyton. "Please don't. It'll be okay." He meant it too, although he couldn't say why.

"Tuna and iceberg lettuce sandwich with no mayo." The waitress slid the thick white plates onto the counter, "And for you, sir, grilled cheese and chips. More water?" She poured without waiting for an answer and winked at Peyton.

Libby's eyes opened wide. She glared at the counter girl. It was happening already. This girl was an advance scout for Saltine's swarm of horny hussies.

Libby softened and spoke to her man. "Whatever you had on you–wallet, bag–it's gone. I'm sorry I can't help, there. But I have all we need and I've been readying our home during this past year since we first met."

"Remind me?"

The hurt returned to her eyes.

"If I could remember, I would. I swear." Peyton felt he should be more alarmed, but he still couldn't find a reason. She seemed to know him, had saved and fed him, and was about to marry him. How was it that he could not remember?

"In a café, at lunch, in Mecca. There were two seats left, next to one another, and we walked in at the same time and the hostess seated us together. You started the conversation talking about the weather...."

Peyton listened. No bells went off. Libby made it up as she spoke, hiding her nerves and barely touching her sandwich. She smiled and flirted and knew nothing she said would jog any memory. "... and now your goat lives in my ... *our* pen. Where'd you find her, anyway?"

Peyton crunched ice from his water glass, and shrugged. "No idea." Though he wanted to, and thought maybe he should grab the goat and leave. But to where?

Libby paid the tab, and again took Peyton's hand, careful not to hang on too tightly. They walked out into a blast of stinking heat and dust, turned up Avenida de las Frutas, and climbed the steps to Stripes's single wide.

Peyton followed Libby to the landing and in. She hollered, "Daddy!"

Stripes came out of the bathroom. "What!" He stopped. "What's he doing here?"

"Don't start with me, Daddy." Libby stood straight, a double-dare-you straight. "Peyton's staying here with you till the wedding."

"The what? No. No. No. You can't...." said Stripes. "He can't."

Libby and Stripes stared at one another, each standing taller and taller in a silent face off.

"Be on time for dinner," said Libby. "That's all I have to say." She spun around and slipped through the door with a wedge of daylight and was gone.

"Aw Hell," said Stripes.

"Sorry to put you out."

"Hogwash."

"I can try to find a room somewhere else."

Stripes took a long moment to study Peyton, who was going to be his son-in-law. "When did all this marriage stuff happen?"

"Wish I could explain it, but I have amnesia."

"You and your buddy amnesia can sleep on the couch," Stripes told Peyton. "You might have to share with Guizar."

"Guizar?"

"My dog." Stripes whistled and waited. "Guess he's out."

"It's dark in here."

"Yeah. So's you can't see the fur balls." Stripes blew on a shelf lined at its back with empty bottles and a cloud of black fuzz burst into his face. "See there?"

"Barely." Peyton peered. "It's warm, too."

"Don't smell so bad when it's dark." Stripes toggled the switch on a table lamp and sixty watts lit the room.

Peyton sensed he'd walked this kind of fence before. His skin itched. The air stank. "I don't want to put you out."

"My daughter will hang me from that tree of hers if I make you leave."

"Two weeks," said Peyton. He wondered if Libby was heir to her father's hygiene. "Appreciate your hospitality. What should I call you?"

"It's Mr. Flagler until Reverend Byle files the papers. If and when that happens, we'll reopen the discussion.

"So this is where you live, Mr. Flagler?"

"Yeah, Payload. Sure do. You got a problem with that?"

"No sir."

"Help yourself to whatever you find." Stripes nodded toward the kitchenette. "There's nothing. But help yourself."

"What's there to do in Saltine?"

"Besides move out?"

Peyton laughed. "Yeah. Besides move out."

"Nothing." Stripes picked up the remote. "Unless you've got money. Then, I'd say, you could move out." He eased himself onto the couch in a slow mushroom of dust, then pressed the ON button of the remote. "Time for *Oprah.*"

Peyton stepped outside and took a longer look around Avenida de las Frutas.

"We'll visit Libby tonight." Stripes hollered. "For dinner."

Stripes's single wide sat on a concrete slab, like the mobile homes left, right, and across the road, all pastel sided with plenty of space around them. No grass anywhere, but across the Avenida, the house had a yard with a plastic deer, two living Joshua Trees as gateposts, and barbed low-growing succulents as a fence. Nothing says Welcome like cacti with four-inch spines.

In Stripe's yard sat clusters of themed objects. The kitchenette window looked out on three garden trolls with ribbons tied to their arms and legs that followed the breeze. Farther out sat a flamingo amputee, only the one leg it stood on remained, followed by a rubber duck, a small naked and headless doll with its feet planted to keep it vertical, and a hand-painted "KEEP OUT" sign nailed to a stick. Someone had planted a modest garden of plastic flowers, ringed by a squat halo of grey rock.

Ten minutes on the hot porch and Peyton felt nauseous. He slipped through the door, closing it fast behind him, and joined Stripes inside.

"Hey sonny. Where'd you get to?"

"On the stoop is all. I started feeling sick."

"Welcome to our little slice of heaven."

Peyton's nostrils were crusty and his lungs burnt, his eyes ran and his skin itched. It felt like a chemical burn. "You ready?" said Stripes.

"Is *Oprah* finished?"

"It's a Dr. Phil day."

"What I'm wearing is all I've got," said Peyton. "Do I have to dress for dinner?"

"Does the Pope wear plaid?"

"Right."

Stripes sprang from the landing to the ground. "Daughter lives on the poor side of Saltine."

At six o'clock the air was dry and, according to the LED on the Magic Lantern Movie House, had cooled to 87°. The two men turned from Avenida de las Frutas and walked the incline a block on Paseo Centro. Glory's Groceries, Hector's Hardware, and Ramble's Drugs were open for another hour, and the Magic Lantern's marquee had just lit up, featuring *Blade Runner*.

Peyton halted. He was looking at the marquee and experiencing a flash recollection: buzzing lights and ringing bells and running and panic.

Stripes slowed. "Something I should know?"

Peyton couldn't have said, even if he'd wanted to.

"Libby loves Harrison Ford," said Stripes. "Take her to the movie if you want to score points. She's seen it several times but she'll still glow in the dark for you."

Peyton wondered if he'd scored too many points already, marrying in two weeks.

"Use to have a beauty parlor and a real estate agent." Stripes pointed to boarded-up store fronts. "Gone now. Gas Station, too. Still got the liquor store."

Peyton felt dehydrated and not brimming with good will. "And what is that unpleasant smell?"

"What smell?"

"What smell?" *Really?* "Oh, let's see ... old fish, carrion. Chemicals or some kind of acid. My eyes burn," he said. "Even before I turn them toward *you*."

"We're 500 feet from the shore."

"What shore?"

"The Salton Sea-shore, Paystub. Where the hell you think you are? Miami?"

Peyton shrugged.

"You're full of complaints, ain't you? Come on, Paydirt. Libby runs a tight ship." Stripes walked faster. "This way."

The homes fronting Euphorbia Road mirrored the single wide mobile model Stripes lived in. Each was raised on a slab but Peyton couldn't fathom why. It was clear from the stubble of vegetation that Saltine was a parch zone. No floods on the horizon, residential landscaping limited to whatever refused to die. Even some of the Saguaros had become skeletal. Most houses lay scattered in no regular pattern, beige or yellow or sun-bleached aqua, all had their curtains drawn to the outside world. In the field between Euphorbia Road and Sidewinder Circle, two boys played one-on-one basketball. For a hoop they used a wire trash bin with a blown-out bottom, duct-taped to a pole. Behind them, a dozen Chihuahuas tore apart a black plastic bag of garbage.

The two men turned from Erphorbia Road onto Sidewinder Circle.

Stripes pointed. "She's in Big Pink at the tail end."

Peyton wondered how a circle can have a tail end. He peered ahead, said. "What's that?"

Stripes stopped and looked at Peyton. "Wax clogging your ears, boy? What I just tell you?"

What Peyton saw from a distance, he didn't understand. Up close, he didn't understand it much better, but at least he could identify what he was seeing. In front of Libby's pink and white double wide was what looked like a tree, but it was made from remnant spans of iron Rebar stringers bound together with copper wire and duct tape, its branches spreading a six-foot radius from the openwork trunk. In place of leaves, Libby had arranged, artistically, some of what she'd foraged: purple plastic Easter eggs, lengths of yellow police tape, wads of silver foil, knots of ribbon, several pair of pantyhose, PVC tubing, gallon containers from milk, aluminum soda cans, a duck decoy, a rubber owl, fishing line, silver filament from broken cassettes, wine bottles in green, brown, and clear, a dozen Christmas ornaments, a University of Nevada baseball cap....

"You'd be hanging there, too," said Stripes, "if she'd stumbled on you dead."

At the base of the tree, a mosaic-in-progress from shards of china, melmac, glass, stone, and plastic lay in adobe-grout. Libby had placed a table and two mismatched chairs on a completed stretch.

"Holy mackerel," said Peyton.

"Maybe," said Stripes.

Peyton gawked in fear and admiration. His betrothed lived in a world quite different from other folks. He wondered what sex would be like, and his body shivered. And what would she serve him for dinner. He admired her industry but considered the possibility that the woman had some inherited peculiarities. Peyton noticed a top branch of rebar with a plastic fish hanging by its tail. The holy mackerel, he thought. His laughter erupted, grew audible, out of control, and unstoppable just as Libby stepped out the door.

"Hi Daddy." Libby waved. "And welcome...." she stopped. She looked at Peyton who was doubled over, then back at her daddy. "Is he alright?"

"Seemed alright enough a minute ago." They stood and waited.

"Peyton Neworth," she said, finally, when Peyton began again to breathe. "If I didn't know you better, I'd take your hysteria as an insult."

"Doll," said Peyton, calming his breath, "with due respect to your lovely self, just how well do I...I mean, I trust we're engaged and all, but that knock on the head or whatever it was.... Well, honey, I...."

Tears bulged from Libby's eyes.

"Aw Doll, don't." Peyton hung his head and breathed. "I'm seeing your house for the first time. And it's like no other house I've ever laid my peepers upon. And I'm not laughing at you. Doll." Peyton began to sweat like a man telling lies. "I'm ... I'm just so, so pleased at your uh-h-h-h-unusual taste." That, he figured, ought to dry her ducts. But, just in case, "and I look forward to our life together. Creating things. And thank you for the dinner invitation."

Peyton looked to Stripes for manly affirmation. Stripes stared back at Peyton, shrugged, and raised his eyebrows.

"And I'd have brought flowers. To my bride. But...."

"Enough," said Libby. "Come inside. Before you – both of you – give me a headache the size of all Frink."

Peyton followed Stripes past the outdoor living diorama and up four steps. Inside, because no way was ten years of collecting hung from that tree, inside was the rest, a collection, a medley, a museum, whatever she would call it, the walls were lined with shelves and curio cases, objects arranged according to type, and always in transition as definition of type changed with each addition: body parts from dolls, baby food and other jars – some still with scraps of labeling, buttons, zippers, hooks, snaps and fasteners, nails, screws, mechanical parts from unidentifiable machinery, kitchen utensils, oddments of equine gear, snippets of fabric, drinking straws distinguished by color, wire, gauze, toothbrushes with bristles, toothbrushes without bristles, sunglasses, combs, pill bottles, CD's, crayons, pens, pencils, printer cartridges, candy wrappers, an unopened set of guitar strings –

"Dinner is free range chicken," said Libby. "Do you like free range chicken, Peyton?"

Yanked from reverie, "Sure do, Doll."

Doll. She liked that.

Free range. He wondered if the chicken was still breathing when she found it.

"Gentlemen, have a seat." Libby had set her table with a daisy-printed cloth, the flat sheet part of the set she took the pillowcase from, and mostly matching thick white plates, bowls, and coffee cups. At the center, a bouquet of plastic anemones shot out of a vase.

"I'm not much for prayers," said Peyton.

"I go either way," said Libby.

"Great. Let's eat." Stripes reached for the platter of chicken pieces and took two. "Got anything worth drinking?"

"Not tonight, Daddy." Libby looked across the table at Stripes. "I thought you quit."

"Most of the time," said Stripes. "Now, I drink only when there's a reason. You've got me sitting next to a big one."

Peyton selected one thigh, spooned out some mashed potatoes, and left the peas. "Never was one for greens," he said.

"Ooops. Forgot." Libby gazed across at Peyton. "Been too long, Sweetcakes." Libby pointed at the paper napkin and Peyton wiped his mouth. She sat amazed at her great fortune.

The chicken was juicy but conversation was dry. Stripes kept his mouth full. Libby worried Peyton would remember his past and didn't want to jiggle something loose. Peyton could remember nothing so he had little to contribute.

"Would you like dessert?"

"With a beer," said Stripes.

"What a lovely dinner, Doll. Please," said Peyton.

Libby excused herself and fussed at the sink. She pulled apart a cellophane package and clattered a couple of small plates, upended a squeeze bottle and shook out the last of the syrup. She turned to the table. "Dessert!"

Two plates, each with one chocolate-drizzled Ding Dong.

"And, for your breakfast tomorrow," said Libby. She handed Peyton a bowl and batted her eyelashes.

"And no beer." Stripes stood. "Come on, Payload. Time to go. What kind of name is Peyton, anyway? You some kind of replicant?"

"Don't let him drink," Libby said to Peyton. "You hear me, Daddy? Go straight home."

Peyton picked up the bowl of mashed potatoes and canned peas, and felt a swelling in his pants. He escaped to the bottom step and wondered, what the hell?

In the desert dusk, waves of hot air lifted off the ground, giving everything an underwater wobble. Peyton examined the Rebar tree and wondered when Libby had planted it. He wanted to ask how fast it grows.

Libby whispered, "Well Daddy?"

"If you're asking me," Stripes licked a spot of mashed potato from the corner of his mouth. "Addled, and he's not one of us."

"Oh, Daddy." Stripes burst out the door, Libby lunging after him, Stripes quicker, jumping to the ground, bypassing Peyton, and walking off before the screen door hit the molding.

Peyton waved goodbye to Libby and ran to catch up. He said, "What's a replicant?"

"What Libby calls the citizens of Saltine." Stripes picked something from his teeth and spit it onto the ground. "They ain't human. You never seen *Blade Runner*? Harrison Ford. Like I said, Libby's favorite."

"Some daughter you've got!" said Peyton.

"In respect to what?"

"Uh ... her design sense? Her cooking?"

"The Lord gaveth man two damn heads." Stripes stopped and turned. "And enough blood to work one at a time."

"Stripes, honest–"

"You know what I'm saying?"

"We've waited–"

"Use the one on your shoulders is all I'm saying." Hook, line, and sinker, thought Stripes. Thank the Lord, just the same. His daughter wasn't yet 30, but the desert was a hard place and lately Libby was looking less spring-chickenish and more free-rangey. "Wait longer."

Peyton squinted in the dark. He did not trust his own directional sense back to the single wide and didn't want to trip and drop Libby's bowl of breakfast so he skipped after the old fart.

They turned the corner onto Avenida de las Frutas and were greeted by a big, black, slobbering mutt with patchy clumps of fur on its legs and none but a fine undercoat on its body.

"Guizar my boy. Hey Payout," Stripes knelt and scratched the dog's scalp. "Meet my boy."

"Fine canine you got there," said Peyton. "Who's his barber?"

"What? You think this is the arctic, sonny? You never took your coat off in the heat?"

Peyton reached his hand and Guizar sniffed. "Maybe he'd like some dinner?"

Stripes stood. "Guizar takes dinner from no man. My boy is a hunter, an alpha dog in a beta body, a top gun, a wolf with killer instincts."

"The hit-man will share his couch with me?"

"Ask him nice. He only hurts folks intent on hurting

me." Stripes aimed his feet toward the single wide and called back, "You plan to find a job?"

Peyton, among the living for two days and having nothing but lint in his pockets, hadn't considered a job. "Anyone hiring?"

"How would I know?" Stripes hopped up the steps. "Might try Glory's."

"Sit," said Libby, pointing to one of the chairs under her rebar tree. "I'll get my scissors. And don't look at me like that."

"I don't need or want a haircut," said Peyton.

"You'd prefer Glory fires you even before you start working?"

Working or not working didn't much matter to Peyton, but he wasn't going to tell Libby that. He didn't need her to start in at him. Anyway, whatever he'd say would get back to Stripes, and living with Stripes was already hard. Maybe he should up and be on his way out of there.

"Just a little at the ears," said Libby. "Maybe tidy up the back?"

"Whatever you like, Doll," said Peyton. She could tell him to hit the rail, if he offended her, maybe even stab him with the scissors.

Peyton sighed. He had no recollection of a past beyond the one Libby provided, even if he reckoned it couldn't be all there was. The only sure thing was to take some time and settle into Saltine. Just being himself was curiosity enough for Saltine's residents, what Libby called the replicants. From the start he'd felt suspected, as the newcomer, of everything from devil worship to training attack scorpions, and he could see the hope in their eyes that their worst fears were justified. Even Glory, who'd hired him to wash out the butcher trays, she'd given him a job only because of her crush on Stripes. Peyton thought maybe he should join the Elks Club.

Libby stood back and admired her handiwork. "You clean up pretty."

"May I see the mirror?"

"And ruin the moment?" Libby's face fell. "Just trust me."

*

The next day Peyton reported to Glory's Groceries at 4:00 PM.

"Nice haircut," was the first thing Glory said. "Come with me."

They walked through the store to the loading dock door. "Here's where you check in." She showed him the time-card punch-machine. "Been hanging off this wall since 1972. Never been used."

She introduced Peyton to the hose, soap, scrub brush, and meat locker. "You need to be done and checked out by 6:50 PM. Think you can do that?"

"Yes, ma'am."

"I lock the front and leave through the back, after you."

"I can handle it, ma'am."

"I like to get home in time for *Court TV*. They're showing the Bill Clinton trial."

*

Libby was so proud of Peyton after his first day of employment, she made her special canned tuna stroganoff with banana pudding for dessert. No greens. They sat at the table for two, under the rebar tree.

"What horrible thing did he do?" Peyton asked.

Libby, like everyone else in Saltine, couldn't say why she hated Bill Clinton, but she did. She thought him horrible, horrible, horrible, horrible.

"I really don't want to talk about it," she said.

"Must be *really* horrible," said Peyton. "Do you think we should bring back hanging?" He winked. "Sorry ma'am but that tuna casserole's a hangin' offense...."

Libby felt a noose tightening around her own neck.

"Do you want pudding, or *not?*"

Meat, potatoes, a pink aluminum roof over his head, sex presumably, and tuna stroganoff. "Where's the pudding, Doll?"

Libby fluttered her eyelashes and headed toward the door into the kitchen.

A waft of cooler air brushed Peyton's face. He had a brief moment, sensory rather than visual, of a large turquoise swimming pool and the urge to dive in.

"You like banana, don't you, Doll?"

"Sure do." He dug into his bowl of yellow pudding. "Tell me. Can a person swim in the Salton Sea?"

Libby had always walked in the opposite direction, toward the tracks. In her 28 years, she had never been in the water. Take her clothes off and expose her nakedness to the sun? Wade into that desiccating cesspool of Central Valley pesticide runoff? And fish poop? Stripes's single wide was as far west as she ventured. She might have to exaggerate a little to keep Peyton far from blissfully ignorant bikini-clad tourists, alcohol, and goodness knows what other temptations. "You cotton to a painful death?"

"Really?" Peyton stared.

"Rotting fish. Mutant birds. Used needles. Trash heaps. Putrid inlets. Vile odors. Chemical spills," Libby said. She raised her eyebrows and flapped her arms. "Scorching sun, burning tires, tourists.... Hardly any water left not glazed in an oily slick and if you do go into the drink, then you'll glow in the dark, get an ear infection, and be sick for weeks while your chronic cough keeps me awake all night."

"Thought I'd ask."

*

On day four after Peyton's arrival, Libby awoke in anticipation. Stripes content with his leftover tuna stroganoff, and Peyton securely employed, Libby got to work.

Eleven years prior, Libby had gone on her only date with Ed Schotz. They were in 12th grade. He took her to dinner at Ramble's Drugs' coffee counter and then to the Magic Lantern to see the new release, *Spaceballs*. Stripes urged his daughter to grab the man while she could. Even at seventeen, Libby knew she and Ed were perpendicular to one another. Fate was not going to align their futures. Libby had considered letting Reverend Byle marry them in Saltine's Our Lady of Succulents chapel. But the thought of Ed in her bed just did not sit well. After their first and only date, she determined to keep herself to herself. Other young women married their high school sweethearts. Libby took up collecting.

Peyton, however, had fueled her romantic engines anew. She hadn't ever attended church and felt no allegiance to Our Lady of Succulents and so chose for her nuptials the Ravine of Righteousness, this side of Salvation Mountain. Not her daddy, not the mayor, and especially not Deputy Ed Schotz, would persuade her differently.

So that fourth morning, Libby struck out early, waited by the tracks, and at 7:00 AM took the trolley to Niland with coins she'd saved from returning empty bottles. With a color photo of Salvation Mountain held flat in a notebook, she boarded and sat under the warming sun. The trip would cost her close to four hours, but walking would have exacted an entire day.

Libby looked out across the scrub. Only a half mile out, like low-hanging beige clouds, the dust and condensation along the desert floor blended up into the horizon. A hand painted sign along the tracks listed the attractions of following the rail north: Elks Club, Sheila's Beer Bar, and long-term UFO Abduction Insurance.

In Niland, Marsha's Dry Goods had a coin-op copy machine where Libby made a half-dozen color prints of her

Salvation Mountain photo. She bought six vanilla-colored sheets of paper with six matching envelopes and an extra-fine roller-point black pen.

Around the corner, Coyote Café was filled for lunch. "Fresca to go."

She carried her paper cup four blocks east to the tracks and caught the trolley home, braving the afternoon heat under her straw hat.

Stripes had taken Libby to Salvation Mountain only once, and that was almost 20 years earlier when he still bothered to try raising Libby right. The Mountain was a testament to faith. Five stories high, half the length of a football field, a foundation of sand and rubble faced with adobe, staircases and passageways, biblical references, all painted in enamel of every color, the Mountain rose from the desert in one man's reverent vision. Stripes had hoped, in spite of his own apostasy, the experience might invest his daughter in religion. It didn't.

What struck Libby at the time, though, was Leonard Knight's unstoppable will to do what everyone said he couldn't. She saw her current matrimonial quest in a similar light, felt kinship with his determination, and thought it correct that she acknowledge this by tying the knot in the Mountain's great shadow. She'd have a Destination Wedding.

Her guests would have to walk. Six years earlier, Jeb Pohler drove a 10-ton delivery van across Borax Creek Bridge and cracked it in half. Since then, nobody can enter or leave Saltine by car without breaking an axle, so nobody owned one. The town was a mile one side to the other so everyone walked to wherever they needed to go, or caught the trolley north or south.

From Saltine, Salvation Mountain was 4.7 miles east by foot. Libby wasn't sure what kind of leverage she'd require to induce Daddy Stripes, Mayor Nuckle, Glory Apodaca, Reverend Augustus Byle, and, of course Peyton, to make the trek. If they started out on foot at 4:00 AM they could be there easy by 6:00 AM for the nuptials, and back home for the wedding bed before the wind changed and the sun reached its morning burn.

Libby sat at her dining table and pasted a photocopy to the front of each folded vanilla-colored sheet of paper. In her finest hand, she penned:

Mr. Maurice D. Flagler has the honor of inviting you
to witness the marriage of his daughter,
Liberty Belle Flagler of Saltine

to

Peyton Neworth of Los Angeles
The 12th Day of December 1999 at 6:00 AM
Ravine of Righteousness below Salvation Mountain
Champagne will be served.

TEN DAYS LATER

Libby peered through the parting in her living room curtains. The yellow bug-bulb and the waning moon offered enough light to see by. The wedding party stood with a lantern, waiting.

Through the open window, she hollered, "Daddy!"

"What!" Stripes spun around. "What now?"

"Do I have to explain again what you're supposed to do?"

"I'm not senile." He turned to the men and one woman gathered for the march to the Mountain, "Peyton," growled Stripes. "In exactly three hours, give or take fifteen minutes, she's yours. Till death do you part. And it better be yours, not hers, and that's all I got to say."

"I sure hope so," said Peyton.

"Daddy!"

"What!"

"What are you waiting for?"

"She has this all worked out in her head," said Glory, "and no good ever came to a man who didn't stand and salute a bride's orders."

Stripes looked back at the window. He said, "Don't get you britches in a bunch." Stripes turned to Peyton. "It's you and me first, Sonny. That's the way she ordered it."

Peyton picked up the knapsack Libby had told him to carry. "Libby thinks you'll like me once we get to know one another. Pop."

"Not much chance, if you ask me," said Stripes.

"I'm not asking."

"Good 'cause it ain't likely to happen." Stripes grabbed the lantern.

Stripes and Peyton walked ahead. Guizar loped along against Libby's wishes, padding between the two men, sticking near and snarling if Peyton walked too close. Behind them strolled Glory, Mayor Nuckle, and Reverend Byle.

Libby had insisted on bringing up the rear. She wore her boots and a floral dress, one with tropical flowers, a dress Peyton hadn't yet seen.

"You wearing that?" Stripes said when she tried on the dress for him. "You look like a fruitcake."

"And you're an old fart," Libby had responded.

"Fine."

"Fine."

"Make sure Peyton takes his vitamins," Libby had said, "He's going to need his strength."

Stripes had put his hands over his ears at this and howled *La Cucaracha* so loud he drowned out everything else.

At the rear of the wedding party, with a promise from Peyton not to look behind him, her bridal ensemble remained untarnished, unappropriated by her betrothed's gaze. She'd dug through storage boxes filled with her treasures and pulled out a blue ribbon to tie tightly around her right thigh. And she'd put her hair in rollers the night before, a pointless ritual. By the time they reached the Ravine of Righteousness, below the mountain, no curl would remain. A dab of lipstick would have to suffice.

*

Libby peeked around the corner of the pink and white double wide to watch five shadows moving away in the scrub. The half-moon was low in the sky but bright enough, with her lantern, to light the ground in front of her. No tripping, no daydreaming, and no picking-up flotsam, she told herself. There'd be plenty of time after. Now, she just had to make it to the Ravine without vermin or snakes biting her ankle.

Gunshots rang in the distance. One, then three in a row. Hunters were already out.

She held her lantern high. She could hear Mayor Nuckle laughing, then Guizar barking and scrambling after a night critter, and Stripes hollering to "Get the hell back here." She hoped Stripes and Peyton were coming around to friendliness instead of putting-up-with-each-otherness.

Pre-dawn had cooled to a perfect low sixties. Libby kept her sights on Salvation Mountain, obscured in the distance, but up ahead. She wouldn't be able to see colors in the dark but understood the mountain as a creation of the most fervent faith. As for artistry, well, there was nothing like it. A real mountain rising up, covered in 100,000 gallons of enamel paint retrieved from the county dump. Fifteen coats, blobbed on by the hand of one man. How could she describe its greatness? Flowers and bands of color and staircases carved into the rock with decorated steps, waterfalls, blue birds, stars and patterns, symbols in orange, turquoise, yellow, purple, green and every color under the Sherwin-Williams sun. A great big red heart in the middle of it all with the sinner's prayer from Acts and a giant Cross at the top: surely a sign from the Man in the Sky himself. This was a site of devotion, *the* place for Libby and Peyton to bind their futures in what Libby called Wholly Matrimony.

Peyton had lain awake for long stretches the previous night, wondering who he'd been and whether the answer to that question mattered. If he was supposed to be somewhere else, he guessed he'd be found eventually. In the meantime, maybe it was confusion, but he felt no pressing need to run.

Libby smoothed her dress and fluffed her hair. She stood straight and said, "Peyton, dear. You may turn around."

"Doll, you look perfect."

"Right," and, "Yes indeed," chorused Nuckle and Byle.

Glory snapped a photo.

"She looks like a juicy piece of fruit," said Stripes, "and too darn ripe."

"Ripe. Right," said Peyton. "Where do you want me to stand?"

Glory handed Mayor Nuckle the snapshot camera. Libby pulled Peyton next to her with the Mountain in the background. The twelve frames were snapped with everyone in a couple of poses before Reverend Byle began. "We gather here, in the sight of our Lord...."

"Not *my* lord," said Stripes. He gulped long from his flask.

"Daddy!"

Guizar growled at Peyton.

"We gather here, in the sight of Salvation Mountain and its Ultimate Creator...."

"Hogwash." Stripes pulled from his pocket a red calico neckerchief and blew his nose.

"None. The. Less." said Libby. She glared at Stripes, then relaxed her face before turning back to the Reverend.

Reverend Byle waited a moment. "To blind, uh bind these two in Holy Matrimony." Byle looked around and decided against asking for objections to the union. "Peyton, you have known Libby for two weeks."

"A year and two weeks," said Libby. Her back broke a sweat, her knees wanted to give way, but she stood firm and straight. "Pardon Reverend. We've known one another a year and two weeks."

Stripes snorted. "Uh huh. About five years not long enough."

"Settle down." The Reverend bent his head left and right to crack his neck. "Everyone."

Libby'd had enough. "We all know what comes next, so can we cut to the chase?"

Reverend Byle blinked a couple of times and shrugged. "I guess."

With that, Libby's words tripped over her teeth. She said, "I *do*."

Peyton said, "I do, *too*." And he did. In the two weeks preceding, he'd grown to like Libby. She was straightforward and wanted to keep him around. He started to have fantasies of his own where she was concerned. He was friendly with Doc and enjoyed his time at Glory's Groceries. And, the bottom line, he had nowhere else to go.

"Well, then, seeing as how– "

Libby flew at Peyton and glued her lips to his.

The reverend smiled. "I now pronounce you husband and wife."

"Let go of her," said Stripes. "You're steaming-up the fruitcake." Stripes looked at Reverend Byle. "Who ever heard of the smooch lasting longer than the ceremony?"

"Okay kids," said the Reverend.

Peyton dropped his arms to his sides, but Libby held tight. Peyton opened his eyes to see Stripes staring, teeth clenched, lips puckered, bottle in hand.

Stripes groaned. "You really gonna make me watch this?" His tone so upset Guizar that he circled the happy couple and growled. Striped bellowed, "Liberty Belle Flagler!"

Libby detached from Peyton. "It's Liberty Bell *Neworth*, Daddy." She pulled back from Peyton. "Darling, Where's the knapsack?"

Peyton opened the small pack, dropped in the camera, and pulled out a bottle of champagne and six plastic cups. "Want me to pop the cork?"

Stripes looked disgusted. "You going to shake her, too?"

"Yes sir," said Peyton. "And let her bubbles tickle my nose."

Stripes said, "Uuuugh" and bent over like he wanted to puke.

Libby handed out the cups and Peyton poured the champagne. He said, "To my beautiful wife, may she find me a worthy husband." The couple bumped cups.

"Good luck to that," mumbled Stripes. He downed his bubbly, then emptied his flask.

"Reverend Byle," said Libby. She handed Peyton her cup.

"Give me that." Stripes took the cup.

"Reverend," said Libby, "would you, Glory, and Mayor Nuckle do a new bride the favor of escorting her back home? I need some time to ready myself for the consummation."

Stripes looked up. "What do you need to do that for? And why do I need to hear about it? Show some respect."

Reverend Byle drank up. "I'd be delighted to walk with the bride."

Nuckle stood at attention, "My honor, Mrs. Neworth." He winked at Glory.

Stripes chugged the rest of Libby's champagne.

"Daddy, you and Peyton wait about a half hour, would you?" Libby flapped her eyelids at Peyton. "Maybe amble on back together. By then the sun should be starting to show."

Peyton looked up. "Stripes?"

"Me and Guizar. And you." Stripes picked up the half-full bottle of champagne. "Yep. One big happy family."

Libby, Glory, the Reverend, and the Mayor walked four astride into the dawn light, lantern held high, and disappeared in the low haze.

Stripes upturned the champagne bottle into his mouth, swallowed half a dozen times and threw the empty against a rock. He turned and moved off into the dark.

Peyton heard the splatter of piss landing on a dry ground. He'd been startled by the shattered bottle. He called to Stripes, "Big bladder for a little man."

From the dark, Stripes called back, "I may be littler than you, butthead, but I'm twice as mean." A gun shot came from Stripes's direction.

Peyton hit the dirt. "Stripes!" he yelled, "You there?"

Stripes walked out of the darkness, pistol in one hand, half a rattlesnake in his left. "Can't be too careful out here."

"Whoa," said Peyton. He stood and dusted himself.

"That's why I carry a pistol," said Stripes. "Never know when you'll run into a snake. Live long enough and you can see 'em in the dark." He glared at Peyton, then threw the tail end of the rattler into the dirt for Guizar to tear apart.

"Let's get the hell out of here," said Peyton.

"What's your hurry, Asswipe?"

"You kidding? Besides," said Peyton, "You're just a little too loose at the moment. And this place gives me the creeps."

"We're in the sight of somebody's God, Sonny," said Stripes. "Sacred ground."

"Yeah," said Peyton. "So now you're a believer. Hallelujah."

"And, just so you know...." Stripes pulled a fifth of

whiskey from inside his jacket, cracked it open, and drank down an inch. "I am not drunk."

The eastern horizon wasn't visible for the mountain, but the black sky above was turning a deep blue and stars were disappearing. Birds had begun to sing, and the rasp of creatures scuttling across the parched earth shifted from bug to mammal, at least that's how Peyton imagined it, with the sound of quadrupeds instead of millipedes: larger, but less creepy.

Peyton wondered where Stripes stowed the gun. He didn't have a belt or shoulder holster.

"Guess we might as well," said Stripes. He and Guizar started walking in the wrong direction. Peyton grabbed the knapsack, and guided Stripes and Guizar toward Saltine. The three had walked half a mile in silence when Stripes stopped and said, "Libby's not like anyone else you know."

"I can see that."

"Don't expect her to be, well, don't go thinking you can change her."

"Never would," said Peyton.

"She's a lady."

"She's my wife."

"She's my daughter." Stripes spoke louder and walked again, faster. Guizar moved from the outside to between the two men.

Peyton kept pace. "She's a handsome, fully-grown woman."

"Careful what you say, Sonny."

Peyton stopped walking. "We waited, Pop, just like she wanted. But now she's my wife."

Stripes turned. "You're talking to the girl's daddy." His shoulders twitched. "Show some respect." He was almost hollering. Guizar snarled. "That's right, my boy," said Stripes, hopping from one foot to the other. "Go on, Guizar. Tell him for me."

Peyton took a step back.

Guizar circled Stripes once, teeth bared, drooling.

"What the hell?" Peyton stepped back again. "Old man, you're drunk."

"I got reason to drink."

"What's that?"

"You're swiping my girl." Stripes started to weep big tears then stopped and, like Guizar, bared his teeth and growled.

"You got it backwards." Peyton shook his head and walked on. "She found me."

He hadn't gone twenty feet before Stripes yelled, "Get him, Guizar."

Guizar whined, then sprang toward Peyton.

The dog leapt forward from his haunches. Peyton, several feet beyond, brought his right foot up to protect himself and caught Guizar in the throat.

The dog didn't even yelp. He rebounded toward Stripes and fell to the dirt with a thud. His eyes were open and he was alive, but the air was knocked out of him and his voice box broken by Peyton's steel-toed boot.

"Oh baby, Oh my boy." Stripes bellowed and dove to the ground at Guizar's side, howled and held the dog's head in his hands, then lowered it to the ground. "What did that fucker do to you?" Stripes looked up at Peyton.

"I had to," said Peyton. "You told him to come at me. I didn't want to hurt him."

"You fucking–" Stripes's hand reached into his pocket, but he struggled and couldn't pull his hand out.

Peyton grabbed Stripes from the back and raised him to his feet to contain him in a choke hold. Stripes freed his hand and waved the pistol in the air, aiming over his shoulder. One shot. Two shots.

Peyton wrestled away the pistol.

Stripes buried his chin in his chest and bit into Peyton's arm.

Peyton pushed Stripes away. "Rabid old fool. I'm sorry, man. I never wanted to hurt your dog."

Stripes clambered to his feet. He twisted to face Peyton. "What you wanted don't matter. You killed my boy." He was breathing hard. "You gonna shoot me too?"

"No."

Stripes edged backwards, then he turned to run, but stopped. He spun around again to face Peyton. He said, "I could've liked you, but instead I got a fuckhead for a son-in-law. A fuckhead!!" With one swift bow, Stripes reached into the lining of his boot, pulled out an eight-inch hunting knife, and, with a war cry, raged toward Peyton.

Peyton raised the pistol and took one shot. Stripes lifted into the air, then fell on his back. The Smith and Wesson 38 bullet had hit Stripes's thigh, but the leg was bent wrong and the pain was bone pain.

"Kill me," hissed Stripes. "Kill me now, you fuckhead. You killed my best friend. And I ain't living on like some cripple."

"I'll run get Doc," said Peyton. "Why'd you rush me, man. Why?"

"You going to kill me or not?"

"I already said I wasn't."

"You said you weren't going to shoot me, and you did. Now, Sonny. You goddamn finish what you started."

"I'm going to get Doc."

"Fuckhead!"

Stripes lay on his back. With his right hand, he lifted the hunting knife and shoved it into his own abdomen, upward from his stomach into his own chest. The blade severed organs and a turquoise-inlaid bone-handle stood from his belly. Before Peyton was able to comprehend what had happened, Stripes stopped screaming and lay dead.

The world around Peyton became very still. He listened for voices, sounds of any kind. But only Guizar's panting and the birds, far away now, were awake. He wondered if anyone heard the shots, but figured no one would know where they'd come from, and anyway, hunters roamed all over these parts, even at night. Peyton stepped toward Stripes and searched for a pulse in his neck. Then he went to Guizar, the dog's eyes still open, scared. "Sorry boy," said Peyton. "Wasn't your fault." Peyton couldn't leave a dog to suffer but closed his eyes before aiming the gun. He fired one more time then couldn't look and walked away.

Peyton walked a hundred yards toward Saltine, the gun in his hand, then stopped walking and sat on the ground. Over Salvation Mountain, the sky was a thinner blue and the air was warmer and the mosquitoes were humming. For close to half an hour, Peyton sat. He whispered to himself, over and over, "What the hell happened?"

Who would ever believe him? Should he run? Turn around and go east as fast as possible? Should he carry Stripes back to Saltine? He couldn't confess to Libby. If he left Stripes where he lay, he was sure coyotes and desert shrews would take care of the corpse before anyone stumbled on it for the desert plain was wide and vast. He considered what story he'd have to tell, tried to see it from every angle, then forced it out of his head. He stood, opened the cylinder, emptied the bullets into the dirt, and put the gun in his pocket. He said, "Forgive me."

He walked the final four miles to Sidewinder Circle. Peyton threw the pistol in the weeds next to the goat pen.

He tiptoed past the rebar tree, up the steps of the pink and white double wide, and opened the door. He'd convinced himself he'd done the only thing possible given the circumstances, and gathered his nerve to face Libby on her wedding day.

"Doll," he called. A scented candle flickered on the table. "I'm home." He looked around and closed the door behind him. The table with the candle, where the three of them had eaten dinner together the first time... Peyton gagged and felt as if he'd swallowed a stomach full of dust.

He'd cursed himself the entire walk home, turned around three times wondering if Stripes was really dead and twice thinking if he were dead, he should at least be buried but in the end Peyton hadn't gone back.

He called,"Where could she be, that beautiful new wife of mine?"

Libby's boots sat on the mat inside the front door. Peyton removed his too and left them beside hers.

A giggle came from the bedroom. Libby murmured in a come-and-get-me singsong, "Oh Sweetcakes...."

The fragrance of gardenia dusting powder drew Peyton's nose, if not at the moment the entirety of his heart, yet nonetheless swelled his groin. "Your Sweetcakes is searching for his lovely bride. Where might she be?"

Peyton stepped into the bedroom with its pink flowered wallpaper, blond-veneered vanity, and striped bedspread. Libby lay across the stripes.

Stripes, thought Peyton. Holy shit. Why *stripes*? He buried the thought and bridled his anxiety. He shivered and couldn't determine if his body was reacting to turmoil or desire. He swallowed and mopped his forehead. He said, "You look like a Goddess."

"Oooo," said Libby. "Then I'm a Goddess awaiting her God."

"I've no doubt been called a lot of things in my life, Doll, but I'd be surprised if it was ever God." Peyton found the boudoir tableau like something from Mustang Ranch, then he wondered how he knew about Mustang Ranch, but decided he'd better say nothing. "I need a shower, Doll." He unbuttoned his shirt but didn't remove it.

In the bathroom, Peyton ripped off his shirt and shimmied out of his pants and shorts, then wadded them into a ball and decided he'd insist on doing his own laundry. He bore the smell of death, not that he believed there was such a thing, but gunpowder did have a smell, after all, and so did Guizar, and maybe the smells somehow stayed with him. And Libby might sense a disturbance in the ether. Like the old fart said, Libby's a different sort of girl.

The shower stall was sized for a double wide trailer, and the water pressure was down to a fast drip. Yet Peyton lathered up, blew out his nostrils, rinsed his mouth, scrubbed his ears, scraped under his short fingernails, and rubbed hard with his hands to remove soap and any other odors that might have found a pore to lodge in. He'd shaved before leaving for Salvation Mountain, and even if he wanted to shave again, his kit was in Stripes's bathroom. Poor old fart. Shit, thought Peyton. Shit. Shit. Shit.

"May I come in?" Libby stood outside the bathroom door.

"No!" Peyton shouted. "I mean, I'll be out in two minutes." He gasped hard from the shock of Libby's voice, creating an upheaval in his own uneasy ether. "You just hold those pretty little reins of yours and your Lone Ranger will be riding 'round the mountain at any moment."

Libby giggled and jiggled the door knob from the bedroom. She had no intention of opening the door, but the jiggling sent Peyton spinning. He kept his voice low. "Just two minutes, Doll." He toweled himself off and looked in the mirror. If she noticed, he'd have to explain his red face as anticipation.

Libby wore a white cotton nightie, a slip of a garment

that reached her knees, so out-of-the-package new that it still had folds and the feel of factory starch. When Peyton poked his nose out the bathroom door, she said, "Hello Sweetcakes."

"I hope I can be that to you, always, Doll." Peyton meant it, too. "Maybe we should have some breakfast first? Keep my strength up?"

"You're plenty strong." She lay back. "First, me. Then, breakfast."

So, he thought, the first thing married life meant was, no breakfast till she said so. The second thing was, before I get breakfast, I have to screw the woman I orphaned. What could be third? "I'm pretty straight forward about all this," said Peyton, though he didn't really know. He had no memory of women and hoped biology would take over. He sat on the edge of the bed and bent sideways, his face inches from Libby's.

"Well," said Libby. "If you look around, you could probably figure out so am I. Straight forward. Just tired of waiting." Libby leaned into Peyton and planted her lips on his.

The last time she kissed me, thought Peyton, just a couple of hours ago, I hadn't yet killed her daddy. Technically though he killed himself, right? Shit. Peyton pulled back from Libby. "Let's take it slow."

"Let's not." Libby's top lip puckered. "We can take it slow next time." She dragged Peyton onto his back across the stripes of the bedspread. The drapes were closed, but rays of sun broke through, enough to get a good look at the man she'd married. Libby untucked the towel wrapped around Peyton's waist. She smiled. "Oh Peyton," Libby said, "I'm rich!"

Panic again rose in Peyton and the rest of him fell.

"The family jewels," said Libby, "jewels to sustain me into our future."

And Glory, thought Peyton. Shit. She'll be crushed.

Libby stroked the hair on Peyton's chest. "Isn't that right, Sweetcakes?"

"What? Oh. Uh huh." The family jewels. He gave in to the moment. "You want me to do anything?"

"Just lie there is fine."

While Libby stroked the hair on Peyton's chest, Peyton thought about the yellow police tape hanging from Libby's rebar tree, and by the time Libby had worked her hands down to Peyton's navel, he was imagining the tape tied into a noose with he, himself, standing on a platform awaiting the hangman, but when Libby started running her fingertips across his balls, Peyton was floating above the rebar tree, the yellow police tape his only tether.

Libby asked, "You liking that?"

"Uh huh," said Peyton.

Libby put her lips on Peyton's hundred karat family jewel.

The yellow tether snapped, and Peyton was afloat, adrift.

Libby snaked her way toward the head of the bed, lying even with Peyton. "How was that, Sweetcakes?"

"Uh huh."

Libby was on her knees. She lifted her nightie over her head. Her body was younger than her face. Pale, bony, but not painfully so. Libby didn't shave anything. She moved so her knees were one on each side of Peyton's waist. She dropped to all fours, kissed her father's killer, and sat down slowly. And then, as if she'd been waiting all her life to come, Libby did.

Peyton, on the other hand, couldn't. No rocking back and forth, no moaning or groaning. "Oooooh Sweetcakes," Libby mumbled. "Where'd you learn to do all that?"

"Beats me."

"What about you?" said Libby. "Did I do something wrong?"

"You did everything right, Doll." Peyton tried to assure his bride. "Everything right, but I was thinking about you, not me. Next time. You'll see." Peyton had returned to earth as Libby clutched and clenched. "I need to take it slow," he said. "Can we eat breakfast now?

*

"Power food," said Libby. She placed a plate of three over-easy eggs, hash browns, and two pieces of raisin bread, toasted and slathered thick with strawberry jam on the table in front of Peyton. "Juice and coffee on the way."

Libby set coffee and juice down for Peyton. For herself, she sipped a cup of coffee with sugar and gazed at Peyton from across the table. Peyton ate like a man starving, shoveling down the salty potatoes, wiping yolk from the plate with sweetened bread, gulping the orange juice, adding three teaspoons of sugar to black coffee before pouring that into his mouth, too. "Wow," he said when he'd finished, and looked up to find Libby's eyes.

"Do you always eat breakfast like that?" Libby was mildly alarmed at Peyton's appetite, but well enough lubed so it didn't matter a whole heck of a lot how Peyton answered.

"Did I do something wrong?"

"You did everything right. Glad you like my cooking."

"Never ever tasted better, Doll." Peyton smiled a big smile. "Not in a lifetime of breakfasts."

Libby blushed.

"What do you say we climb back between the sheets?"

"Now?" Libby sat up straight.

"If you say yes, I'll wash dishes later," said Peyton.

"I never heard of.... It's past noon...." Libby looked at Peyton's crooked smile. "Well, if you say."

"Wife," said Peyton, "It's the power food!"

Peyton took Libby's hand and led her into the dizzyingly pink room. He lifted the nightie over her head, gathered her in his arms, whirled her once around in a waltz, then flung her, on her back, onto the bed.

"Oh, Peyton," she said. "You're such an animal."

Peyton agreed. He was a killer animal but forced himself to ignore the fact and rather concentrate on what was in front of his eyes. He tore the towel from around his waist, and dove onto Libby as if nothing was amiss. The bed creaked and the wood struts sounded a precarious crack, but it all held together while Peyton snuggled his family jewels between Libby's pink thighs and hoped biology would maneuver his hundred karat carrot.

Libby said, "Oh!"

Peyton cried, "Ah ah aaaaaaah!" and collapsed. "Sorry. I couldn't wait. See what you do to me?" Peyton rolled off and lay flat on his back, as Stripes had in his dying breath.

"And you'll wash the dishes?" said Libby.

Libby had tied her apron around Peyton, naked but for a pair of her socks, and handed him the dishwashing liquid.

"I was hoping you'd forget."

"I never forget." Libby grinned at Peyton and waited for the third ring to pick up the phone. "Hello? Yes, Deputy. Thank you. Yes. No." She rolled her eyes. "I don't keep tabs on him." Libby nodded her head. "Yes, I will do that." She put the receiver down.

Peyton turned to face Libby, pink rubber dish gloves, a floral hostess apron, chest and shoulders of brown fur. "Should I be jealous?"

"Ed Schotz can't locate Daddy," said Libby. "The senior replicants meet for coffee every morning at Ramble's."

Peyton stopped washing and looked over at Libby.

"He wasn't there today." Libby thought for a moment. "You don't mind, do you Sweetcakes? I invited Daddy for dinner tonight."

Peyton held his breath and tried to look like a man telling the truth. "Great." Peyton turned back to the sink and scrubbed dried egg off the spatula. "You can interrogate him then."

"I'm not going to interrogate him," said Libby. "It's just that Ed was looking."

"A man's got to have his own life, Libby."

"And that means–"

"Nothing," said Peyton.

Oh God, thought Libby, Peyton wants his own life. "This morning. When you left him?"

"Don't ask."

"I'm asking," said Libby. "You know something I should?"

Peyton put the spatula down on the counter. "Okay. I didn't want to tell you, but he'd been drinking."

"I knew it."

"Heavily."

Libby blew breath between her teeth and hissed. "I'm going to beat the daylights.... He *promised*."

"I'm not trashing your Daddy." Peyton ordered himself to remain calm. After all, he told himself, he hadn't been the one to hold the bottle to Stripes's mouth. "But he downed the rest of the champagne and opened a fifth of whiskey after you left." Peyton added, "I tried to take it from him, but he backed away and," Peyton considered his next sentence, "he pulled a knife." Shit, though Peyton. "I didn't want to bait him."

"That's so like Daddy." Libby puckered her top lip. "Ed said he'd swing by tonight. To check up." She looked at Peyton. "Darn him anyway. Why can't things be normal?"

Normal. Peyton was flotsam from the trolley. Normal to him meant grabbing a buoy in a sea of Imperial County sand. He hovered among the grounded, he was a deserter amid the enlisted, claimed by a woman he'd never before seen. He stood now in a pair of Libby's blue socks, his balls against the wall with suds between his fingers, his brain not able to recall a past or focus on the lifetime of strings Libby was attaching with epoxy. "What's normal?"

"You serious?"

"No." Stabbing oneself in the gut isn't normal. Shooting a paralyzed dog isn't normal. He didn't know if lying was normal or not. Peyton thought better of answering. "Do me a favor, Doll? My clothes. In the washer– "

"I'll hang them," she said.

Better them than me, thought Peyton.

"When Glory pays you, buy a second set." Libby stood and pinched Peyton's bottom as she passed by to the laundry room. "Normal," she said, and giggled. She pulled Peyton's jeans, shorts, shirt, and socks from the machine, which he'd set to Hot, with a double rinse. "Let me do the laundry from now on," Libby called. She dumped the damp clump into a plastic basket, rotated the knob to Cold and simple rinse, and stepped out the back door.

"Wait," hollered Peyton. He remembered the weeds where he'd thrown Stripes's gun. Libby would be standing right next to it. "Maybe you should, or maybe I should..." Peyton breathed hard. "What I mean is, I don't want to make more work for you, Doll."

"No problem, Sweetcakes." Libby left her wooden clothes pins on the line. She hung Peyton's jeans and his shirt, then looked around to the spot where she'd buried the roll of twenties she'd lifted from his pocket that first day. She'd put the roll in an empty green beans can and hidden it in a shallow hole next to the tree growing up against the goat pen, which now contained Nanny. Maybe she would surprise Peyton with a vacation on their anniversary. And, she thought, Daddy will show up. He always does. Libby turned to the clothesline, sighing and contented, and hung Peyton's shorts and socks.

Libby had kept chickens in the goat pen. But feed was expensive and there were rumors circulating about some kind of deadly bird flu. A year ago, an itinerant came through Saltine, looking for work. Libby had spied him from afar but up-close determined he was not husband material, so she fed him lunch and paid him to slaughter all 18 of the fowl, gut, pluck, cut, bag and put them in the deep-freezer on her back step, which she padlocked at all times.

She dropped the empty laundry basket, dialed the freezer lock combination and pulled out a bag with half a chicken. "Six birds left," she said, then let the top of the top-loading freezer drop, and snapped the lock closed, giving the dial a spin. She sang, "*Tonight I'm Gonna Party Like it's 1999.*"

If she left the basket on the landing, the wind would take it. If she put the chicken in the basket and left it outside to defrost, Guizar would snatch it as he'd done before, and then the basket would blow away. She brought both inside.

"Thanks, Doll," said Peyton. "You didn't have to."

"And you'd go out? Dressed like that?" Libby ran her hand up the inside of his naked thigh. "Yeeeeow!" Peyton spun to face Libby. He dropped the dishrag on the floor.

Libby picked it up and handed it back. "Just wanted you to know I like you." She laughed and put the frozen half chicken in a bowl on the counter. "I'm going to run to Glory's. Your clothes shouldn't take an hour to dry and I'll be back."

Peyton stood with his jaw hanging.

"Want me to relay Glory anything?"

"Nuh-uh."

"That you'll see her tomorrow maybe?"

"Oh." Payton blinked. "Sure."

Libby slipped off her mules and pulled on her boots. She waved and was out the door.

Peyton dried his hands and hung the dish towel over the knob on the oven door. He looked around. He was naked. He couldn't go out for a beer. He had no buddies. He couldn't insult Stripes. Stripes was dead. He contemplated contagion from a dead chicken. He hoped Libby would give him his pants before Ed swung by that evening.

"I don't like it," Deputy Ed Schotz had told Doc two weeks earlier after dumping Peyton on Doc's office couch.

"Not one bit."

"You're paid to be suspicious," said Doc.

"I don't know," Ed said. "A man unconscious next to the rails."

"And besides," Doc has said, "everyone knows you're sweet on Libby."

Ed Schotz grumbled something like denial.

It was true. Since high school, Schotz had been constructing a fantasy life with Libby as his bride. He never dreamed what Libby had in mind as he pushed the wheelbarrow to Doc's. Then, without talking to anyone about it, without knowing much about Peyton or introducing him, two weeks later she upped and married the creep. To Deputy Ed Schotz, something smelled as rotten as the tilapia farms in the Salton Sea. Of course no one expected to see Stripes the day of the wedding. But the day after? That was another ball of fur. Morning coffee wasn't the same without Stripes. Schotz was prepped for malfeasance, and he went looking for it.

Deputy Schotz began to sweat before he stepped outside the Sheriff's air-conditioned office. He knew Libby would come after him and inflict pain were she to learn of his personal investigation of her husband. Truth is, Schotz was afraid of Libby. When he wore a uniform, he could affect the air of legal authority. He didn't want anyone to see him as weak, surely not Libby, the object of his desire. He checked his holster, cleared his throat, lowered his voice half an octave, and walked out onto Paseo Centro.

He talked to each downtown merchant. None had seen

Stripes for two days. Glory'd said only, "I wish." Schotz struck out perpendicular to Paseo Centro into the scrub toward the rail. He had four hours until, as promised, he'd swing by Libby's, but only three of good light. So Schotz followed what he thought must have been the wedding party trail two nights earlier. He hadn't been invited to the nuptials, but he knew what was happening. And where.

The wind had erased the party's footprints but Schotz approximated their path as closely as he could. He didn't know what he was looking for, but figured he had two search options. One: pace a zigzag back and forth across the territory, cover a wide swath, but make little forward progress. Or, two: go straight for the deep interior, toward The Mountain and miss the periphery. Schotz chose to go deep. He commenced a fast walk, taking in what he could, left and right, following the straightest line to the Mountain, the shortest distance. He walked for precisely one hour and twenty-five minutes. He didn't make it all the way to the Ravine of Righteousness, and knew he should keep going, but he wanted to be at Libby's by six o'clock. He'd give himself ten minutes to catch his breath before turning back.

Schotz stood and looked at his own footprints. He could shift twenty feet left or right for the return and search different ground. He flipped a mental nickel, rested another four minutes, then moved to his right to begin his return 20 feet north of, and parallel to his own prints.

Had Schotz chosen to shift to his left and walk ten paces to the south, the Deputy might have noticed a glint of light refracting off a silver blade leaning upright against a skeleton already picked so clean that buzzards no longer circled, the corpse torn by coyotes and shrews, and consumed down to bone in 30 hours. Instead, Deputy Ed Schotz saw no glimmer of light at all.

*

Peyton found he liked roaming the house naked. He wished he could do it outside. Chickens and goats roam naked, he thought, so why, oh why, can't I?

The gun! Peyton bolted upright. The backs of his thighs stuck to the Naugahyde dinette chair. He peeled himself free. He ran to the bedroom and pulled the yellow daisy sheet from the mattress, wrapped it around his torso, and used the belt from his jeans to fasten the sarong to his body. At the front door, he stepped into his boots.

Peyton walked back through the kitchen and onto the back porch and folded the floppy torso of his sarong down over his belt. He thought, better they wonder if I'm wearing a skirt than a dress. He moved at a deliberate pace, not wanting to appear in a hurry. He walked to the clothesline, pulled off his jeans, shirt, shorts, and socks. He'd dropped the gun into a large clump of browning Buffalo grass. He pretended to pick up something else, too, just to throw off track anyone who might be looking, then sauntered into the house through the back door.

He grabbed the roll of duct tape he'd noticed in the shelf above the washer. He kicked off his boots by the front door and unbuckled his belt. He moved into the bedroom and stretched the sheet back over the mattress, then put on his shorts and socks, then shirt, then jeans, winding his belt through the loops.

Peyton looked around the room. He duct-taped the gun to the underside of Libby's blond veneered vanity and ran his fingernails over the tape to make sure it adhered.

"Yoohoo! Sweetcakes, I'm ho-home." Libby put her bag of groceries on the table.

Peyton walked out. "Hi Doll."

"You're dressed!" Libby cocked her head.

"Want to get undressed?"

"How'd you get your clothes? Are they dry?"

"You work too hard, Doll. Thought I could lighten your load just a bit." Peyton leaned over and kissed Libby. He kissed her because he really wanted to, but also because he knew he'd be less likely to have to defend himself. "And, yes, they're dry."

Libby smiled and melted.

"Might have scandalized the replicants, though." Peyton took Libby's hand. "I went out there wrapped in a sheet."

"Don't you pay them the time of day," said Libby. "It's all water over the bridge." She gazed at her husband.

"You mean under the bridge."

"No. Borax Creek Bridge, before it collapsed, water went under, but now the water goes over. Water over the bridge, Peyton."

*

"I can't invite you in, Deputy. My husband is not yet home from work."

"I'm only here to discuss your Daddy's disappearance, Mrs. Neworth." Schotz was sweating.

Libby reddened. "Please sit." She gestured to the chairs under the rebar tree. Inside her kitchen, Libby placed two orange cups on a blue Melmac tray, along with a Tupperware pitcher of lemonade she had planned for supper. She took the refreshments out to the patio table. She sat and poured.

"Thank you, Mrs. Neworth." Ed straightened.

"Oh, Ed. For crying out loud. I'm still Libby."

"Libby." Ed's voice softened and his eyebrows pinched together.

"Don't!" said Libby. "So help me, Eddie. If you start drooling like some old St. Bernard...." Libby put her cup of lemonade on the table.

"But Libby –"

"I said, *don't*." Libby sat straight.

Schotz looked down into his lap. He took a deep breath, then spoke in a voice half an octave lower. "You are right." He cleared his throat and looked up. "I've come by because I'm concerned about your father."

That's more like it, thought Libby. "What exactly is it that concerns you?"

"Well, he seems to be missing."

"Ed." Libby fluttered her eyelashes. "Wouldn't I be the first to know if my Daddy went missing?"

Schotz couldn't respond to this, but wasn't it just like Libby to flummox him this way?

"He's invited for dinner." Libby sipped her lemonade. "I'll ask where he's been."

"Okay. But, in the meantime, would you mind if I have a look around?" He thought he should be scoping out the scene but couldn't take his eyes of Libby.

"Why yes I do, Ed." Libby thought a moment. "It would be unseemly, under the circumstances."

Which are? Ed wanted to ask but held back. He understood present circumstances was another way of saying, I'm married. "I understand." Schotz stood. He gazed up at the rebar tree, then again at Libby. "I'll be going, then."

"Oh. So soon?"

"If you see Stripes –"

"*When*, Ed. *When* I see Daddy...."

"*When* you see Stripes, let him know all us guys are wondering what hole he fell into." Schotz used his red calico handkerchief to dust off his badge. "Thanks for the lemonade."

"Anytime." Libby watched Ed move away down Sidewinder Circle. "You take care, now." She put the orange cups on the blue tray with the pitcher of lemonade and carried it all into the double wide. Law enforcement. Humbug. What could Ed possibly think he'd find?

Schotz didn't look back. He walked slowly and zigzagged back and forth across Sidewinder Circle and pocketed a tuft of Guizar's fur.

Libby let the oven door slam closed. "Daddy's never late for food." She put the pan of baked chicken on the counter next to the sink then turned to look at Peyton who'd just come through the door after walking home from work.

"Do I have to ask you every time to take your boots off?"

"I always –"

"Never mind. Nobody gives the time of day for all I do around here." Libby threw her hands into the air. "He must be on a binge. Maybe he's up in Frink. In any case," Libby stopped. "What is it now?"

"Doll, I –"

"Eddie stopped by, looking for him, and –"

"Schotz was here?"

"Didn't I just say that?"

"Eddie?"

"Yes, Peyton. Eddie."

"You call him Eddie? I've never heard you call him –"

"Dinner's on the table, Peyton, and did you not hear what I said?"

"Yes, I heard." He shook his head. "I'm just not sure what you want me to do."

"So you won't help me look for him?"

"Of course I will. I'll do anything. What is it you want me to do?"

"How am I supposed to know? Daddy's never been late for dinner. Unless he's on a bender. He promised to stop drinking. Sort of. Though he's promised other times before, too."

Peyton set his boots next to Libby's at the door. He plopped down on his Naugahyde chair at the dinette.

"Tell you what, Doll." He thought calling her Doll might assuage his beloved. "It's too dark to see anything tonight. First light tomorrow? I'll go by his house and look around. He keeps a key –"

"I know he keeps a key."

"How about I let myself in and check around. Ask his neighbors."

"Eddie's already been there."

Again, Eddie. "Maybe they'll tell me something they wouldn't tell the law."

"More likely some replicant will call the law to report a snoop." Libby sat across from Peyton.

"They saw me coming and going with Stripes for two weeks." Peyton wished things were back to normal. Normal.

"And that makes you *not* a stranger?"

Peyton's world was spinning. "Well, what did Schotz suggest?"

Libby leaned back in her chair and sighed. "He wanted to look around."

Peyton's insides burst into flames and his bowels turned to water but he sat perfectly still and maintained eye contact with Libby. "Okay by me."

To be fine with another man looking around was a betrayal of the first order. Libby's jaw dropped and her eyes filled.

"*Now* what did I do?" said Peyton. "Doll, I'm horribly confused."

"I told Eddie," a tear escaped. "I told Deputy Schotz it would be improper, with my husband not here, for him to look around." Tears dripped down Libby's cheeks. "I only did what I thought you'd want."

Peyton felt he should put his arms around her, comfort her, but he genuinely didn't know if his back door would hold. "Would you wait right here, Doll? Just wait? I'll be right back. Would you?"

Libby blinked and nodded.

Peyton stood, carefully, and held onto the table. He grimaced and Libby, mistaking the grimace for a smile, smiled back. He clenched his muscles and walked to the bathroom as if his knees were glued together.

Libby waited, and heard the bathroom fan go on, but she was antsy so she rose and set three places. She served the chicken along with a bowl of rice and dessert cups of canned peaches. Peyton liked canned peaches, and Libby liked that he felt randy after eating them.

"I'm sorry Sweetcakes," Libby said when Peyton returned. "I don't mean to be rough on you. I'm worried about Daddy, that's all."

"May I give you a hug? I wanted to hug you earlier," he said, "but didn't know if you'd let me."

Libby's tears left a wet patch on Peyton's chest.

"Aw Doll," said Peyton. "I wish...." Peyton didn't finish his sentence. He was thinking about Schotz. *Eddie*, rooting around. He could have come by when I was here. Something's off.

"We might as well eat," said Libby. "No use letting it get cold." She pulled back from Peyton and sniffed. "I hope Daddy's eating dinner."

More like he was eaten for dinner, thought Peyton. Shit. He kissed Libby's forehead, "He's missing the best baked chicken this side of Salvation Mountain." Peyton picked up a thigh and gnawed at it. "Mmmm," he said, mouth full, knowing Libby's gaze would scold if he opened his mouth to say, "Delish," as he almost did.

"You sure make a girl feel like she knows what she's about."

In Peyton's mind, nobody knows what he's about because nobody knows anything in advance of it happening. He would never have guessed he'd have shot his father-in-law. We're just animals, eating, screwing, pooping, and passing on. Reverend Byle would claim different. But look at old Stripes. Thinking he knew what he was doing, with his dog and his pistol. A half bottle of champagne later, that's all it took.

"Canned peaches taste sweeter when they come from you, Doll," said Peyton.

"I add cinnamon." Libby blushed.

"How about I wash the dishes in the morning, and you come to bed with me now."

"What if Daddy walks in?"

"We can only hope." Peyton grinned big. He stood. "Race you to the bed."

"No way I'd win," said Libby, smiling up. But she watched for an opening, as she often did, without even knowing it. When Peyton closed his eyes to stretch, Libby pushed off like a swim racer. She darted past Peyton and was first to dive onto the yellow daisies.

The following morning, Deputy Schotz walked from morning coffee at Ramble's lunch counter, nervous over Stripes's absence, to the pink and white double wide, up the steps to the screen door.

"Hi Eddie," said Peyton without looking up from the sink and last night's dishes. He recognized Schotz's walk. Peyton had taken to washing dishes in the buff, wearing only Libby's apron, and he stood there awaiting Schotz's salutation.

Schotz peered inside through the living room, into the kitchen, then looked away. "I'll come back." He clomped down the steps and walked without veering, back the way he came. He knew which days Peyton worked. He'd questioned Glory.

"Someone at the door, Sweetcakes?" Libby called out when she stepped from the shower to dress in the bedroom.

"Eddie."

"Eddie?" Libby wrapped the towel around her body and walked to the kitchen door. "Did he find Daddy?"

"Didn't say."

Libby padded barefoot to Peyton's side. "How could he not say?"

"Done," said Peyton. He turned from the sink to Libby. "Doll. I swear, you'd have to ask Eddie that. My guess is no."

"You going to Daddy's house?" Libby watched Peyton's hairy bum leave the kitchen.

"Yeah. I suppose it's time we get worried."

*

The secret key to Stripes's front door was not in the stiff grey diaper hanging from the plastic amputee yard-stork's beak. Peyton thought the wind might have blown the key across the yard and he'd never find it. Imagine, he thought, the show I could put on for the replicants, searching for that key. He walked around the side of the single wide, turned the corner at the rear of the house and bounced backward after running face-to-face into Schotz.

"Mr. Neworth," said Schotz.

Peyton caught his breath. He couldn't hide his red face. "Deputy."

"Might I ask your business here?"

With this ambush, Schotz had evened the score. Peyton could let it slide, or he could ramp up the ante. "Libby. You know, my wife? She sent me to look around."

"Well," said Schotz, hand on his holster, "if there was something to be found, I already found it."

It had been three days and Peyton was sure there could be naught left of Stripes on the desert floor but his bones, and if the good deputy hadn't the nose to follow a carrion scent when it wafted or the eyes to notice vultures when they circled overhead, Peyton might once again breathe free. He said, "Maybe there's nothing to find."

"Maybe," said Schotz, "you just didn't look hard enough."

"What are we talking about here? I wasn't looking at all." Peyton's half-smile grew a tiny bit. He added, "*She* found *me*, Eddie. Remember?"

Schotz remembered well enough that it was he who toiled the wheelbarrow to Doc's. He took his hand from his holster and pulled a notebook and pencil from his chest pocket. He wrote something, then spoke. "Mr. Neworth, I am informing you that this house and its contents, the yard and its surroundings, are a potential crime scene. You must remove yourself from the premises immediately." Shotz stood very straight and still. "Yellow police tape will demarcate the perimeter."

Peyton shook his head. "My poor Libby."

"Do you understand what I've told you?"

Peyton slouched and scratched his head. "Clear as Saltine tap water. Eddie."

"I'm not horsing around here."

"Deputy," said Peyton. "How could you even suggest something so contemptible?" Peyton clicked his heels together, saluted, thought *touché*, and began his amble back to Big Pink, as he'd begun calling the double wide. He really did wish things were otherwise because Libby was going to suffer. But, given that they weren't otherwise, Peyton was relieved to think he'd not be exposed. He had to be at work in two hours. Enough time for lunch at home. Stripes is missing. How was he going to tell Libby?

*

"Another unbeatable lunch." Peyton wiped his mouth with the paper napkin Libby had set at his place. "Let's talk."

"I have to do the dishes." Libby jumped up and scooped the place settings from the dinette table. "Bones and gristle. Chicken salad makes a mess." She hadn't asked about what had happened at her Daddy's. She hadn't said word one about anything other than lunch.

Peyton followed Libby to the sink. He put his arms around her from behind. He said, "Come sit."

"I really should tidy up." She squirmed out of his embrace.

"Wait."

"Just let me." She stood facing the sink.

"Can't, Doll." Peyton stepped to Libby's side. "You need to know."

Libby dropped her arms, sighed, then grabbed a towel. She squeezed a dab of hand lotion from the dispenser on the counter and applied the balm as if wringing her hands. She followed Peyton to the dinette table and sat. She said, "I already know."

How could she? He took a breath. "What do you know?"

"You'd have told me if you'd found Daddy."

"Well, he does seem to be missing."

Libby gazed past Peyton and out the window by the screen door. Peyton tried to find Libby's eyes with his.

"Strange," said Libby. "The birds are missing, too."

Peyton waited for more.

"Have you noticed?" Libby turned and looked at him. "There aren't any birds. They always come to winter at the Salton Sea. Thousands of them fly over." She stared back at the window. "This year there aren't any."

"Doll?" Peyton reached out to touch Libby's cheek and she jumped as if he'd pinched her. "You hear what I'm saying?"

"What's to be done?"

"Deputy Schotz is on it," said Peyton. "Considers the disappearance suspicious."

"Eddie wouldn't know a pigeon from a gull."

Peyton wasn't so sure. "Doll, I'm telling you, Deputy Schotz thinks Stripes might have met his end." He watched for tears.

"We even had pelicans. Can you believe that?" Libby looked back at Peyton. "Do you want to bother with a Christmas tree?"

Peyton wondered if he should call Doc but decided to give Libby time. Maybe this was how she reacted to bad news. Take another day. Wait and see. "I could forego the tree."

"Me too, given the bird situation." Libby puckered her top lip.

Peyton's brow creased as he flipped through his mental note cards for a cause and effect between pelicans and Christmas trees.

"I'll finish tidying up now," said Libby, "if that's okay with you."

"Sure, Doll." Peyton stood. "I'm off to work."

"Poor Glory," said Libby.

"Because of me?"

"No, Peyton." Libby shook her head and wondered, Do men understand nothing? "Because Glory has it bad for Daddy."

It was too easy, thought Peyton. While he hosed down the meat trays on the loading dock behind Glory's Groceries, Peyton had time to contemplate the previous several days, which made up the better part of his known life. He couldn't quite grasp, in one go, all that had happened. He'd awakened at Doc's in a town full of replicants and married Libby at Nightmare Mountain, then engaged in mortal combat with Stripes after the nuptials, a boot to the chops of poor Guizar, hired by Glory to clean meat trays and goaded into a nasty tangle with Deputy Eddie Schotz. All of this a hazy web of disconnected events held tenuously together with panic and duct tape, and, in sum, bewildering enough to erupt in a headache so Peyton let it all go, back to wherever thoughts disappeared to when he stopped thinking.

The foaming green disinfectant corroded the tender skin between Peyton's fingers when he didn't wear protective gloves but he never felt a good grip through the rubber, so he rarely wore them.

Had he actually killed Stripes? Maybe he'd provoked it, or he was an accessory of some sort, but he had wanted to run for Doc, hadn't he? Okay, so maybe he was teasing his new father-in-law, but he wasn't the one who'd gone and got nasty, was he? He was ready to head home for the honeymoon. It was Stripes who was drinking, Stripes who baited him and wouldn't let him go, wasn't it?

Peyton's hands were clean. He stacked the aluminum display trays in the cold case ready for loading the following morning, then he stepped into the freezer and, without thinking, grabbed from the bulk package one modestly-sized T-bone steak, wrapped it in a paper towel and stuffed it, frozen stiff as it was, between his belt and his backside before punching out at ten minutes to seven so Glory could lock up and make it to her easy chair before *Court TV* began its daily coverage of... what was it again?

Peyton lay in bed the following morning, his brain still working to make a simple narrative out of two weeks that seemed operatic in complexity. He made a fist and punched himself in the chest a couple of times to wake up but rolled over and put the pillow over his head.

"Sweetcakes," Libby called from the kitchen. "Breakfast."

The aroma of steak and eggs leaked through the synthetic fiber of his pillow.

"Peyton?" Libby poked her head into the bedroom.

Peyton grunted.

"Feet on the floor?"

"Coming." Get up, he told himself. She cooks. You eat. He sat on the edge of the bed and pulled first his shorts then his pants to his knees, wiggled into a tee shirt, then stood to fasten everything in place. "Coming," he said again.

If Peyton closed his eyes, his stomach demanded food. If he inhaled, opened his eyes, and looked at the plate in front of him, he wanted to hurl.

"You don't look healthy," said Libby. She jumped up to feel his forehead. "No fever."

A fevered conscience, thought Peyton. Would it register on a forehead? "Could you take the steak away?" Peyton kept his eyes closed. "I'd love the eggs, Doll. And some toast, maybe? But you eat the steak."

Libby'd found it defrosted on the counter and fried it up. She said, "It's a big piece of cow, Peyton."

Peyton could think only of a dead animal. "It's yours, Doll."

"I could save some for dinner. Make a pot roast with potatoes?"

Peyton left for work early. And when he arrived at the back door, Glory was checking the time cards. "What's this?" She looked at her wrist watch. "You looking for more hours?"

"Not punching in yet, Glory, not until it's time, but some extra disinfecting needs doing," he said.

There was no returning the steak, and he hadn't yet been paid so he couldn't pad the till with what he owed. Maybe an extra hour's labor would repay his debt, if not quite make right the red ink in Peyton's karma account.

Each afternoon, Glory rewrapped the unsold display meat and returned it to the big cooler so that when Peyton arrived at 4:00, he could pull the trays out for cleaning. It was no different this day, but instead of taking the trays to the back of the store and washing them down, he deposited the trays on the loading dock outside and returned to the display case. Peyton used a scrub brush to disinfect every crack and corner. He polished the glass inside and out, polished the aluminum ribs, then cleaned and oiled the sliders at the back. He looked up to see Glory watching. "Notice a difference?" Peyton said.

Glory nodded.

Outside, on the loading dock, with a brush full of foaming green disinfectant, and without rubber gloves, he sanitized the trays, scoured the aluminum to a dull shine, and turned the hose on them to rinse. Peyton sat on the stoop for the three minutes it took the trays to air dry and checked in with his conscience. He contemplated his clean hands and returned the trays to the cooler.

A couple of hours later, Peyton called, "Thanks, Glory," as he did each night to let her know he was leaving. He punched out and stood silently on the rear dock of Glory's Groceries. He inhaled the evening air, still warm in late December, and looked across the field to the collection of single wides parked on their foundations, pioneer wagons circling against the unknown. Peyton picked up the end of the hose he'd coiled and lifted the nozzle to drip on his head. Then he turned the tap and let cold water run down his face and neck, down his body and his backside.

*

The following day, Glory stopped Peyton at the punch-out clock. "Peyton," she said. "Your internship here has ended." She handed him an envelope. "Your pay."

"Thanks, Glory." Peyton wondered if this was severance or down payment on future employment. He was eye to eye with the woman. He blinked first. "So – "

"Stripes was right about you." Glory stood in her mother pose, hands on hips.

Peyton nearly broke into tears, his face a quick crimson.

"See you on time, Tuesday afternoon."

Peyton's mouth turned up on both sides. He nodded. "Thank you, Glory," he said, and walked out through the back door. On the step he took a look inside the envelope. Bless her, thought Peyton. She'd paid him in cash. One week's pay, $60 in twenties. Peyton took the bills, rolled them tightly, and slid them into his back pocket. He stopped where he stood. Twenties. Twenty-dollar bills. He wondered why that should mean something. For a fraction of a second, a more agile Peyton was running full tilt from loud voices and neon lights, someone yelling, "Stop!" He shivered.

Señor Hector senior had said, "Of course," when Peyton asked if he'd keep his dry goods store open an extra ten minutes the evening he got paid. So after work, money in his pocket, Peyton walked next door into the hardware store and Hector turned the sign to "Closed" behind him. Peyton placed three twenties at the register and Hector gave Peyton one large shopping bag with new clothing in it and one small silver-wrapped box which Peyton placed in his chest pocket. All of this Peyton had selected the day before and awaited only the cash to pay for it.

Hector returned $3.78 to Peyton and opened the front door for him.

Peyton had done well. "Thank you, Mr. Ramble."

"To my customers, I'm Señor Hector senior."

"Señor Hector senior." Peyton held out his hand.

"Me and Glory," said Hector Senior. "We're glad you married Libby."

"I take that as a high compliment, Señor Hector senior."

"Good night, Peyton."

Libby sat at the dinette table and cried.

"Aw Doll. Give me a clue, would you?"

Libby wept and heaved. She squeaked and whispered, "It's just so unfair, not knowing."

Peyton's conscience wasn't clear. He thought Libby must have realized he'd stolen the steak or maybe she found the pistol. "I'm so sorry. I couldn't bring myself to tell you."

Libby sat straight. "Tell me what?"

"I don't know," he said. "That's what I couldn't tell you." I'm an idiot, thought Peyton. A paranoid idiot. "Did I do something wrong?"

"No. No." said Libby. "It's Daddy. That old fart. He doesn't deserve me," said Libby. She blew her nose. "Or you."

"We could debate that." Peyton saw two cups in the sink and figured Schotz had come back. He'd said he would. Timed it right, too. "Did Ed have anything enlightened to say?"

"Enlightened?" said Libby. "Like about God or something?"

"Like from doing his job. Like information about Stripes."

"Nuh-uh." Libby sniffled into her tissue.

"Then why'd he come by?"

"Peyton, I swear. I don't know why he comes by or what he wants. Maybe he's been eating his own Tilapia and become delusional."

Peyton gazed at Libby. The detour Peyton walked each day to and from Glory's Grocery took him within view of

Stripes's house. "You know he sealed-off your Daddy's property?"

From a slump, Libby again sat straight. "He what?"

"Doll. Let's take a stroll." Peyton stood and offered his hand to Libby. "You need to see this." Then he lied, "This is what I couldn't bring myself to tell you." Damn, he thought, I didn't need to say that. Why do I do things like that?

Peyton and Libby walked down Sidewinder Circle and, before reaching the Polk property, cut to the left across two yards. In the alley, about 20 feet away at another intersection, something in Peyton's peripheral vision moved. He swung his head around and caught sight of a tail – "No way," Peyton said under his breath. The matted fur on the non-wagging appendage hung heavier than a desert dog should have to carry, but, at its tip, the tail was bald. Guizar's tail.

Libby spied the yellow police tape up the road. Her steps quickened from a stroll to a trot. "Who does he think he is?" She panted and said more loudly, "What does he think he's doing? He has no right – "

Libby grabbed a piece of the caution-barrier and tore it apart with her hands. She stormed past the tape and into the yard and up the steps and pulled at the locked door in frustration. Libby turned to Peyton who stood just outside the barrier. She clenched her hands into fists and howled like Guizar would have – if he could have. Libby bellowed, "Daddy!" And again, "Daddy!" her cry loud enough that Stripes, in some distant ether, surely heard.

Peyton did not want to cross the line. "Libby," he called. "Please. Come out."

Libby stood in place, fists tight. "I can't make my feet move."

Peyton conferred with himself. Crossing the line meant Schotz had cause for arrest, and Peyton was certain Schotz would relish jailing him. "Lift your right foot," said Peyton, "and put it down closer to the steps."

Libby was crying again, her head shaking, tears flying about her eyes and cheeks. "I'm stuck," she said.

Doc had been on a house-call across the road and heard Libby's cries. He was too out of condition to run, wheezing as he came closer and wagging his finger back and forth at Peyton. "Stay out of there," Doc said when he reached Peyton. "Let me catch my air." He bent over and rested his hands on his knees. He inhaled, then exhaled loudly. He straightened up. "Ed's just waiting...." Doc said, and gasped one more time. "But I suspect you know that."

The word 'suspect' hit Peyton in the bowels. "What's happening here make my stomach go wonky," he said.

Peyton's reaction wasn't new to Doc. "There's an outhouse, just beyond the property." Doc reached into his bag and handed Peyton a pocket-sized pack of Kleenex. "Go." He watched Peyton waddle around the side of the yard, then he turned to Libby.

"Libby," he said. "I've known you since your Daddy moved to town when you were too small to walk up those steps by yourself."

Libby stopped wailing and looked at Doc.

"But now I want you to walk down those three steps and over to me."

"I can't." Libby was whimpering. "I'm stuck."

"Aw Libby, I've seen you make magical things happen."

Libby sniffed. "Like what?"

"Well, like marrying a fine man like Peyton, for one," said Doc. "So I know you can do something as simple as move your feet."

"They're frozen."

"Libby, dear. It's 80° Fahrenheit."

Libby looked at her boots. She lifted her right foot, as Peyton had suggested. Put it down. Lifted her left foot and placed it on the first step. "I can do this, Doc." She stepped, one at a time, to the ground and tiptoed across the yard to the outside, where Doc stood.

"Honey," said Doc.

Libby burst onto his shoulder. She howled, a grieving daughter, and when Peyton walked up, his eyes watery, too, Doc lifted his forefinger to his lips in a "Shhhh."

*

Mayor Nuckle investigated and could find no evidence of foul play.

"It doesn't smell right," said Deputy Schotz. "In fact, it stinks." He prowled around, eyes squinting from under his brow and delayed three days before he agreed to sign the certificate of death. "I'm signing," he said, "under protest, and you can make my job as hard as you want, but I'm not done looking."

"Go right ahead, Ed," said Nuckle. "But you're pissing upwind."

Nuckle tore down the yellow tape, rolling it up as he went, and Libby, Peyton by her side, waited to take it home. Ed stood behind them, across the road, in the neighbor's yard. He hid behind one of the neighbor's Joshua Trees at the side of the gate but stood wider than the tree trunk and wasn't at all hidden.

"I can't give you all of it," said Nuckle. "Never know when I'll have to use it again."

"A scrap, then?"

Nuckle unfurled an arm's length and cut the tape with his pocketknife.

"Thank you, Mayor." Libby held the scrap in the air and let it fly in the breeze. "And Eddie," she called, without looking behind her. "Don't you follow me or I'll report you to the Lord himself."

"Okay, Mrs. Neworth."

It wasn't Libby whom Ed planned to follow. Peyton, who'd said nothing during the tape-removal, could almost smell his own burnt backside, singed under the searing stare of Deputy Ed Schotz.

*

Deputy Schotz held Scooter Polk by his remorseful short hairs. Six years earlier, Scooter had convinced Ed to invest in Off World Tilapia, an aqua farm north of Saltine, and the following year the Salton Sea receded ten feet along its perimeter, and the years since as well. Last year, the farm went belly-up after the FDA found levels of pesticides in the fish four-hundred times the allowable level.

Libby heard about this. "Explains a lot, doesn't it? I mean," she said, "replicants?"

Ed lost his savings and never really forgave Scooter. A guilty man feeling beholden has a hard time saying, "No."

"I'll pay you a dollar a day and I'll be there a couple of weeks," Schotz had said.

What could Scooter say but, "Yes."

Marge and Scooter were to ignore what appeared on their property overnight. It looked like an old porta-potty, an upright box, small windows punched out near the top, screened and dark, the structure tall enough for a man to stand in and wide enough to furnish with a chair. From the inside, Ed had poked ventilation holes at eye-level for viewing the Neworth pink and white double wide. He had requested his accumulated vacation and intended to use the extended time-off for surveillance.

He was going to see Peyton in jail.

*

The following Saturday at 9:00 AM, Mrs. Byle tolled the church bell–audible throughout Saltine–as if it were Sunday. Glory, the Reverend, Mayor Nuckle, and a dozen of Stripes's buddies from the morning coffee klatch gathered at the pink and white double wide. They stood quiet and reverent around the rebar tree.

"Welcome," said Libby. "If he even knew the words, he'd never have said them, so I will: Thank you, every one of you. Your friendship was a gift for Daddy." She looked around at the mourners. Where the heck was Eddie? "Before I begin, would any of you like to say a few words?"

Glory raised her hand, stepped forward, but couldn't speak. She stepped back. No one else moved.

"Well, I know how you feel." Libby walked to Glory and put her arm around her shoulders. "There just aren't words." Libby offered Glory the box. "Tissue?"

Peyton held a long rod of bamboo with a tumbleweed wreath from Libby's collection, adorned with a bow fashioned of yellow police tape. He said, "For Stripes. We hope you can see this from your roost in heaven...." Peyton imagined he heard Stripes holler, "Fuck You Asshole." "... or," continued Peyton, "wherever you are."

Libby glanced over. "What's that supposed to mean?"

"Well, Doll, maybe he's in between."

Libby had grown to love Peyton, but why did he have to say things like that? "Just place the wreath."

Peyton maneuvered the pole into the rebar branches, settling the memorial into a crotch between two rebar twigs at the summit.

Libby beamed. She said, "Please join us graveside."

"Graveside?" Glory looked to Reverend Byle. "But...."

Libby walked toward the chickenless goat pen. She had selected a site at the far end, ten feet beyond where she'd buried the roll of twenties she'd found in Peyton's pocket that first day by the tracks. "Reverend?"

"Let us pray." The Reverend bowed his head. "Lord, Maurice Flagler, Stripes to his friends, of which (in spite of his profound and recurring efforts to the contrary) you certainly have been his *best*, Stripes may challenge your throne in the sky, but he was a good man here on earth and may, in time...." Reverend Byle glanced up to see fifteen pairs of eyes directed toward him, and Libby was fidgeting, "yes, notwithstanding his rare ability to laugh at others to their faces, and his cantankerous disposition that might have you rethinking all creation, yes, well, but trust me when I say that in time, you could coerce him, or, show him the way...." Reverend Byle paused to regroup.

"Amen," said Libby.

"Amen," said everyone else, just as quickly.

Reverend Byle shrugged. "Amen."

Libby had written an epitaph, which Peyton had chiseled into stone and then embedded in the dirt at her chosen site. She read from the stone:

Here lies Maurice Flagler
In life and death he was a haggler
Lived in Saltine but came from Frink
And in the end what killed him was drink
1926–1999

Glory applauded. "Well," she looked around, "in my book that man, and these tributes, deserve a round of applause." Mayor Nuckle was next, then everyone stood clapping at the stone.

"Glory, thank you. Thank you, everyone." Libby blushed. "Please stay for coffee and cake."

Skulk was the word Libby used to describe Ed Schotz's movements. He wasn't stalking her, exactly. But she couldn't call him friendly anymore, either. He was lurking.

"Aw, Doll," Peyton said. "It's because you married me and broke his heart."

What killed him was drink? Ha! thought Schotz. The Deputy Sheriff spent his banked vacation time on the Polk property in his fabricated porta-blind noting the comings and goings of Mr. and Mrs. Neworth.

Just up the road that evening, at the pink and white double wide, after a dinner of baked chicken, fried rice, and Apple Betty, Libby took Peyton's hand and gazed into his eyes. She said, "Sweetcakes, you'll never guess."

Peyton nodded. "Tell me."

"You don't want to guess?"

Peyton's bowels groaned. He guessed replicants were invading, or she wanted him gone, or someone scary from his past had turned up, or that *Eddie* had found Stripes's remains, or–"

"I'm pregnant."

Libby might as well have told him the fridge was on the fritz.

"Peyton, are you listening?" She squeezed his hand. "We're having a baby."

Peyton sat and stared, smile forming on his face.

"Earth calling Peyton," said Libby. "Hellooooo?"

"What?"

Libby giggled. She said this slowly. "You are going to be a Papa."

Peyton paused, then he smiled, then he laughed. His laughter grew and he couldn't stop. He took his hand from

Libby's and jumped up out of the dinette chair, laughing too hard to breathe. He gave Libby a skinny-man bear-hug, bumped open the front door, and leaped down the steps into the moonless night. Libby followed to the landing and watched Peyton rip off every piece of clothing he wore and waltz naked in the dust under a new moon. He sang, "*Rock-a-bye baby, on the rebar treetop....*" and started again to laugh. "Get your pregnant body down here, Doll," he said, "and dance with the Great Inseminator."

For six weeks, Ed had sat in that box sweating and thirsty, cursing the universe and reciting the Pledge of Allegiance to stay awake. And now, while Peyton jiggled his jewels on public display under the stars in the warm evening air, Ed, on his first night back at work, missed the show.

"What on earth are you doing?" Libby stood next to the freezer on the back stoop and watched Peyton working a shovel into the ground.

"Planting a garden." Peyton had started turning over soil, such as it was: dry, saline, devoid of biomass. He was shirtless and sinewy, laboring as if his life depended on it.

"It's not even light yet."

"Our baby is going to need fresh vegetables." And Peyton wanted Libby to see he was taking care of their family.

Libby admired this kind of industry, but she was confused. "I don't think babies eat fresh vegetables."

"Well, when he's older, then, he will."

"He?"

Peyton stopped digging and turned to Libby. "Maybe I'll learn to like green beans, Doll." He grinned big.

Libby thought, I've always wanted to taste fresh green beans. "You're going to need a tall fence to keep out the critters."

"Yep." That was common sense. "Already talked to Señor Hector senior."

"You've been to town?"

"Stopped by before work yesterday," said Peyton. "He'll put in an order."

"But–"

"Eight or ten trolleys from now."

I should be pleased, thought Libby. Peyton planting vegetables. Some men would get drunk. "Don't hurt yourself, Sweetcakes."

"Mr. Universe doesn't get hurt."

"Mr. Universe," said Libby, "doesn't plant beans."

It took the full two weeks but Peyton broke up a patch of ground, hacking chunks of petrified earth into rubble, pounding rubble into fine grains of recoverable dirt. He dug a flat-bottomed hole, three feet deep and about two thirds the size of a single wide, starting from the center and working outward in all directions. He'd envisioned the plot so that dirt, manure, and peat could be pushed in from the perimeter.

"We could fill it with water," said Libby, "and make a swimming pool."

"Or a pig sty."

With the credit Glory extended him until his regular pay day, Tuesdays and Fridays Peyton bought groceries and meat other than chicken. Depending on what hadn't sold and was about to expire, ribs or steak or pork chops, whatever had been defrosted and displayed, was discounted so Peyton took it home. Libby ate animal protein. Glory broke even.

And when Deputy Schotz blustered around the loading dock and inquired of Glory, "Has that skinny-ass given you any flack?"

Glory had only good things to say. "He works hard. He don't steal. Now go away."

Frustrated, Ed one day knocked on the double wide door and said to Libby, "Your husband. What's he doing? Digging Stripes a grave?"

"You are a cruel, cruel man, Deputy," Libby said, "and I won't dignify your accusation with a response." She slammed the door and burst into tears. "Hormones," she told herself.

He'd returned to work, but before his shift, Ed sat in his blind, swallowing the skin that formed on his cold coffee. He watched Peyton wrestle iron staples from wood uprights and separate rusty chicken wire from an abandoned corral.

"Evidence," he said. "I need evidence," Ed's mind parboiled by the heat of obsession.

Peyton slid the staples in his seat pocket and rolled the wire as it came loose. Four feet wide and with an inch grid, he estimated, it would do just fine to keep out most any burrowing animal and was probably of sufficient length that he wouldn't need to buy additional in order to line the bottom and sides of the garden hole. The deep ground may be hard as rock, but Peyton wasn't going to let some resolute creature tunnel its way under his vegetables and invite the brood to share a banquet of tender roots.

During Libby's fourth month along, Maevis Deeler, the Niland midwife, delivered a baby in Frink then continued on the spur to Saltine for an initial consultation. "Not the best time to be pregnant," she said, "the world's in sorry shape. Climate Change. Overpopulation. Dead fish." She sniffed her chamomile infusion. "So tell me," she looked across the dinette table at Libby, "how've you been feeling?"

Libby blinked. "A little scared, I guess."

"Houston, we have a problem." Maevis laughed. "Just kidding. First time's always scary."

"But I'm trying real hard to do everything right."

"Everybody does, Hon," Maevis said. "Usually works, too. This tea–it *is* tea, isn't it?–it won't make you puke, will it?"

"Hasn't yet."

While Peyton sprinkled manure onto the ground over the chicken wire, layering it between fill dirt, using his shovel to mulch the strata with peat, Maevis examined Libby and pronounced her normal. "No cervical dilation. You're looking good."

Another five months, thought Libby. Five months. I need to *stay* looking good. But she was always tired and her ankles were swollen by noon. She'd spit venom at Peyton several times when he'd tried to caress her breasts that seemed to grow heavier and more tender daily, and she couldn't hold her bladder. At least once a day Libby collapsed and wept. She'd turn up the radio, hoping her baby heard easy listening instead of her moans.

Peyton watched Maevis walk the trail back to the tracks and the pumpers who smoked cigarettes and waited. He kicked debris off the shovel and leaned it against the back stoop, then stepped out of his rubber garden boots and into the kitchen. Peyton said, "Hello, beautiful."

"Oh *please*." Libby sat at the dinette, eyes puffy. She moaned.

"What's wrong, Doll?"

"Here we are, adding to the problem."

Peyton stood at the sink and washed his hands. "We have a problem?"

"It's totally irresponsible."

"You lost me." Peyton sat down.

"The cat's out of the bag, Peyton, and there's no putting Humpty Dumpty back together again," Libby said in a squeak. "Do you understand nothing?"

Peyton reached for Libby's hand. "I understand some things."

Libby pulled her hand back and dropped her head into her arms. "Like what?"

"Like I should get a move on if I want to be on time for work."

"Okay. What else?"

"Well, like how a person won't turn into a replicant if he eats fresh vegetables." Peyton grinned.

Libby lifted her head. "How do you know?"

He grinned even bigger. "It's a well-known biological fact, Doll."

Libby pursed her top lip and looked at Peyton for a long moment. She said, "I need to put my feet up."

Peyton had done a bit of counter-surveillance of his own to learn which evenings Schotz was on regular sheriff's duty. He'd asked, in casual conversation with Glory, about Ed's route, if he ever varied his patrol.

Glory had said, "You're talking about Ed, here, Peyton. He'd have to develop an imagination first."

So before work one afternoon, Peyton stopped and bought a bag of dry plaster. "Got a couple of dents to fix in the kitchen walls," he told Señor Hector senior, who nodded his approval.

"I admire a man who takes care of things," Señor Hector senior said.

"Yes, sir," said Peyton. "A man's got to take care of things."

And that night, after dinner, when Libby took her shower, Peyton prepared to take care of things. He filled a small bottle with water, grabbed a spoon from a kitchen drawer full of two dozen unmatched spoons, and, from the rear of the cupboard a large coffee cup that neither he nor Libby ever used. He hoped she wouldn't miss the pieces and put the lot into a plastic bag with the pound package of plaster. He stashed the contraband amid the clump of buffalo grass where he'd once hidden Stripes's gun.

The following afternoon at work, Peyton asked Glory if she would excuse him fifteen minutes early. "I have a surprise for Libby," he said. "It's kind of just between her and me, but it's our six-month anniversary, and I need–"

"Oh Peyton," said Glory, "you old romantic. Say no more. Leave *twenty* minutes early if you need to."

At 6:40 PM Peyton punched out. He slipped through the loading dock door into the twilight, trusting that Deputy

Schotz was enjoying his coffee break before patrolling the far side of Saltine. Peyton cut across one alley and two yards and down Sidewinder Circle then tippy-toed into the buffalo grass to retrieve his provisions. Libby would be in the kitchen. Peyton crouched and poured water from the bottle into the coffee cup. He remembered a rule: dry into wet, and sprinkled plaster powder into the water and stirred with the spoon. He added a bit more powder for a gloppy consistency, then hightailed it a hundred feet back up Sidewinder Circle to the Polk place and Schotz's blind.

Peyton stood in the dusk, visible to Libby if she looked, but hidden from Polk's front window. He'd counted the day before, and now, with the back of the spoon, he pushed a lug of wet plaster into each the six peep-holes Ed had drilled to surveil the pink and white double wide. Peyton worked fast, hoping coverage was complete. If ever he'd wanted to dance wildly, naked in the night, it was then, but Libby would have dinner ready and part of Peyton's glee was the anonymity of his subterfuge.

Peyton camouflaged the bag and its plunder with his garden tools, then ran back around to the front door and entered with a grin. "Happy Anniversary, Doll," he said. "Six months!"

"Oh, Sweetcakes." Libby smiled. "To you, too. Guess what?"

"Uh, Dodgers won the World Series?"

"Nooooo. The baby kicked today."

Peyton put his arms around Libby from the back and placed his hands on her belly.

"Feels so strange, something alive inside me."

"You know, you can call Glory's anytime I'm there."

"She'll wonder. And if I go telling people, well, I just don't do that kind of thing. It's bad luck."

"Think of it," said Peyton. He leaned into Libby and

rocked her back and forth. "Beans in the dirt. A baby in the oven." And, yes, Schotz losing his marbles.

Peyton still didn't know where he'd come from just over a half year earlier. He guessed it wasn't Los Angeles, a suspicion that counseled caution about stories Libby told of his past and a shake of skepticism when confronted with her notion of truth. Neither of these, however, was any longer of much consequence. Nothing in the past was. He wondered occasionally where he found Nanny, if he had family elsewhere, and why he wasn't more driven to find out. Were he a believer, Peyton might have thanked divine providence for all he'd received. As it was, he felt fortunate to have landed in Libby's pink and white double wide, reprieved that the Township of Saltine hadn't charged him in Stripes's disappearance, and euphoria in anticipation of Papahood. Peyton was proud to serve as proof that the American Dream lived. He grinned. He said, "I've got a surprise for you, too, Doll."

Libby struggled free of Peyton's embrace and turned around from the sink. "Where?"

He said, "Close your eyes." The gift had been hidden in his garden tools, and now Peyton pulled from his pocket the small foil-wrapped box he'd bought from Hector two months earlier. "Okay." He held his hand out toward Libby. "Open your eyes."

Libby looked at the box in Peyton's hand and her jaw began to wobble. She couldn't make her hand reach or her feet budge toward Peyton. She met Peyton's gaze and then everything went blurry and she was tasting her own tears. The only force that could move her was gravity, and, light though she was, even at five months pregnant, Libby's world spun for a moment, then went dark as her knees gave way and she crumbled to her bottom. She caved backward, her belly a small mountain rising, and banged her head against the linoleum.

"Libby! Libby! Oh, Doll," Peyton said her name over and over as he crouched to her side and worked his hand under her head. He could see a vein in her neck pulsing in regular rhythm. He brought his ear close to her mouth. He said, "Thank God you're breathing."

"Of course I'm breathing," Libby said loudly into Peyton's ear. "What is –. What are you doing?"

"Doll," Peyton pulled back. "I think you fainted."

"Impossible," said Libby. She moved her eyes to look around. "I've never fainted in my life and I'm certainly not about to start now."

"I should get Doc," said Peyton. The last time Peyton wanted to get Doc, it was Stripes hurt and horizontal.

"Would you look at that molding?" said Libby. She'd turned her head and was eye-level with the vinyl kick-board under the sink. "It needs serious scrubbing."

"Please, not right now," said Peyton.

"I didn't say *now*, Peyton."

"Let me carry you to the bed." Peyton slid his arm under Libby's neck and reached with the other arm to cradle her knees, but Libby stopped him.

"I'm not an invalid." Although she didn't exactly feel in control of her body, either. She struggled to sit and he propped her up. "I'm okay. I had a moment, but it's passed. Just help me stand, will you?"

Peyton stood. He and Libby each held onto the others' wrists, like slipknots, and Peyton pulled Libby to her feet. He steadied her until she could balance, then led her toward the bedroom. He pulled back the spread and helped her get situated. He asked, "You want me to find Doc?"

"Peyton, I'll be fine."

"You sure?" He straightened the blanket. "Maevis Deeler?"

"Would you stop?" Libby inhaled. "No!"

"Anything?"

Hadn't she just said, No? Men should go through this, this bodily insult, thought Libby, and let's see just how long they remain cheerful and composed. Libby wiggled around until her pillow felt right. She said, "Well, I suppose there's still the matter of my anniversary present...."

Consistent with Peyton's determination to live for the moment, he erased from consciousness Libby's spill and found the tiny foil-wrapped package under the dinette table. He sat on the bed and watched Libby pick at the tape then flatten the wrapping paper. She looked up at Peyton with the slightest of flirtatious smiles, then opened the box.

Peyton said, "I hope you like it, Doll."

Libby's lower jaw wobbled again.

"I thought you should have a ring from me...."

"Oh Sweetcakes..."

Peyton took the box from Libby and plucked the thinnest silver band he'd ever seen from the satin fold. "It's not much. But *I'm* not much either–"

"Don't you *ever* say that."

"Okay. How about, the ring is even skinnier than I am." Peyton grinned. "I like rings."

"I'm glad, Peyton."

"I mean love, the circle never ending," said Peyton. "Like that. And now a baby."

Libby held out her left hand.

"It's our angel's halo." Peyton placed the wire-slim ring on Libby's finger, next to the chunky gold one from her collection, the ring she'd married with.

"Perfect," said Libby.

"Isabella Katherine Neworth," said Libby. She listened to the room as if it would say the words back to her. "Audrey Inez Neworth." Again, she paused. "I like that. Audrey Inez Neworth. I'll have to run that past Peyton."

Peyton stood at the door to the kitchen, listening. "Mitchel Maurice Neworth," he said.

Without turning, Libby laughed and said, "Anna Rose Neworth."

"Noah Benjamin Neworth," said Peyton. He didn't move. "Even Maevis Deeler said the baby is a boy."

Libby looked around at Peyton, then turned back to the table. "What does she know?"

"Geoffrey Jonathan Neworth," he said.

"Bella Marguerita Neworth," Libby said.

"I like that one," said Peyton. "You writing these down?"

"I've got all the good ones saved in my head." Libby pointed at her ear.

"Marshall Ambrose Neworth," said Peyton.

"Ambrose?" said Libby. She again turned. "Ambrose?"

Peyton shrugged. Within two minutes he was back raking dirt into the hole and struggling to mulch it well with peat and manure. Along with reading the headlines, the sports page, and the "Ask Aggie" column in the *Imperial Register* during his ten-minute break at Glory's, Peyton had discovered in her dry goods aisle a paperback, copyrighted 1967 and unopened, on backyard gardens. He studied growing cycles, and was determined to put squash seeds into the ground before spring and harvest the first crop in fall.

With shovels full of manure, heavy as bricks, the work of mulching made Peyton sweat but he liked the feeling a manual labor, of having built something he could feel and results he could see. The chicken wire had been a happy miracle of proportion and sufficient to line the floor and walls of the ground-level planting bed. With the addition of peat and manure, though, there'd be more fill-mix than there had been packed dirt chopped out of the hole, so Peyton planned to use several lengths of the fencing he'd ordered to raise the bed.

Ed closed and latched the corrugated aluminum door from inside the blind and slid down onto his folding chair. He set his cup of coffee at his feet but sloshed it over the lip against his trouser leg. "Crap," he said. "Wouldn't you know." It usually took a moment for his eyes to adjust, but the box seemed darker than usual. "What in Jeeber's name...." He blinked and opened his eyes wide. His breath came hard and strained. "Where are my holes?" Ed ran his right palm over the wallboard in front of him and bumped over low, rough mounds where his peep-holes used to be. "Goddamnmotherfuckingsonofabitch!" He twisted up and kicked through the latch on the aluminum door. He tripped over his coffee and cut out of the blind and around to the outside wall facing the pink and white double wide to find shallow knobs of plaster swelling from that surface. "He deserves to die," said Ed. "That lying, murdering, evil-scheming, woman-stealing, bastard, deserves to die."

If Ed had held a grenade, he'd have hurled it at the double wide. He stumbled back around and pivoted his folding chair away from the clogged peepholes. The aluminum door, he let fly loose. He sat in the chair facing out of the blind and stared at the peeling windowless section of the Polk house.

Just that morning, over coffee, Mayor Nuckle had heard Ed grumbling and watched him as he sat shaking his head. Nuckle said, "Stress getting to you, Deputy?"

Cold, thought Ed. After ten years of service. Just so cold. He sat in the blind and fumed. And now *this*. It was the final insult, yet Ed couldn't exactly report filling-in peep-holes as a crime.

Sitting there with the door hanging from one hinge, Ed said with a bitterness that surprised even him, "As if Nucklehead ever knew how to crack a case." He kicked the aluminum door and it rebounded, pushing hot evening air back at him. *He* hadn't changed. Oh, no. It was all of *them* who'd changed. Libby found some loser deadbeat on the tracks and half of Saltine tripped over itself to do him favors.

Glory had cautioned Peyton that Ed might be losing his balance, that something might be seriously wrong and that he, Peyton, might want to keep an eye out.

"I can take care of myself," Peyton had said.

"Then do it for Libby. Ed's the straightest arrow that goes the worst off-course."

Peyton enjoyed shifting Ed's course, and since the pranks seemed to him more playful than cruel, he looked forward to gumming up Ed's works whenever they exposed themselves. He cottoned to subversion, didn't know why, but he enjoyed it and would try to maintain a light touch.

Ed, on the other hand, reacted with all the levity of poisoned fish lying belly-up on the surface. Patrolling the streets or attending to a call, he managed a studied calm. While in uniform, his ironed-and-creased surface betrayed nary a ripple from the turmoil raging in his gut.

So, instead of roasting in the blind, Ed turned to hunkering down in his recliner in front of the television with the sound muted so he could hear if an intruder neared. He had begun to keep the apartment locked and dark, the mini blinds drawn, and the air conditioner on. The phone might ring, but he was certain that Peyton had a bug in the line, so Ed no longer answered. Ed worried Glory might put drugs in his ground beef. He stopped eating anything that didn't come canned: creamed corn, grapefruit juice, spam. He kept his pistol loaded on the coffee table and, on the rare day-off when Ed ventured out for other than work, he'd take the trolley to Frink, even as far as Niland, to interrogate locals hoping to find someone who might provide a key to the misdeeds and transgressions of Peyton Neworth.

The morning was clear and warm. Peyton was at his garden early and he watched, sitting on the ground behind the raised bed, as Ed walked across the scrub toward the rails. The raised bed was full, the surface sat a foot off the ground. The height gave Peyton cover until he raised a fence. It would also give carrots and other roots more room, and the crop would be much easier to work. Peyton smiled.

Libby stood on the porch. She said, "Holy tomatoes, Sweetcakes." She took a deep breath. "Guess you'll have to learn to like vegetables."

"I can feel the power, Doll. I'm a believer. Earth Goddess reigns golden. It's ... it's like...."

"Should I find Reverend Byle for a benediction?"

Peyton threw his hands into the air. "I'm connected to the soil, Doll. I Am Earth!" Peyton jumped up and danced in the dirt under his feet and the sun in the sky. "I Am Earth."

Libby cradled her belly in clasped hands. "Peyton, don't you go getting naked."

At that moment, in a true flash, Earth sent Peyton a blazing epiphany. He needed a fence taller than the one he'd planned: not just a critter repellent, but a barrier, through or over which, no man would be able to see.

While Peyton recalculated his board requirements, Libby stepped into the kitchen and lowered herself into a dinette chair. Two days earlier, her insides had cramped, then relaxed. She'd timed it, and the cramp had lasted for over a minute. And now, again, a cramp. She sat as bent over as her girth would allow. She moaned and she rocked, the pain shooting from her spine to her bladder, then, like that, it eased and she was able to straighten up. Libby felt as though a hand had reached insider her and yanked on her cervix. The spasm lasted barely a minute and left her slightly weak but nothing more. She thought, I'm seven months along. This is practice. The baby is fine, she told herself, and so am I.

Libby pushed herself off the chair and inched to the porch. She said, "Peyton?" But he was at the far end of the raised bed, on his knees with a pencil and tape measure. Libby decided to drop it. The cramp had disappeared.

Peyton looked up. "I'd better get cleaned up for work." He held a package of green bean seeds. "As soon as I get the trellis marked off."

Peyton had spent two week's salary for new fence boards, most of which hadn't arrived yet. He'd planned to drive posts and attach the boards at the windward side of the garden, then use chicken wire elsewhere. With his new plan, however, he was going to have to scavenge for additional wood. The region still had dozens of abandoned shacks in the scrub just outside the town boundary with enough sun and wind-carved timber to make an interesting, if not downright artistic, enclosure. He'd ask Glory if scrounging were legal, and Señor Hector senior if he could cancel the order for undelivered planks. Peyton would save the money. He'd buy something special for Libby.

When Peyton came out of the bedroom, showered and bursting with love of peat moss, mankind, Mother Earth, and Libby, she was spreading Miracle Whip on sandwich bread.

"It's egg salad with pickle relish and minced banana," she said.

Peyton stared at his wife. This must be what Glory had warned him to expect. "Sounds adventurous," said Peyton. "I'll pour the milk." He made a mental note to buy a pound of salami, then wondered if his beloved would serve it doused in canned peaches.

*

Three weeks later, Peyton was walking what he figured would be his final foray into the scrub for raw fence material. He'd scoured semi-circles in a progressively wide radius from the pink and white double wide and had amassed three large piles of usable wood, though Libby made it known she was not exactly pleased. "Why can't we go ahead and buy the boards," she'd said. "They'd be so much more neighborly."

This, Peyton thought, from a woman whose home is filled with multiples of junk that won't fit on her rebar tree.

The gritty wind had eroded the softer surfaces on the secreted planks, leaving knots and sun-bleached striations of grain that Peyton, when he looked closely, thought quite beautiful, mystical, even. The swellings he associated with a pregnant belly. The arcs and swirls he thought of as life's random deviations. He favored the found wood, but for durability-sake would insert a plain, new plank at odd intervals. Older pieces would have to be overlapped and nailed together to make a tall enough barrier, but nails were cheap. The more Peyton thought about it, the more he liked the improbability of it all. The question was: should the better-looking side face inward, or outward?

"Why can't we go ahead and buy new boards," Libby said. "We have to think about curb appeal."

"Doll, relax, Give it a chance. If you don't like it, I'll change it."

"I like to present a polished face to the world, but you, Peyton, are not quite so particular. I mean… it's not something I would have imagined of you, but...." Libby sighed. "It's your project and only my public humiliation at stake."

When Peyton began work in the garden that Saturday, he noticed Ed's blind was gone. "Point," he said. Peyton sunk posts and sequenced his planks around the perimeter. The bed itself was 20′×20′, and the enclosure he planned was to be 30′×40′. Peyton wanted five feet of access aisle on left, right, and far sides of the fence, and fifteen feet open space near the house where he'd keep a small shed for his tools, and the gate padlocked.

On his fourth morning of fence work, while he was nailing fragments of wood together, Ed walked up. He stood several feet away, waiting for Peyton to hammer down, hoping to see fingers pounded. Peyton knelt to fit one piece of wood with another. He'd decided to keep the top edges uneven, which might give Libby a migraine, but was in harmony with the natural irregularity of the planks. The sides, however, had to be impervious to peepers. Peyton fitted the fragments and slivers carefully, then slammed the hammer down.

Ed said, "You got a permit?"

Instead of bringing the hammer down again, on his fingers, Peyton let go of the handle mid-air, tossing it clear over and behind him.

"Goddamn it, Neworth."

"Whoa, Eddie," said Peyton. "You surprised me." He jumped up. dusted his palms on his thighs, smiled, and held out his right hand. "Sneaking up on a fella like that."

"Damn you, Neworth."

Peyton pulled his hand back. "Seen Libby?"

Ed snapped to. "She'd better not be missing." Ed wondered if he could prove in court that Peyton had provoked the punches he desperately wanted to deliver.

"That's not funny, Ed." Peyton took a moment to look at the ground. Then he looked up and laughed. "She's just the most pregnant lady in Saltine."

Ed forced his breathing into a regular, cool rhythm. "I'm here simply to see the permit for your fence."

Peyton looked at Ed. "Well then...." Peyton signaled Ed to follow, but the Deputy went only as far as the back porch while Peyton walked into the kitchen. He opened the silverware drawer. "Nope. Not there." He opened the condiments cabinet. "Not there either."

Ed stood at the screen door and watched this piece of theater scripted just for him.

"You on the clock, Ed?" Peyton opened another drawer. "Hmmm."

Ed watched Peyton's every move, every shift in gaze. He heard every sigh.

"Lib-by," called Peyton. "Doll, could I trouble you?" Peyton held his index finger up to Ed, One moment, *please*.

Libby scuffed barefoot from the bedroom into the kitchen. She wore a floral house dress and her hair was pulled back in a ponytail. "Why all the noise, Peyton?" Then she saw Ed. "Oh, my. Peyton, you didn't tell me–"

"He wants to see my Permit."

"The fence permit, Mrs. Neworth."

Libby shook her head. "A permit for everything nowadays. Why do we need a permit, Ed?"

"I don't make the laws, ma'am."

"You just choose which get enforced," said Libby. She waddled back into the bedroom.

Peyton looked at Ed and shrugged. "Hormones."

"The permit?"

From her night table, Libby grabbed a piece of paper and handed it to Peyton. She said, "It cost us $8.00. It's signed by Mayor Nuckle. It had better be legal."

From Peyton, Ed took the dot matrix-generated receipt. He held it up to the sun and turned it obliquely for a true ink signature. "Looks real, but you never know." He handed back the paper. "What is it you expect to plant, Mr. Neworth."

Not that it was Deputy Schotz's business. Peyton reached into his back pocket and pulled out an empty, crumpled seed packet. "Beans."

They were, in fact, already sewn. Furrows had been dug, the trellis built, the self-timed soaker hoses laid. Beans, carrots, potatoes, tomatoes, and zucchini were labeled atop the moist brown soil. Peyton would see sprouts by the time he finished his fence, and maybe even sell some of his produce in town.

SNAKE IN THE GARDEN

That evening, Peyton jogged home from work, excited to see his Eden. He'd spent three hours scrubbing Glory's meat trays and walk-in cooler in reverie over the fence. It would be a work of art, a unique expression of his creative self. He arrived home and stood at the side of Big Pink to admire the work-in-progress. Maybe he ought to extend the trellis around the north side. But then it might block the sun, well, nothing really blocked the sun. He could decide later. He hopped onto the back porch, stepped out of his shoes next to the door, and walked in through the laundry room to find Libby curled up on the kitchen floor. Peyton dropped his pound of sliced salami and dove to her side. "Doll?" He held her head in his hands.

Libby shook and moaned.

"Doll, can you hear me?"

Libby knotted her forehead. "You! *Ouuuuuh.*" She cried out and swung a limp fist at Peyton. "You did this." She let out another shriek of pain, then her eyes rolled back.

"Oh God." Peyton watched for breath. "Oh God." He lowered Libby's head and ran out the front door. "Help!" He raced up Sidewinder Circle toward the Polk place whose steps he took in one leap. He pounded on the door. "Help!"

Marge Polk opened. "Mr. Neworth?"

"The baby. Something's wrong." Peyton couldn't breathe. "No phone. Call Doc. We have no phone. Call Glory. Tell them to come. Please, please. Just do it, please."

Peyton jumped to the ground before Marge Polk could respond and ran back to Libby. He flew into the kitchen and lifted her head. "Doll. Doc's coming. Just hold on. Hold on, Doll. Oh God."

Libby exhaled a deep, tortured groan, then let out another scream splintered by spasms. Her forehead dripped with sweat, her eyes were rimmed in red.

"I can't move," she said. "Peyton...."

"Libby. Oh baby." If only he hadn't stopped to gaze at his own work.

Libby exhaled a cry of contraction, then one of pure anguish. "I'm sorry, aaaaaaahhhhhh." The floor underneath her was glazed with spilled orange juice and her water broke to pool under her left hip.

Peyton grabbed the apron and wadded it up with his free hand. "Libby, Libby, put your head on this and let your body relax. I'm going to turn you on your back then get pillows." Peyton leapt for the bed pillows and slid back to arrange them on the floor. "Try to breathe, Libby, don't let go. Stay with me. Here, roll into my arms. Keep your knees bent."

"Mr. Neworth." Marge Polk was at the door. She cracked it and looked in.

Libby tried to let her abdominal muscles relax, but she convulsed in a cramp. "The baby...." She howled, choked on her own saliva, then turned her head and gagged to the side, over and over.

"Oh my God," Marge said. She stood and watched. "I called."

Peyton nodded without taking his eyes off Libby. From his knees he reached a hand into the refrigerator for the bottle of apple juice. He flipped open the top and put the bottle to Libby's lips. "Drink."

Libby took a sip but choked again and coughed. Her eyes closed and her body seized.

*

Glory ran from the Grocery Store, charging up Sidewinder Circle, breathing hard, forcing herself to keep moving forward. She mounted the steps, pushed Marge out of the doorway, and rushed to Libby's side. She said to Peyton, "Where's Doc?"

"Coming."

"When did this start?"

"I don't know. Oh God, it's my fault. I stopped to look at the garden."

"Put water on a burner," she said. "It's not your fault. And bring me towels."

"Should I call Maevis?"

Glory shouted at Peyton, "Towels, water, *now*."

Glory knelt low to the floor. "Libby," she said. "It's Glory. I'm here to help."

"My baby," choked Libby, her face wet with heat and pain.

"Breathe," said Glory. "Deeply. Exhale all the way and try to relax, and when you have a contraction, breathe quick and shallow."

"I'm one big contrac–ahhhhhhhhooouuuuuuuu...." Libby trailed off.

"Shallow quick breaths," said Glory.

"It's. All. Contraction." Libby pushed out these words, one between each shudder, before her eyes closed again and her body loosened.

Glory had delivered five babies in her lifetime. But this wasn't like anything she'd seen, Libby's abdomen looked angular and lumpy. Glory had a bad feeling she didn't dare share with Peyton. Glory gently examined the birth canal and felt something that couldn't possibly have been the crown of a head. She put her hands on Libby's stomach and tried to figure the baby's position. The head was in the wrong place, up against Libby's rib cage, so what was it she'd felt?

Libby, on her back and propped with pillows, whimpered.

"Peyton," said Glory. "Listen to me." She had to yell. "Peyton!"

Peyton stopped fussing with the tea kettle and stared at Glory.

"Run and tell Doc to hurry."

"But–"

"Now!"

Peyton backed out the door, then sprinted down the road. He tore across two yards and the alley toward town. Dogs barked and window shades parted. Tears ruptured from his eyes to blur his sight. When he ran into Doc, Peyton was able only to pant and weep. Doc handed his bag to Peyton and followed, keeping up the best he could but arriving minutes after Peyton.

Peyton had flattened himself against the kitchen wall. His nose dripped. Tears mixed with saliva. He clutched at the door molding behind him.

Libby lay on the floor and convulsed. She screamed in pain and pushed with her contractions.

"Get down here and talk to your wife," ordered Glory. "Tell her what you've been meaning to tell her. She can hear you."

Peyton dropped to his knees and carefully lifted Libby's shoulders into his arm. He stroked her forehead with his free hand and put his cheek against hers. He whispered in her ear, "You've given me everything. Stay with me."

Peyton could see only Libby, white as bone. He held his breath for a moment, then sobbed, Libby in his arms, his trembles shook them both. He rocked her, calling her name until again her muscles seized. Libby shrieked and Peyton could envision nothing but breaking bones and tearing flesh.

"Push. Come on," said Glory. "Push!"

Libby let out a cry and then took a breath and growled,

but she pushed and Glory pulled a baby, feet first, from Libby's body. She straightened the rubbery little arms, scooped mucous from the baby's mouth and nose, and patted his back until he let out a squeal.

Libby collapsed. Peyton's eyes ran tears. "Thank you."

Glory took the kitchen scissors, cut and tied the umbilical cord. She sat in shock on a dinette chair, holding a tiny baby boy who breathed perfectly and slept, wrapped in a towel, against her shoulder.

Doc climbed the steps and let himself in. Orange juice and afterbirth covered the kitchen floor, table legs, and everybody. "My God," he said. "What happened?"

One of Libby's arms escaped Peyton's rocking embrace.

Doc's eyes widened. He looked at Glory.

"The baby's alive." Glory's jaw quivered.

Doc looked at Peyton, who sobbed and held his wife. Doc grabbed his bag from where Peyton had dropped it on the kitchen counter. He knelt beside Libby and put the stethoscope to her chest. "She has a heartbeat." He positioned her head, pinched closed her nose, and began mouth-to-mouth.

Libby lay unconscious for what seemed to Peyton an eternity, but Doc kept breathing into her mouth and in less than a minute, she blinked and took air on her own. Doc wrapped her in blankets and spoke. "Make yourself comfortable, Libby. Don't try to get up. I'll be right here."

"My baby," she said.

"He's fine," said Doc.

"A boy," breathed Libby.

"Peyton," said Doc.

He looked at Doc for a moment, then shuddered and began to breathe more normally.

Doc gave him a mild sedative anyway. He offered Glory something, too, but she shook her head.

Doc raised Peyton to his feet then led him into the bedroom. He sat Peyton on the edge of the mattress. Peyton kicked off his shoes and, without a word, lay down and slept.

"Where's Peyton?" said Libby.

"Peyton's okay and so is the baby."

Libby lifted her head to look down at her body. Her eyes widened.

"Your son is perfect." Doc kept Libby on her back. "We need to make sure you're okay."

"You'll want to check him, too," Glory said to Doc. "And the tie off."

Doc spoke to Libby. "Are you fully conscious?"

Libby nodded and rubbed her eyes. Doc helped Libby to scoot to where she could lean against the cabinets. "Are you in pain?"

"I'm sore." She looked around.

Doc lay the baby against Libby's chest, showing her how best to cradle him.

"He's so beautiful." She looked beyond the infant. "Oh my goodness." Libby's eyes grew wide at the sight of the floor.

*

Peyton didn't wake until the next morning. He opened his eyes to see Libby's back under the sheet and thought, I must have dreamt the whole horrible event. Peyton eased out of bed feeling dizzy. He walked out to the kitchen.

Doc sat at the dinette table. The two men locked eyes. Doc said nothing but watched while Peyton's brows narrowed and he shifted his head the slightest angle.

Doc cleared his throat. "I gave you a mild sedative. You slept."

"No." Peyton began to panic. "Oh no. Ooooooh no."

"Get hold, Peyton." Doc stood and braced Peyton by the shoulders.

"What–" Peyton swallowed.

"Breathe, Peyton," said Doc. "All the way in and all the way out. Your son is with Libby, in your bed."

"Are they okay?" He turned.

"Yes." Doc restrained him. "Everything's fine. Everyone slept, except Glory and me."

The night before, Doc had held the newborn while Glory gave Libby a sponge bath before putting her to bed. She threw all the bloody clothing and towels into the washer and scoured the kitchen. When she left to go home, after midnight, she carried the trash bag. She used her store dumpster, then let herself inside the grocery to pick up a package of diapers, two cans of formula, and a bottle before walking back up Sidewinder Circle near dawn.

"I only remember ... well, I ran to get you, and Marge Polk, and Libby screaming more than I could bear, then holding her." Peyton looked around, unfocused. "We tried to do everything right..."

"And you did," said Doc. "Do you hear me?" He watched Peyton for signs of shock. "Your son wanted to land on his feet is all."

That morning, Peyton gave Libby a kiss and held his son in his arms. He stared at the round head and the apple face, the pursed lips. He pushed the blanket back and one of the baby's hands reached and curled itself around Peyton's pinkie finger. "He doesn't cry. Is that normal?"

Peyton gazed at his wife as if this miracle were the first of its kind. Libby's pale face and quiet body ... she was the Libby he'd married, but somehow didn't look at all like the woman he'd known a day earlier, and he caught himself wishing Stripes could be there.

The child made a noise that Peyton would have sworn was laughter. "Doll," Peyton murmured close to Libby's ear. "Maybe he's hungry."

Mayor Nuckle stood behind his desk. He clutched his Stetson and ran his fingertips over the rim. He looked up. "I hate having to be the one to tell him."

Doc balked. "Hey. Don't look at me."

Deputy Schotz stood in the doorway in pressed uniform, hand on holster.

Doc picked up his bag.

"Stay," said Nuckle. "Ed, you come in and sit down."

Schotz walked in then leaned at the edge of the desk.

Nuckle looked at Doc, then turned to Ed. "Libby gave birth to a boy last night."

"Yep," said Schotz. "Another population explosion."

Doc watched Schotz's mouth twitch. She'd been pregnant for nine months. A birth was inevitable. "She's your friend, Ed."

"She was. That's right."

"Deputy," said Nuckle.

Ed nodded. "I'm late for my patrol."

"I could to arrange for someone if you want to talk," said Doc.

"Talk? About what?" Schotz stared, waiting for an answer that didn't come. He walked out and closed the door of the air-conditioned office behind him. He cleaned his sunglasses, peered around, then headed down the Paseo.

"He's hurting," said Doc. "You might keep an eye on him."

Schotz walked into the scrub and straight to the rails in time to wave down the trolley. Two hours later, at the south end of the spur, his uniform dusty and sweat-stained, Schotz occupied a stool at Calipatria's *c-Bar-s* making fast work of his third beer.

The guy on the next barstool said, "A man with no plan. That's me." He turned to Schotz. "You got a plan?"

Schotz raised his index finger into the air between them–one moment *please,* and he took that moment to consider. He pondered the question, sat straighter, and tweaked his head to the right. His shoulders tensed and his forehead creased, and by the time he turned to look at his inquisitor, Schotz's eyes were sharp. "I am working on one."

It wasn't enough Asshole murdered Stripes. But then marry his Libby and knock her up? "Bartender!" Schotz pointed at his empty beer glass.

In his seedling of a plan, Ed had quit his job and closed out what remained of his retirement account. Just the thought made him smile and dulled the pounding in his head. He would use his law enforcement skills to track down the God's truth about Asshole Peyton Neworth and prove to Libby his everlasting devotion.

The owner of the *c-Bar-c* respected the law and, because of the uniform, he ignored Ed's grumbling and heavy sighs. He pitied the guy for whatever tragedy must have come his way and lost count after serving Ed's fifth beer and sixth shot of tequila. By closing time, Ed had started talking about murder and revenge. The proprietor wanted no trouble and put Ed to bed on the upholstered bench of a corner booth.

The following morning, he found Schotz back on a barstool.

"Whoa, man. You might slow down."

"Hair of the coyote. Just this one," said Schotz. "And I'm gone." He swallowed a final mouthful of beer and slapped five ten-dollar bills on the bar. "Thanks for the hospitality."

"You got somewhere to go?"

"No."

The morning was cool by local standards. Ed took deep breaths to clear his head and walked north along the spur back toward Saltine composing, as he went, his letter of resignation. It recounted every imagined offense committed against him by anyone ever, and the words of apology that should have been offered him but weren't. He repeated–verbatim he'd have sworn–accusations of laziness Saltine citizens had hurled at him and their comments of a personal nature about his growing gut. Each of his suggested improvements to civic and cultural life had been unconscionably ignored. He credited himself with maintaining order in an essentially lawless town and listed what he saw as miscarriages of justice where criminals were let go and innocent people were fined. His resignation grew long with allegations and digressions, and, by the time he'd compiled what must have been page eight or ten, he could no longer remember what he'd alleged in his rambling on page five. So, as he entered Saltine and walked up Albatross Avenue to his apartment, Ed decided on, "I quit. My final day was yesterday."

He was done. Done with humiliation and rejection and bullshit. He unlocked the door of his apartment and entered the curtained room that smelled of beer, microwaved spillovers, and a sour bathroom. He washed his face and underarms, noticing for the first time how frayed his towel was, and hummed a country song from the radio, what was it? *Take this Job and Shove It.*

Ed folded shirts, jeans, socks, jockey shorts, and a small blanket into his old Kelty backpack. He ripped the wad of cash–his retirement account–from under the silverware drawer where he'd taped it, rolled and slid it in a toothpaste box, and threw it into a canvas duffel with toiletries. He dressed in Wranglers, a belt with a silver and turquoise buckle, a blue, short-sleeved polo shirt, and a western style hat—had to have the hat. When he'd bothered to dress for the outside, he'd worn jeans and a polo shirt just about every off-duty day for years, but, for the first time he could remember, he felt comfortable. He called the church and told Mrs. Byle to come and collect what she could sell at the annual flea market. He advised his landlord, "Keep the cleaning deposit," and handed over the key.

With his resignation notice, Ed stuffed his beer-stained and slept-in uniform into a plastic grocery bag and left the package at the Mayor's door, who'd pass it on to the County. With that, Ed sprung himself from the tyranny of an ill-fitting straightjacket of routine, released from another minute among folks with no respect.

After high school, with Stripes's urging, Libby had agreed to eat lunch with Ed then go to the Magic Lantern for a matinee.

Encouraged by one date and Stripe's approval, Ed pursued Libby for years, writing off the rebuffs as playing-hard-to-get which is what Ed's mother had said Libby was doing, and expecting one day she'd relent. Then Ed's mother fell ill. He was offered a job by Imperial County in his hometown of Saltine. He'd stayed another ten years. But, no more.

"Damn," said Ed, excited about tossing his uniform in the lap of the law, and how different the world outside was going to be. No need to say farewell to any of the locals, he walked once more across the shrub to the rails.

The trolley left Calipatria every weekday morning more-or-less at 8:00. He'd catch it north as it came through Saltine.

"What are you doing?" said Glory.

"It's four o'clock," said Peyton. "I'm punching in."

"With Libby and a newborn at home you're going to clean out the butcher case?"

"Libby told me to go away. She's not feeling well."

"How is she not feeling well?"

"Slight fever. Belly tenderness. Won't let me touch her. She's tired and told me to go."

"You should call Doc."

"She forbid me to." Peyton smiled, but he looked as if he might start to cry. "She said, what did I expect? She'd just had her insides ripped out."

Glory considered calling Doc herself. No, it wasn't her place. "Did you hear?"

"I've heard nothing for days."

"Ed's gone."

"Gone?"

"He quit his job and left town."

"He what?"

"Nuckle told Doc, who told Hector, who told me that his note gave no reason, so I can only guess."

"What would you guess?"

"Plain and simple? Ed lost."

"Yeah," said Peyton. He nodded. "I might have rubbed it in."

"And now the little one. That man never did get it." Glory thought for a moment then shook her head. "So, what are you going to name the boy?"

Peyton spoke normally, but because of Ed's sudden disappearance, he could feel his intestines turn liquid. "Libby wants to name him Deckard."

"Deckard?"

"Deckard Maurice Neworth. She said it's a heroic name."

Glory sighed. "She always was different."

"As long as he's healthy and happy."

Peyton excused himself for the bathroom and wondered how much a part he had played in Schotz's exit. They'd had two, three small exchanges since he'd plastered the peepholes. Peyton played a low-key but maybe a little bit serious game of gotcha. Who could know what went through Schotz's head.

"I'll be putting together some baby things to send home with you."

"Glory – "

"Don't argue. If I couldn't afford to do it, I wouldn't."

*

Two shopping bags sat by the punch-clock. Glory had filled one with baby bottles, Pampers, corn starch talc, Q-tips, Johnson's baby oil, wipes, Desitin, a recipe for a casserole with the required can of tuna, mushroom soup, and egg noodles. Señor Hector senior figured Libby had all the spoons and bowls she'd ever need, so he pulled from stock a Disney mobile for above the crib and an assortment of Tupperware and cleaning supplies, then wrapped a bow around a new, boxed Bottle Warmer.

"Glory." Peyton stood, holding his time card, looking at the bags. "Glory, this is way too much."

"No one asked your opinion."

"Thank you." Such kindness. His recollections had been frustratingly vague, but somewhere in the past, along the way he'd experienced generosity because Glory and Hector's actions resonated. Precisely what community life *should* feel like.

He slipped his arms through the hand holds so the

bags dangled from his elbows while his hands gripped the bottle warmer. Peyton walked his normal route, bags bumping against his hips and thighs, the box resting like Deckard on his forearm. Peyton spoke to the rhythm of his steps.

Beloved son,
You fully-baked bun,
Today you breathe,
Tomorrow you'll teethe....

Peyton mounted the steps to Big Pink. "Doll...." he called. "Deckard.... You won't believe what Glory and Hector did...." He set the gifts on the kitchen table and walked into the bedroom. "Libby?"

Libby lay on her left side, curled around Deckard who slept in his own blanket. She opened her red-rimmed eyes then closed them again. Peyton moved closer. He didn't sit. "Doll?" Libby shuddered. He felt her forehead. "Oh, oh no." Her face was burning. Peyton fell to his knees and wrapped his arms around her shivering body. "Libby, Doll, you're feverish." He changed the damp blanket for a dry one. "Don't move. I'll get Doc."

Peyton thought to take Deckard with him, then didn't. He ran through the kitchen, leapt off the landing, and tore across the dry field toward downtown, oblivious to window shades curling open, dogs barking, and the rising smell of dinners cooking. Peyton wheezed and called, "Doc! Doc! Help!" Peyton stumbled in without knocking, grabbed the black bag, took Doc by the arm and pulled him along. Through his gasps, Peyton said, "Doc, it's real this time."

*

Peyton crouched, his back against the bedroom wall, wondering how his wonderful life and perfect moment could unhinge so quickly. He begged the God he didn't think he believed-in for an explanation.

Doc slid a thermometer into Libby's mouth then listened to her lungs and heart. "Her lungs are congested. Temp's 102°. We have to get her fever down. Peyton! Wake up! Get a towel, wet it cold, wring it out, and bring it to me."

Peyton did what he was told.

"Hold your son."

Peyton reached across the bed and gathered a squirming Deckard into his arms.

Doc snapped the twisted towel flat and draped it along Libby's back. "I'm giving her antibiotics." He emptied a syringe into her shoulder then wrapped a cuff around her upper arm. Libby's blood pressure had always read below normal. It now registered 200/113. Doc glanced up at Peyton.

Peyton rested Deckard on his forearm and rocked gently. One tiny hand escaped the blanket. "You hungry?" Had Libby been able to nurse? He nudged the cotton blanket away from Deckard's round apple face and looked into his large brown eyes.

"No nursing after the antibiotics," said Doc.

Two hours earlier, Peyton had left work full of gratitude. "I don't understand."

Doc closed his eyes for a moment and when he opened them he gazed down at Libby. He'd been her physician since she was a youngster. He'd substituted as a father-figure when Stripes went on week-long benders. He'd watched Libby grow up. After it collapsed, he'd argued in favor of repairing Borax Creek Bridge, offering a dozen crisis scenarios as reasons, but the County never came through with funding.

"Stay here," said Doc. "Warm a bottle of formula. I'm going to make a call."

Doc hurried up Sidewinder Circle to the Polk place and pounded on the door.

"Marge!" said Doc. "We have an emergency. I need to phone Mecca. I'll pay you." Doc knew where the phone sat. He pointed at the TV. "Turn it down?"

"Yes," said Doc. "I'm the GP in Saltine. We have an emergency. I'm calling for your life-flight helicopter." He was put on hold. "Yes. We have an emergency in Saltine...."

"What is your emergency?"

"A new mother with sepsis, barely responsive."

"The copter is on its way to Los Angeles with two injured in a car crash. I can put you on the list."

If only they'd fixed the bridge....

Peyton hugged his son to his chest and sat next to his wife. He spoke in a whisper.

Come back to us, Libby, and stay awhile,

Deckard and I, we need your smile.

Doc put his hand on Peyton's shoulder. "Some women develop a uterine infection after giving birth, if the Penicillin works to bring down her temperature... well, let's wait together."

"Where did you go?"

"I called for an emergency helicopter."

"You did what?"

"Without success. Let her rest now."

Doc wanted to give Deckard a quick check-up so Peyton wandered into the kitchen. He looked into the gift bags. Along with the makings of tuna casserole, Glory had included two cans of baby formula. Peyton poured a couple of ounces into a bottle and read the bottle-warmer instructions. Then shoved the second can into a drawer and shut it. He did not want to think about why he needed formula.

By 10:00 PM Peyton had cooled and wrung out the towel a dozen times, and opened and warmed formula for Deckard who sucked it down and now slept again next to Libby. All his gurgling and restlessness had not roused her, nor had Peyton who sat on the bed, holding her hand. "Stay with us, Libby."

Libby didn't stir. She wouldn't take liquids. By midnight, Doc could see ... what would he say to Peyton?

*

Inside of a year, the man had arrived, married, lost his father-in-law, welcomed a son, and now was about to become a widower.

At 2:00 AM Doc touched Peyton's shoulder to wake him.

He sat straight up. "What?" He'd fallen asleep on the bed with Deckard between him and Libby.

"Peyton," said Doc. "Wake up."

"I'm awake."

"Son, I don't know how to say this. I've done all I can." Doc's eyes were bulging with tears. "Libby has an infection that neither I nor medication can control. I'm afraid infection will stop her heart not too long from now."

"What about the antibiotics?"

"It's rare, but in a difficult birth like Deckard's, amniotic fluid gets into the mother's bloodstream sending staphylococcus throughout her system."

"Okay so give her more penicillin!"

"She isn't strong enough."

"Strong enough?" Peyton stood frozen. "She's young. She's healthy." The two men stood and stared at one another.

Deckard squirmed and let out a squeal.

Doc said, "Lie back down, embrace your wife and child, talk to her and let her go in peace, with love. Your kindest gift to her..."

After an exchange of silent stares, Peyton did as Doc said. He held his tears. He reached across the space occupied by their son and draped his arm over Libby's waist. It was more true than the day before, she didn't look like the Libby he'd known. She was pale and still. Her breath was shallow and her eyes remained closed. Peyton stroked her hair.

*

The following day, Peyton did little but feed Deckard and change his diaper, rock him and lie by Libby laid out on her back on the bed and stare at her. He could hear Mayor Nuckle and Jim Polk digging her grave which they sited next to Stripes's memorial a dozen feet from Nanny's tree. They let themselves into the kitchen for glasses of water, then let themselves out just as quickly.

Peyton was numb. He did what was required of him, his fathering automatic and unconscious but sufficiently nurturing to keep Deckard serene. Only when the infant slept did Peyton let go of the boy. Then he put his head down and let the tears come. The loss overwhelmed him. The emptiness was deeper than he could comprehend, as if he grieved not only Libby, but his own failings still hidden from memory.

On the second day, Glory arrived in the early morning to feed and bathe Deckard while Doc put Peyton in the shower and got him dressed. Nuckle and Jim Polk wrapped Libby in a new white sheet and carried her graveside. Reverend Byle presided with very few words. Peyton held Deckard to his chest and said, "No, no, no," as Libby was lowered into the ground.

*

Peyton walked downtown and automatically punched-in for work.

"What are you doing?" Glory stood in the doorway.

"I want to work."

"You look terrible."

"Nobody tells you what a newborn is like. I've got him here, with me." Peyton moved the blankets from over the sling.

"Well, for heaven sake, your son is not going to spend three hours in a meat locker. You can't expect an infant to grow normally if he's surrounded by cold dead animals and disinfectant." She took the newborn in her arms. "Even if he's asleep." She looked down and grinned. "Oh, isn't he just the perfect image of his–" Glory choked. "Mother? Why are you here, Peyton?"

"To do something. Anything. I really don't want to bother your routine. I can ask Marge Polk to watch him. If you don't want him here."

"Do I look like I don't want him here?" Glory stared at Peyton. "Libby calls Marge a replicant, from Off World. No-way no-how she'd let Marge take care of her baby. I just wish Stripes could see his grandson."

Peyton closed his eyes, a reflex to screen his guilt.

"Ed isn't here, thank the Lord, but I do wish Stripes.... oh well."

"If Deck is any bother–"

"Oh, stop." Glory lifted the bundle to her shoulder. "I never had babies of my own. Being an honorary Grandma is a gift."

"If he's trouble, just –"

"Stop!"

Over the next months, Deckard became a regular at Glory's Groceries and shoppers asked about him when he wasn't there.

Glory doted on Deckard and, when he slept, read cookbooks.

The boy grew fast and strong, and Glory bestowed time and gifts so that her little guy had more than he needed. Libby had arranged a crib and a rocking chair. Glory provided diapers, lotion, powder, rash ointment, a thermometer, clothing, bibs, formula, baby food, instructions on how to use it all, and, often when Peyton worked, personalized day care.

Deckard sprouted like a watered dandelion under sun. The first time Peyton opened a jar of infant food, he dipped a finger in the mush, and tasted. "Yech!"

But Deckard waved his fists wildly so Peyton spooned a tiny glob between pink gums into the open mouth. Deckard swallowed, laughed, and opened his mouth again. Peyton wondered at what age taste buds develop and hoped they would in time for the first crop of fresh vegetables.

"How would I–I don't know what to call it," Peyton said. "I want to make baby food. Purée fresh carrots, mash steamed zucchini, that sort of thing."

Señor Hector senior sold Peyton a blender and threw in, gratis, a large sun umbrella.

Peyton spent mornings tending his wandering bean trellis and baby zucchini, and assembling the final slats of his fence. Deckard sat in his Bouncy Baby Bungee Chair, under the umbrella and out of direct sunlight, and listened to Peyton's stories.

"Your mamma and I by a railroad tie
found love we could not have foreseen,"

"This is not food." Peyton pulled a volunteer out by the roots and held it up for the ten-month-old to see.

"We wed by-and-by then you came just shy
of my trellis of beans turning green...."

Doc made regular house calls. He listened to Deckard's heart and lungs, tested reflexes, hearing, sight, length, weight, and smiles on the faces of father and son. He said, "What are you feeding this little guy?"

"Mostly what Glory tells me," said Peyton. "Why?"

Deckard, at birth weighed five pounds, at three months weighed thirteen, at eight months had Glory chasing him up and down the aisles, and now at ten months was all muscle and brain. His grasp was iron and his jaws gummed anything that came near enough.

"The boy's shooting upward like ice plant used to, around here," said Doc. "You're doing it right."

Doing it right, thought Peyton. *Except* for Libby. *Except* for Stripes. *Except* for Schotz who vanished without a word. *Except* for the knot of guilt in his belly. These events left a foul essence in the Saltine air, invisible but as psychologically corrosive to Peyton as methane rising off the Salton Sea. He saw himself covered in a residue of ignorance and misdeeds.

Ed sat on the edge of the trolley, legs over the side, boot-heels dangling only inches above the ties, pack and duffel settled on his body, his baby blues gazing squarely at the future. At 11:30 AM Frink was coming into focus through the dust.

Years earlier, before his mother fell sick, Ed read that when a traveler enters a new town, to get his bearings, he should find a place to sip a coffee and think about what's next. From the Frink trolley stop, Ed loped across the sandy field. He walked three blocks remembering a place, but not a name.

"Eureka!" He pulled open the swinging door to the Coachella Café.

The waitress noticed Ed the moment he walked in. She said, "Hey stranger."

Ed was taken up short. "Have we met?"

"It was only a matter of time till we did. I'm Luna. Luna Boreanaz."

"Ed." He wiped his palm on his thigh. "Ed Schotz."

She tilted her bronze chin, and fluttered her thick, black lashes. She ignored his hand and said, "Follow me." She winked, turned, and walked with a pronounced va-va-voom. "You on vacation, cowboy?"

Ed watched and followed the swaying rump to a window booth.

"Coffee?" She was already pouring. "What brings you to Frink?"

He had to think. "I guess you could say I'm searching."

"Noble. Have you found what you're looking for?"

"Well, not yet."

"I won't take that personally."

Ed drank down half his coffee. "Think of me as Imperial County's, uh, *Magnum PI*."

"Wouldn't take much imagining," Luna stood back and watched him. "That was a compliment."

"Oh. Thanks."

Magnum. Ed liked the image of himself, the best-looking hunka-hunka burning love on the Salton Sea, the all-American hero.

She handed him a menu but made him pull it from her fingers. "Take your time, cowboy."

Ed gulped down his coffee and wondered if he could grow a mustache. He'd never tried, but it suited this new Magnum chick-magnet thing.

Luna, gone for less than a minute, appeared again at the table. "Warm up?"

Ed was jolted from reverie as if Luna had bent over and licked his ear. He looked up at her.

She asked, "Top you off?"

"Top me off?" Ed's face turned bright red. He couldn't believe the cheese omelet she was making of his brain.... was she even eighteen? This is a test, he reasoned, he'd been sent a test. Must focus. Focus, focus, focus.

But Luna stood by his table again. "I can't afford to wait forever so I guess I'll ask *you*. You free later?"

If this was a test, then it was also a Godsend standing right in front of his eyes. He'd waited a decade, and now it was happening. In every one of his travel fantasies, seduction and sex had pushed his foot hard on the gas pedal and, now, the promise of wild thrashing and moist carnality lay at the bone of each conversation with this girl. She wants me. At least I think she does. He sighed to appear casual, and said, "My evening is yours."

Luna stood looking into Ed's eyes, one hand resting on her hip and the other pouring coffee to the rim of Ed's cup, skill and surface tension keeping it from overflow. Then she shook her head and walked away.

Now what had he done? The chills on the back of Ed's neck came from deep down and raised the hair on his arms. He beat his head against the padded seat back. My evening's yours, that's all I said, and she walked away. This would *never* happen to Magnum PI. Are there bugs in my teeth? Focus, man. Focus. Zip your zipper and don't be a fool. After Libby, his mother had warned him ... never, ever, *ever* let a woman turn your head–"

Luna knelt in the booth behind Ed and leaned over the padded seat back that separated them until her face was close to his. She whispered, "I'm off at seven."

Ed bumped the table and spilled coffee out of the cup and over the saucer onto the white paper placemat. He pulled a mop of napkins from the dispenser, then turned the head he had just resolved not to turn, wide-eyed, to look at her.

"Seven." Luna looked him straight in his blue eyes. "Seven o'clock. Here." Then she jumped off the seat and, without taking his food order, without another word or look back, she strutted and swayed into the back room for her break.

*

At the 24-HOUR BUY-IT-NOW, Ed purchased a six pack of Miller Lite, three cello packs of Little Debbie's doughnuts, four cans of Spaghetti-Os, a roll of peppermint breath enhancers, and a map of the region stretching geographically from San Bernardino to Las Vegas. He walked to the Tip Top Motel, thinking maybe he should buy a car to simplify his travels, give him more flexibility, something economical and reliable, a newer model station wagon maybe.

The motel clerk welcomed him. "We're running a special." Ed paid.

He pulled open the cellophane and slid a doughnut into his mouth. He walked along a row of empty parking spaces, used his card key to enter room 139, hung the Do Not Disturb sign on the outside knob, and bolted the door from within. He flipped on the light, turned up the air conditioner, checked the smoke alarm, scoped under the bed, flushed the toilet, then popped a beer and put it and two pop-top cans of the Spaghetti-Os on the night table. From his duffel Schotz pulled a camp spoon and polished it on his elbow. He flung himself onto the newly made bed and situated the pillows, clicked the remote and tuned in to *All My Children* in time for lunch and a nap with Susan Lucci.

*

Ed awoke hazy but resolute. At 3:00, he roused himself and thumbed through the Yellow Pages. He stepped into his boots, put on his hat, looked in the mirror and wiped tomato sauce from his chin. He left the cool darkness of his motel room and walked straight ahead out into searing heat through the parking lot and kept going to *U-Neek Auto Sales* at the edge of town.

He'd never owned a car but had always maintained a driver's license. He stopped and looked both ways before crossing the street. "I'm gonna buy me some chick magnet wheels. Woohoo!" Ed threw his hat into the air. It flew like a Frisbee, but he didn't mind a chase. The wind was blowing in the direction he was headed.

Ed test-drove a 1986 Bronco and a 1991 Chevy wagon, neither of which quite fit the image he wanted to cultivate. A Ferrari was out of the question but surely Magnum deserved something sexier than a family station wagon. Between a Falcon and a rusty Comet sat a 1967 Barracuda.

The salesman popped the latch and propped the hood upright. "You got a good eye for the classics."

"How long's she been here?"

"Last owner was the first owner. Lost all the original paperwork in a house fire. But ain't she a beauty?"

"What about gas?"

The salesman opened the driver side door then looked at Ed. "Man, you don't buy a honey like this for gas mileage. If you want economy, buy a Yugo. Or a Schwinn."

The Cuda was orange, rear-end raised, good tires, acceptable upholstery, modified carburetor, and had a broad white racing stripe running from the front grille, over the black roof, and down the trunk.

Ed stood in the sun, squinting from under his Stetson. The car called to him, whispered in his ear, "I'm your girl, I'm the one."

"How much you asking?"

"Do you want to drive her?"

"Yeah. Off the lot."

"Okay then. Let's go back to my office and see what we can do."

After 30 minutes of initialing boxes and signing on dotted lines, Ed handed over six 100-dollar bills. In return, he was given the title and registration along with two keys: one for the door, and one for the ignition.

To Ed, it seemed as if God had finally answered his prayers. True it may have taken Ed a long time finally to have had enough of life's bullshit, but today, he'd taken the step. Lo and goldarnit behold: he bought a car and made a date.

Off the lot, the Cuda bucked like a bull and ran the road like a tank without shocks. It would get fewer than 12 miles to each gallon and burn through a quart of oil every three tanks of gas. But she turned the heads of Babes and gave Ed options.

Ed drove around the block four times then went back to his room and gazed out the window at his new girl. He pulled closed the drapes, popped another can of Spaghetti-Os and a beer.

When Ed woke, Geraldo Rivera was attempting to interview a Senator, the Washington Monument in the background. Ed kept his eyes on the television but rolled off the bed and stretched to touch the ceiling then reached for the drape to peek at the Cuda. Ed smiled.

"Six o'clock," he said. "What would Magnum do?"

He took the wrapped soap bar from the sink and dropped it into his toiletries. He unpacked his razor and shave cream, he laid his clothes on the bed, and stepped under the shower. Ed placed his hand on the wall and looked at his trimmed fingernails against a square of tile. It was all so very white, even the grout. The world felt new. He liked it, and he liked not being tied down. He massaged the scented soap into the washcloth, rubbed for a lather, and scrubbed his parts.

At 6:55 PM, Ed stood on Main Street, waiting to open the Coachella Café swinging door for Luna. He wondered if dinner was expected. He hoped he had correctly interpreted Luna's suggestions, which seemed clear earlier but became confused by his lurking lesser-self while he napped.

Ed checked his watch. 7:10 PM. She'd probably gone home an hour ago. He peered in through the plate glass. "I am such an idiot."

"Are you a peeper?"

Ed swung around. "What?"

"The way you were looking through the window," said Luna. "A voyeur."

He'd been standing at the door for twenty minutes. She couldn't have gotten past him. "Where'd you come from?"

Luna wore tight black jeans and a pink camisole with lace. Ed stood frozen in place with his jaw limp. She was really pretty, and that pink camisole revved Ed's engine into the red.

Luna stared back at Ed, then reached for his hand and talked while they walked, telling him about her whacko customers. She turned one corner and another then looked up at an old marquee: "Live Music Every Night". She bumped his hip with hers. "The drinks are worth the green. You dance, cowboy?"

Ed couldn't balance on a horse, or a skateboard. In childhood, his mother had told him, he regularly fell out of bed. Ed had no rhythm. After two hours on the dance floor with Luna hanging onto him, and also those awful line dances which Ed never had the coordination for, Ed's feet throbbed, his heart pounded. Wow, he thought. And this is only the first day.

"Jeebers, Luna." He quieted his breath. She was so pretty, and that pink camisole....

Luna grinned. "Where are you staying?"

*

"That's my Cuda," said Ed. He combed through his wallet for the card key, Luna looking on, the Do Not Disturb sign still swinging on the knob.

"Room 139. The perfect number," she said. "One plus three is four, and four plus nine is thirteen, and one plus three is four again, and four is the perfect number."

He smiled; she knows how to add. "What makes four so perfect?" Ed worked the card key into the slot and the button changed from red to green.

"Oh, four corners of the earth, four Gospels, Four-H Club, two arms and two legs, all that. I'm going to take a shower." Luna threw her purse on the dresser and walked into the bathroom without closing the door.

Ed sat on the bed. Then he stood. Then he sat.

First jeans, then the pink camisole flew from the bathroom to the bedroom floor. Ed heard Luna tinkle. He waited for flying underwear but there wasn't any. Was he supposed to undress? Should he join her? How old was she, anyway? He had no legal cover any longer, he felt feverish and sweaty. Was there going to be sex?

The tap shut off, the shower curtain slid open, and out walked Luna.

Ed stood. "Wow."

"It's the genes. Cahuilla Indian mother. Romani Gypsy father." She handed Ed a towel. "Dry me off."

Ed took the towel. The woman was everything Libby was not. Brown with thick and wild black hair, voluptuous, seductive.

"A new experience?"

"Heck no. Heck, heck, no."

"You're funny." She turned around. "My back."

Ed patted her with the towel, neck to ankles and he was on his knees when she spun around. He fell backward. She looked down at him. "Now I watch *you* undress."

Ed scrambled to his feet. "Aw, come on."

"Fair's fair, cowboy." Luna put her palm against Ed's chest and pushed gently. "Stretch."

"You want me to touch the ceiling?" Ed looked upward.

Luna dropped her hand. "Like I said. Funny." She slipped a couple fingers behind Ed's belt buckle and tugged on his tucked-in shirt.

Nerves did to his nuts what cold did to his nipples. He turned his back, stripped down to nothing, and dove between the sheets. He leaned back against a pillow and grinned. "Enough watching?"

Luna laughed and crawled across the queen bed. With the blankets between them, she lay on top of him.

Ed looked up into dark brown eyes. Luna's hair hung down and brushed the sides of his cheeks, his ears. She raised herself on her arms, arched her back so her breasts brushed Ed's chin and put added weight on his groin.

In all his years of brown-paper-wrapped magazine subscriptions, Ed had never imagined an encounter quite like this. He'd spent his life avoiding Kryptonite, working for truth, justice, the American way and, Jeebers, this went against everything, *everything* he knew to be true and decent. His mother would be mortified. Luna was a coffee shop pickup. A complete stranger. He should not trust her. Damn it, his skin prickled. He knew better. He was terrified of diseases and couldn't bear the thought of disrespecting his own moral code – it was the only consistency in his life. But he had lust in his heart. He said, "Okay."

Luna eased herself down the length of his body, pulling her hair across Ed's chest. She slithered toward the foot of the bed, then off onto the floor, taking with her the blanket and top sheet. "I studied Chinese medicine," said Luna. "All your nerves begin in your feet. I'm removing your tension."

"That's nice. I'd like my tension removed."

Luna bent Schotz's foot inward and outward, and from the underside wiggled a finger between each toe. With the heel of her hand she pushed against the ball of his foot in a circular motion.

"That sure feels good." Ed's chest rose and he exhaled a sigh. His fists loosened.

Luna moved to the other foot.

Ed's scalp tingled and his balls dropped.

She stood, then sat on Schotz's ankles and massaged upward through his calves, knees, thighs. She leaned forward and pushed her hands under his buttocks, dug her fingers into the muscle until Schotz began to twitch. She dug deeper. "Don't fight me."

"I'm stretching. I'm stretching." But as Schotz spoke, he felt like Luna had slathered him with Icy Hot and the heat spread from his buttocks through the organs of his pelvis to his belly and groin, and as the heat grew so did Little Ed. Before Schotz could apologize for his rattle and buzz, Luna leaned forward and, and, and.... Jeebers, thought Ed. This is illegal in some states.

He melted. He stopped worrying except for what if she laughs and please, please let me hold back until.... Dead puppies. Dead puppies. Dead puppies. Oh OH NO!

"Oh Luna I'm sorry. I'm so sorry oh God I'm sor-reeeeeee."

Luna sat across Schotz's thighs and shook her head. "Damn." She rolled off his limp body. "I'm thirsty. You stock the fridge?"

Ed tried to leap up. She stopped him. "Yes or no will do."

"I think there's a Beer." He reached and pulled the sheet up and over himself.

For almost 30 years, Saltine and its ways had been the only normal Ed had known. His monthly mail deliveries of *Loaded Chamber* and *Geeks Get Naked* provided a glimpse of modern city life, but his expectations of a life well-lived didn't push much beyond small town morality. He was due–no, he was *owed* another stretch.

From her large purse Luna dumped her waitress uniform and two pair of panty hose, one worn, the other a back-up. She shook them out and held them up. "See what I mean? It always happens. Four. Four legs." Then she bit one pair in the crotch to start a rip, and tore it in half. She did the same with the other. Luna walked to Ed's side of the bed and dropped to her knees. She held his eyes with hers, found his left hand which she pulled toward her. "You ready for a real stretch, cowboy?"

Ed would have agreed to sequential Novocain-free root canals from the woman.

Luna tied a slip knot around Ed's left wrist with the nylon's toe and fixed the other end to the metal bed frame.

"Hm. Okay." Ed said it, but he didn't mean it.

Luna nudged him toward the center of the bed. She pulled the sheet to the floor again. He reached out his right hand for Luna to tie, the way she had his left.

"But now I can't touch you," said Ed.

She slip-knotted his ankles and finished him off, spread eagle.

Ed was higher than he ever in his entire life could remember being and jumping out of his skin with prickly hankering. He was also terrified, as much by the ease of his own surrender as by the situation itself. He'd let his focus blur and his head be turned. While he looked cross-eyed at a pair of cheerful breasts, this girl had pinned him to the bed the way he and his childhood buddies used to pin bugs to the dirt.

Ed winced. He didn't want to give her any ideas. Then he figured he probably couldn't give her any ideas she didn't already have.

Luna lay on her stomach between Ed's legs, her breasts pushed up against his balls. In a friendly sing-song she said, "Don't you dare come." She took his rattle and buzz in her mouth, but only for a few seconds. "I said, don't come."

"I won't. I promise. I won't," pleaded Ed.

"You're going to cut short the fun," said Luna. "Aren't you?"

"No cutting. I won't. I promise. I've just never been tied up before." Ed wiggled his feet and hands, each tied to the bed frame. He wasn't sure he should talk, but quietly said anyway, "Will you untie me now?"

"Now?" Luna rolled over on top of Ed and slid him into her. "You want me to untie you *now*?"

"Or maybe marry me."

Luna laughed and rocked back and forth. Ed came first, silently, but Luna came second with a battle cry like Ed had never heard and he grinned with pride. She collapsed and curled up in the small piece of bed under Ed's arm. She lay next to him for a while before sitting at the edge of the bed. "I should go."

Ed tried to sit, but was yanked back by the nylons ties. "Are you leaving?"

She wiggled into her waitress uniform and slipped on her sandals, stuffing panties, bra, camisole, and jeans into her bag. Luna dropped to her knees beside the bed. She held Ed's eyes with hers. "It's been nice knowing you."

Ed looked up at her. "Okaaaay. Same here."

"I won't take everything, but I need something." Luna picked Ed's wallet from his jeans.

"Awwww."

"Darlin'.... Coyote is always hungry."

"Untie me!"

"You crazy?"

"Untie me!" Ed strained. "I cannot believe you are doing this."

"I'm taking your 50s, five of them. Blame my thieving Gypsy blood."

"Damn it, Luna. I'll get you for this."

"No. You won't." She smiled at him. "It has been fun though, Cowboy, hasn't it?"

"Untie me!"

Luna turned the TV on low. "Do you have a favorite channel?"

Ed ground his jaws and flared his nostrils.

"No?"

The clock, bolted to the bedside table, read 5:12 AM. He twisted and turned but, with each pull, the slip knots drew tighter. And they were nylon, no way would they rip. "Damn my eyes," said Ed. "Damn them."

Should he yell for the maid? Let her find him like this? He could holler for help, but he could also envision Nuckle, Doc, Glory, Polk, and Asshole, not to mention the minions of semi-literate replicants ogling the headlines on the following day's *Imperial Register*, "Former Deputy Arrested in Frink BDSM Tryst." Holy crap. He'd rather have those root canals.

"*Señor?*" It was 9:45 AM. He heard a knock at his door. "*¿Es libre?*"

After a night in lucky room 139, unable to hold his bladder and dreading his imminent discovery, Ed hollered, "I am a U.S. deputy. Do you understand me?"

"Yes sir," said the maid.

"Are you alone?"

"Uh, yes sir. Why do you ask?"

"A bad woman tied me to the bed. Nothing will happen to you if you come in and help me."

The maid entered the room, laughing. She covered Ed with the sheet. "Honored guest, I would like to help you further. Your hands?"

Ed exhaled, grateful. "Please."

"Yes," she said. "Indeed I would like to, if you could see your way clear, in return to...."

"To what?"

"Perhaps financial assistance of a modest sum?"

Too tired, too humiliated, too helpless to argue. "How much?"

"A man of law." She pursed her lips.

"How *much*?"

"How was it that a bad woman tied you to this bed?"

"How. Much." Ed burned hot enough to melt the nylon pantyhose.

"For you," she said, "a man of such honor," she picked up his billfold and peeked in. "Your twenties. One hundred dollars. For my daughter's college fund."

"Take it."

The maid removed five twenties, the last of the bills from Ed's wallet.

He watched her stuff the bills in her pocket, such a generous man.

She untied his hands, told him to take care of the rest of this nonsense by himself, and be out in thirty minutes so she could deal with his nasty mess.

"Remember I am a Deputy and if I ever hear or see one word about this in any way, shape, or form, in the *Register*, on TV, or from the lips of local folks, I'll have you deported."

The maid looked at him and snorted. "I am a citizen of the United States of America." She hung the Do Not Disturb tag on the inside knob for Ed to see, certain he would not understand her meaning and would nonetheless go forth to disturb the outside world.

Ed cleaned himself up, loaded the car, checked out, and swore that if, in the future, he ever again had the grave misfortune to find himself in Frink, it would be only for as long as it took to get out.

FIVE YEARS ON, 2006

Ed pressed the gas pedal hard at the bottom of the on-ramp. His left blinker didn't work and he edged the Cuda into the lane, cutting off a Hummer going eighty-five miles per hour. Ed waved. The Hummer came within inches of a rear-end crash but the driver jerked left and sped by Ed with a stubby middle finger in the air. Ed maintained an easy 45 in the right-hand lane. Cars with trailers raced by with horns blaring. Some yelled from the window. "Pedal to the Metal, Asshole!" or "Who gave you a license?"

Fear for his life was not among Ed's dreamed-of discoveries. He'd long ago realized he wouldn't find information on Asshole Peyton while racing Hummers so three off-ramps later he exited the highway and rolled along a side road.

Ed spent his time wandering California's inland scrub from one Slab City to another–planned neighborhoods that never got built, the poured-and-abandoned foundations instead drawing collections of itinerant mobile homes. He met retired couples who spent years on wheels, traveling from one houseful of grandchildren to the next, whole families who'd gone under financially and now lived in an old Airstream on Dad's disability, stoners with tents and backpacks who sat half-naked and fully-baked staring at grains of sand until the baggie of weed ran empty. Most everyone got along. Few to none of the squatter camps had utilities or telephones or mail service, but each community named itself: Concrete Corners or Slabber's Nest or Misery Flats. No gas, no rent, few single women, he existed on Cheetos and beer but lived on the cheap.

Ed put down roots in these places for three or four months hoping to blend-in. He arranged his lawn chair, camp stove, tarp, and ice chest of beer to share with folks who might know something and be willing to tell him. He talked to hundreds of people, heard enough shit to fill all the bullrings in Mexico, and learned the intimate histories of people he didn't care about, but essentially nothing about Peyton. Finding incriminating evidence still mattered, but less and less. Ed was worn out. He'd spent his days avoiding snakes and mosquitoes in these human clusters hidden in plain sight.

After several years living like this, it came to feel normal. On the other hand, he needed new shoes and wanted food, real food, *hot* food–food he didn't remove from cellophane.

In Hesperia, Ed drove past the Main Post Office. Maybe he should send Libby a note. He dismissed the thought. Maybe she'd written to him at general delivery. Ed made a U-turn, parked, and walked in. He leaned against a wall in the draught of a ceiling fan.

The clerk stared.

"I'm passing through."

"So, you need stamps or something?"

Ed had lost track of time. He'd spent years wandering. He'd stopped at a post office only once, a couple years earlier, to wait out a dust storm. He never before thought to check. "Do you ever get letters for folks in general delivery?"

"All the time. Name?"

"My name? Ed Schotz, ma'am."

"Wait here."

No line formed, no one came in.

The clerk returned. "Here you go." She handed Ed one square pink dog-eared envelope with no return address. The postmark, Palm Springs, was dated four years earlier. "After a month, we're supposed to toss them into Dead Letters, but I keep mine."

"Thank you."

"I don't get too many like that. Used to be perfumed," she said.

Ed took it back to the Cuda and sniffed the envelope. Libby would never use pink unless she'd found it. And perfume? Ed slid a pencil in at the fold and ripped a line along the top. He flexed the envelope to look inside at a single sheet of folded pink paper. It read, "You have a daughter. She was born nine months after our rondayvoo in Frink. Northern Lights lit the sky the night she was born so I named her Aurora." Signed, "Luna."

Ed read the note again. Jeebers. There was no return address, no demand. "Naw," he said to himself. "Naw, impossible." Ed wadded-up the note and envelope together. "Out of sight...." He tossed the ball of pink onto the pile of clothes and old food wrappers filling the back seat.

Ed had acquired a tent, sleeping bag, cook set, propane stove, Coleman lantern, gas cans, and miniature gadgets of all kinds, hooks, bungees, buckets–there was always some new toy. Hesperia Hardware announced, *SALE*, so Ed stopped and was waved-in by the salesman who didn't have to work too hard to convince Ed he needed a Sun Squirt: a three-gallon black PVC pouch to fill with water to hang from the roof rack. A plastic hose and gravity provided the spray, and Ed could wash off the day with water warmed by the sun without dropping quarters into KOA public stalls.

"Some people around here use it for regular bathing," the salesman said. "Practically a shower."

Ed had grown up where "practically" was normal for water pressure. He told the salesman "Sold, if you keep the packaging and fill the thing for me."

Ed tied the Sun Squirt to the roof rack, happy with his

new domestic acquisition, and took off for the nearest gas station. He parked at the pump and walked inside to prepay. "I wonder," he said, "if I could ask you about someone I'm looking for." Ed had repeated that line so often, he had to remind himself to speak it with sincerity.

The pimpled young attendant twitched his nose and listened to the description. He shook his head and took Ed's twenty-dollar bill.

An old man sat outside the gas station door. He turned his head and yelled in, "I might know the guy you're looking for."

"Excuse me?" Ed faced the man who couldn't have weighed much more than the spindly chair he sat on. The old coot was bald with a ponytail and wore a threadbare plaid shirt and jeans that—were it not for suspenders—would fall around his ankles. "You know Peyton Neworth?"

"Might," said the man.

Ed's jaw hung slack. He'd begun to think Peyton had manifested out of the sand. "Lopsided smile, sandy hair. Underhanded son-of-a-bitch?"

"Sounds like him," said the man. He knocked dust from his knees. "Name's Rib."

"Rib?"

"Yeah. On account I'm skinny as one."

"Ed." He held out his hand.

Years earlier, Ed had vowed his pursuit to the ends of the earth. By the time he'd reached Hesperia, though, he'd driven hundreds more miles than he'd kept count of. What was left of his rage had become habit.

Ed quieted himself. "Well now, buy you a cup of coffee?"

"Will you spring for breakfast?"

At Trudi's Breakfast Stop, the two men slid into a booth. Ed drank coffee and made small talk while Rib cleaned his plate and sucked the last egg yolk from a finger. The $7.99 Sunrise Surprise would be money well-spent.

"So," Ed began the interview. "Where'd you meet him?"

"Who? Oh Yeah." Rib lifted his coffee cup. "Well, it must have been near five years ago." He took a swallow. "I was working in Laughlin, Nevada. You know the place?"

"Yes."

"Payson and me– "

"Peyton."

"Right. Peyton. Him and me worked in maintenance at the casinos in Laughlin."

"Which casinos?"

"A couple of them."

"For instance?"

Rib thought a moment. "The Silver Nugget was one. Oh, and the MGM, I think."

Ed pulled a small notebook from his chest pocket and wrote the names. "What was he like? I mean, to work with?"

Rib looked at Ed, sizing him up. "Rotten. The guy didn't carry his weight."

"Did you socialize together?"

"Socialize? No."

"A beer after work?"

"I said no."

"How about, did he ever do anything you thought might be dangerous? Immoral?"

Rib thought a moment and slowly nodded. "Banana cream pie."

"Banana cream pie?"

Rib signaled the waitress for more coffee, and "Banana cream pie. A large slice."

Ed nodded.

"I think he gambled with his money."

Ed made a note in his book. "So, how long did you know each other?"

"Who?"

"Peyton. Peyton Neworth." Ed had his first eyewitness. So what if the name escaped him. Some folks are better with faces.

"Maybe four months is all." Rib glanced from his pie to Ed. "Yeah. From Christmas to Easter, or thereabouts."

"And afterwards?" Ed sat forward, pen poised at the notebook.

"The guy just disappeared. Never saw him again. Hey man, I got to go now."

"One more question. Did you ever see him do anything that might have been, you know, questionable or even illegal? This is life and death. Think hard."

"Well...." Rib scratched his jaw and thought seriously hard at the ceiling. "I think he might of drove without a license."

Rib walked across the street, past the Cuda to his chair outside the gas station office. Ed wrote down everything he could remember from the exchange and left money on the table. He had a destination.

From Hesperia, Laughlin would be 40 gallons to the northeast, which translated give-or-take into only five hours in the Cuda, whose top speed was down to 40 miles per hour, if he drove straight through.

Ed didn't drive straight through. Along the way others might know something, and he told himself he wanted the complete picture before confronting anyone. He would not rush. Besides, he now had a Sun Squirt.

The Cuda's stuffing had begun to sprout through the upholstery and the driver's side window no longer opened. First gear was harder and harder to get into, but the tires were still good. Goodbye great west; hello exotic north, as he defined it. He had a named destination and a renewed his sense of purpose, though Ed did not want to miss out on any new leads. North meant an incursion into the Mojave Desert environs. The map was clear: Victorville-Barstow-Roach-Paradise-Laughlin. Ahead lay acres and acres of sand, cleaved by miles and miles of flat, straight asphalt, dozens of campgrounds and communities not notable enough to warrant a dot on the map but full of people, maybe some with information. Ed fastened his seat belt, checked the mirrors, and pointed the Cuda up the on-ramp of Interstate-15 toward Barstow.

*

Ed meandered along, one hand on the wheel and the other in a family-size bag of Cheetos. An orange right hand had become a lifestyle. Compared to the trailer towns where he'd put-in, Barstow was a happening place. Its population of just over 20,000 supported grocery stores, hardware and discount outlets, nail salons and insurance agents, bars, every kind of fast food, a couple dozen gas stations and car mechanics whom Ed hoped could fix a gas leak and replace the 'Cuda's radiator, though he needed money first.

He celebrated his return to civilization by swinging the Cuda into the drive-through of Maria's Taqueria. He ordered two chicken tamales, two carnitas flautas, three shrimp tacos, one beef enchilada supreme, a pint of chili verde, a side of guacamole–chips included, and a 64-ounce root beer. He paid by credit card, and didn't look at the total, even while adding a tip.

A public park beckoned at the south edge of town; he'd noticed it on the way in. So much green! He hadn't seen such shrubbery in weeks and finding himself surrounded by trees and grass provoked a shot of glee. He parked, slid off the seat and out, breathed-in the plant-based surplus of oxygen. He pulled off his boots and socks and threw them into the back seat, hopped barefoot over the blazing asphalt to the passenger side, quickly wrapped one arm around the double-bagged hot food and the other arm around his half-gallon of icy soda pop, used his hip to close the door, and hurried to the turf. Two black oaks spread toward one another and offered shade over a picnic table. Ed dug his toes into the green as he walked.

The year 2004 had seen severe drought and Barstow wanted to do its part to conserve water so instead of turning on the sprinklers, the City had contracted with the Harvel's Paint to spray the public grass a springy emerald.

Yes, Ed thought, beautiful. He sat and opened the first wrapper he touched, bit in and mumbled "Mmmm. M ... *m ... mmmmmmmmm.*" He pictured Libby's hands dipping into a bowl of water, then picking up a ball of masa, patting it into a soft mound to flatten and wrap around a chunk of braised meat. She lifted the tamale out of the steamer then covered in it sauce and cheese, olives and cilantro and said, "Just for you."

After a tamale, the enchilada, chili verde with guacamole, and a quart of root beer, Ed laid his head on the table for a quick snooze. In his dream, Libby spoke Spanish. She leaned out smiling, batting long eyelashes, taking his order at Maria's drive-through, but kitchen machinery behind her had begun to growl. She said it was the grinder for dried corn, but the growl grew loud and Ed found it harder and harder to hear her words. He strained toward Libby and listened, trying to read her lips but, still at the drive-through window, his foot had become wedged under the gas pedal and, as he tried to twist it free, the other foot got caught under the brake pedal. His toes felt gnawed and both ankles smarted. The harder he struggled to loosen them, the more lodged – and painful – his feet became. He would have sworn, too, that his arms and neck were being stung by a hundred hornets. "Help me," he said. Libby responded, "I'm married now and it wouldn't be proper."

Ed jerked his head upward. "What the hell?!?" Something had swiped his ear, and Ed – still half asleep and with a sugar-headache – hoped it was Libby. But then something sharp pierced the other. He swatted but missed and blood trickled down both sides of his face. Fogged-in by carbohydrates, Ed raised himself amid the noise and screamed, "What the hell?!" The growling and barking grew shrill and Ed forced his eyes to focus in the bright sunlight. The surface in front of him writhed with critters and in an ellipse orbiting the picnic table he saw a pack of snarling, feral Chihuahuas.

They had upturned the root beer, torn apart and finished off what was left of Ed's lunch, ate the wrapping, too, and had begun to eat *him*. Ed waved his arms to free himself. He beat about his head and torso and stamped his feet. He should have moved slowly and deliberately, but lost control and wrenched himself from the bench which brought the entire pack nipping into skin and bone at his hamburgered ankles. The tamale, beef enchilada, and chili verde weighed heavily in his gut. He twisted and fell over, then shot up and zigzagged toward the parking lot amid a school of canine piranhas fierce enough to devour him whole. Ed, still barefoot, raced around the Cuda, thanking Jeebers he hadn't locked the doors. He was too panicked to feel pain from the actual puncture wounds, but razor-sharp incisors had ripped his skin dozens of times.

Ed kicked and banged his bloody legs against the running board to tear the creatures off his pants legs.

He slammed the door, enclosing himself in safety, and breathed hard.

"Joseph, and Mary," he yowled. "I'm in hell."

Ed calmed himself and blew his nose only to see blood on the tissue. He sweat profusely and his mouth ran dry. He couldn't quite process what had just happened but scared himself, looking at his face in the rear-view mirror. His earlobes and nose were bleeding. He felt a throbbing burn in his ankles and blood pooling at his feet.

He'd passed a hospital on the north side of town. Now, if he could find it again.

*

Nurse Carole, tall and brunette, dressed all in white, was using her ten-minute break to offer helpful hints to the ER receptionist. Carole's eyes widened when Ed hobbled in. She looked at the receptionist and very slightly shook her head. She turned and said, "Sir?"

"Can you help me?"

"We'll have to see. What happened?"

In the examination cubicle, Nurse Carole asked about allergies, took his pulse to be 86 beats per minute, his height at 6′1″, his weight at 234 pounds.

"Any history of violence in the family?" she asked.

"Pa and me used to go hunting," said Ed.

Nurse Carole stared at Ed. "Mr. Schotz, if you think domestic violence is a joke...."

"No joke," he said. "No ma'am." Domestic violence?

"You need to tell me the whole truth," she said.

"I'm not sure what you mean, Ms. Carole."

"*Nurse* Carole," she said. "When was your last tetanus shot?"

"Three years ago. I swear, Nurse Carole," said Ed. "There must have been two hundred or more Chihuahuas."

She opened a low drawer and reached in, then twitched

a subtle smile, changed her mind and opened a higher drawer. "Remove all your clothes, put this on, and – " She tapped the examination table, "wait here." Nurse Carole walked out of the cubicle into the hallway and pulled the curtain shut.

Ed peeled off his shirt and trousers. He debated keeping his shorts on, but she'd said "all your clothes" so the Jockey shorts came off, too, and he donned the hospital gown made of paper. It would not reach to close over his butt. He used the step-stool to ease onto the examination table and lay back at a 45° angle. He stretched out his legs and rested his feet on a large, disposable, plastic-lined absorbent pad. The trauma had so fatigued Ed that he dozed. In his daze, Nurse Carol, with generous mouth, adequate bust, and soft hips, ministered to his wounds.

The doctor snapped open the curtain. He looked at Ed. "Good afternoon, young man. Let's take a gander." The doctor looked in Ed's eyes and down his throat. "Say, AHHHHH." He checked lungs and reflexes but ignored Ed's ears. "I understand you met with some kind of attack?"

"Chihuahuas," said Ed.

"Chihuahuas, yes." The doctor put on safety glasses, rubber gloves, and a mask. "So I heard." He selected long tweezers from a stainless-steel tray and carefully lifted flaps of loose skin at Ed's ankles. He prodded scratches that had already started to form scabs and checked for any additional bruising. "Hmmmm...." said the doctor. Then to Nurse Carole, "A consult, please." They stepped into the hall, his back to Ed.

Ed lay on his table and thought he heard the doctor whisper, "domestic," and "insurance," before Nurse Carole slipped back through the gap.

"For the bite wounds, a rabies series is required," she said. "But stitches are not. I'll clean the wounds. Do you need anesthetic?" Ed would rather have died on the table than admit to her how squeamish he was about his own blood. "I think I can handle it," he said. Then added, "I can handle it fine, Nurse Carole."

Ed tried to relax and breathe normally, but he gazed at Carole while she dabbed him with antiseptic-drenched cotton swabs, starting at his toes, bandaging as she went, working her way to his ankles and calves. By the time she washed her hands and pulled on a fresh pair of gloves and rolled her tray of medical ministrations toward Ed's head, he'd convinced himself this angel of mercy wasn't just performing her job. She was full of ardor and commitment. Ed could feel it. He concentrated on yapping dogs to keep his private parts slapped down.

At the end, Carol said, "You'll survive, Mr. Schotz. If you have any more trouble, you know where we are."

*

Ed needed no more of an invitation. Ed left the hospital, his hands orange from both Cheetos and Betadine under the batting and tape, his head wrapped in gauze to protect his chewed-up ears, a bandage across his nose, and his ankles and feet packed and stabilized in wadded cotton shaped into soft knee-high booties with thin rubber soles peeled from their paper and self-stuck on.

The driver's side door of the Cuda was smeared with blood, and the interior had a puddle underfoot and blobs over the wheel and dashboard, sticky or brittle from the heat. Ed turned the key and headed out to find a car wash, and a florist.

This time, with Nurse Carole, things would be different. He could make a move or move on, the choice was his. That Carole had already, literally, bound him up–at least the extreme edges of him–never occurred to Ed, whose purpose in life had just changed.

His ankles were held stationary at 90°, so accelerating and braking were a matter of lifting his right knee and lowering his entire leg onto the pedal. Ed's palms, though, were free to grip the wheel. He ran the Cuda through a *Speed Cleen* then crept along commercial streets with one thought in mind: find a florist. He drove the length of Williams Street and back up Mountain View, was given directions to a Bridal and Flower shop but couldn't find it. He finally stopped at Safeway, blood, bandages, and scabs scaring the girl at the checkout half to death, and bought a bouquet and a card to deliver himself.

The cellophane-wrapped bunch was a springy mix with lots of baby's breath. The card pictured a spray of irises and was printed in silver, "For a Very Special Someone." Ed wrote, "You are my Angel of Mercy, Nurse Carole. Would you honor me with your company at dinner?" He signed it, "Your Ed," and sealed it–hoping it was all legible. Anyone would be touched by this small splinter of sentiment. He would drop the card and flowers with the receptionist, personally, after which he had a Rabies series to fulfill so he'd have to hang around Barstow. More than just hang around. Ed cruised the residential streets with their grey cement and brown grass, children took their basketball and cleared to the sidewalks to let him pass.

On a side road, Ed found a ground-floor studio apartment that required no security check. After more than five years of wandering, Ed had no one to call for a reference. The manager looked Ed up and down, took pity, told him, "No parties," then took Ed's check.

Early the second morning in his Barstow convenience-with-kitchenette, Ed was roused by scratching at the door.

"Oh my God." Ed sat straight up. Had the Chihuahuas followed him?

The sound was faint and masked by air conditioning. A curtained sliding glass door provided the only access from outside, no window in the bathroom to climb out of–not that he could have. He sat frozen. Nothing. Then, a scratch. And another, barely audible. Ed didn't dare reach over and disturb the curtains.

The next time Ed opened his eyes, daylight streamed through the cracks in the drapes. His watch said 9:00 AM. The sun blazed low in the sky and its heat, already at that hour, penetrated the walls. A car ignition, then singing in Spanish from a radio. The only growl came from Ed's own stomach. Ed brought his right hand to his head, the gauze was still in place.

He'd strewn his pants and shirt across the brown couch, his boots lay useless on the linoleum near the glass slider. He stood and dressed. At the door, through a gap where the curtain panels separated, careful to stay far enough back so as not to alert anything to his presence and imminent exit, he peered left, right, and straight ahead. Ed slipped his left hand to the toggle lock and flipped it open. He listened. He pushed past the drapes and into the hot haze. He locked the door behind him and again looked around.

His legs and feet still bandaged, he wondered how long before the hot pavement would melt the glued-on rubber soles. If he removed the gauze and found he couldn't put his feet into his boots, he'd have to go barefoot. Not to mention what Nurse Carole might say. So he stepped one foot at a time, Frankenstein-like, his body stiff and swaying back and forth, down the concrete walk. He glanced under cars, wary of what might be hiding, then turned in between an SUV and the Cuda but stopped short.

Ed stared, mouth open. There couldn't be two of them. "Guizar?"

Guizar stared too. *Yeah Ed, it's me. I tracked you down. Something try to eat you?*

The dog was still mottled pink and bald around the middle with matted ashen fur on his legs and tail. A long thread of thick drool hung from his muzzle. His bark came out a rasp, the upshot of Peyton having damaged the dog's vocal cords, more a cough, Stripes's cough. He twitched his ears back from his yellow eyes. He rasped again, shook his bald head, and the string of viscous saliva wrapped itself around his furless muzzle.

"Guizar. Boy." Ed walked slowly forward. If Guizar were alive, maybe so was Stripes, and, if Stripes were alive.... "Where's your pop?"

Dead, Ed. And you walked right by what bone and gristle was left of him out by the mountain.

Ed couldn't make his sore body kneel to face Guizar eye to eye, but he opened the car door for the animal, who raised his head and sniffed. Ed said, "Go on."

Guizar looked from the car to Ed.

"Oh," Ed retrieved the remains of a three-day old hamburger. If the dog was anything like Stripes, he'd follow the food. He broke off a piece of brittle beef patty and dropped it on the upholstery.

Guizar jumped to the shotgun seat and swallowed the burger-jerky, nosing the catsup-crusted crouton of a bun to the floor. *Okay for now, Ed, but you're going to have to do better.*

"So." Ed gingerly climbed in and started the engine. "Any good smells in Barstow?"

Guizar looked at Ed and flared his dust-caked nostrils. *You're still a dufuss, aren't you?*

"Want to meet my new girlfriend?"

Guizar rested his snoot on the rim of his open window. *Nope.*

Dog riding shotgun. Breakfast at del Taco. Nurse Carole at the hospital. Ed tried to whistle a happy tune but the pull on his jawline was intense.

"Deck, leave the tuna alone."

Deckard, at five years of age, was on his stomach, rolling cans down the center of the aisle.

"No harm," said Glory. "He's discovering the world."

"Will he stop at six?"

"It gets worse every year for the next I don't know how many." She stroked the fair-haired head of the boy. "You teach him to think. This is what happens."

Peyton nodded and shrugged. "Hey, Deck. Ready to go home?"

"I'm not done."

"What? You're not hungry?" He scooped up his son and carried him down the steps of the loading dock then put him on his own two feet. Deckard skipped alongside his papa down Paseo Centro and toward home.

The trip used to take ten minutes but with Deckard walking, it now took close to thirty. Peyton taught Deckard how to bust clouds. They walked, then stood, stared, and concentrated on a cloud until the high whip of white broke apart and dissipated. It worked more often than not. They stopped to name plants until Deckard knew all of them. From Deckard's first toddler steps, Peyton had insisted the boy walk part of the way home, no matter how it slowed them. Peyton wanted his son to learn self-sufficiency. Like busting clouds, Peyton didn't know where he'd picked up the idea, but it had served him well and he hoped it would his son.

*

Peyton woke the next morning at dawn. He left Deckard snoring, which the boy had done from infancy, and took his coffee to the back porch. A coral haze raked across the weathered surfaces of the garden fence and its wood grain stood in high relief. The shallows snaked around knots and the patterns looked to Peyton like aerial photographs he'd seen of Asian rice terraces. He raised his arms and stretched left, then right, and sighed.

"Good morning, Sweetcakes."

Peyton froze. His scalp prickled.

"A beautiful life you've made."

Peyton swung around.

Libby sat on the lid of the old freezer. She had the same brown hair and eyes, she wore the floral dress she was married and buried in.

Peyton's knees gave way and he plopped to his bony bottom onto the concrete stoop. Was this a trick? His jaw hung open and his eyes filled with tears. "Libby?" Peyton wiped his eyes with his sleeve. He pushed to his feet and fell with arms outstretched toward this apparition.

"Oh, no, no, noooo." Libby held up her palm.

Peyton again froze, his breath tremulous. "What is this?"

"I love the way you love our boy. And, Sweetcakes," said Libby. "Your garden is Eden itself."

"What.... What?"

"I had to spin quite a yarn to get the okay for this, this, what did they call it?" She closed her eyes. "Inter-dimensionality." Libby looked pleased.

Peyton felt unfamiliar anger bursting from his chest. "If you can come back, why didn't you stay in the first place?"

"Do you think I'd have left you and Deckard if I'd had a choice?"

Peyton stared at his dead wife sitting on the empty freezer. "I had to explain death to a four-year old. What do I tell Deck now? Oops?" Peyton knew from experience how easy it was to offend the woman, and confused as he felt, he wanted her to stay. "Doll. I don't understand."

"Don't you want me here?" Libby's eyes turned moist.

Peyton ground his teeth. "To sit on the back porch and tease me? Can Deck see you?"

"Even spirits have to get through the red tape. And no, Deck can't exactly see me. Children know things, even if they don't have words to make sense of it."

Peyton had a thought. "Is Stripes hanging nearby? Is he coming, too?"

"Why?"

Peyton had just about vanquished the memory of his fight with Stripes and now, once again it took front and center. "Just wondering."

Libby smiled at her beloved.

"I want to hold you." Peyton took a step toward Libby.

"Sweetcakes, it can't happen. You can see me, but if you touch me, I'm gone." She sounded apologetic. "Apparently it's a variation on a very old theme and rules are rules."

"Are you real?"

Libby tucked her skirt around her thighs. "I had this bread-box freezer for ten years but now is the first time I ever sat on it."

"Papaaaaa!"

Peyton jumped.

"Ah, of course," said Libby. "Go."

Peyton edged around the porch and grabbed the door knob without taking his eyes off Libby. He hesitated.

"Go."

On Deckard's bed, Peyton held the boy close, chest to chest, and patted his back. "Deck. The most wonderful thing just happened." Was this the onset of dementia?

"I'm hungry."

He looked eye-to-eye with Deckard then ticked his ribs until the boy laughed.

"Please."

"Ah, the magic word." Peyton smiled and they both stood. "Breakfast of Champions?"

While Deckard concentrated on pouring milk into his cereal, Peyton quietly backed into the laundry room to peek out the screen door onto the porch.

"Papa. Did you forget?"

She was gone. What had just happened? Peyton eased back into the kitchen. "You're a demanding fellow, you know that?"

"I want what I want is all."

Peyton felt light-headed, but he laughed. Every morning for the past year or so, over breakfast he told Deck a continuing story. "Where did we leave off?" He thought a moment, then began the next chapter of the epic which felt less like invention and more like discovery with each new episode he narrated. "Okay. So....

Two brothers we met the day before,
Who early in life each other adored,
They came to blows while in their teens,
Till playing together and talking it seems,
Had grown from a pleasure,
To rage of full measure,
So that life as brothers,
Was over forever!"

"In fact," Peyton dabbed a drip from Deckard's chin.

"Those close-knit brothers,
They left one another,
One kind and respected,
One mean and rejected. But,"

Deckard finished his orange juice. "But what?"

"Let me think....

The mean one went off,
His fortune to find,
The kind one moved on,
Leaving all behind.
While one ran amok,
Engaging in brawls,
The other pushed luck,
By walking through walls,
In truth no one knew,
What became of the two...."

Peyton placed the dish and spoon in the sink. He said, "More tomorrow. What do you say we hit the dirt?"

"No."

"What I expected." In faded jeans and tee shirts, together the royalty of Eden marched out the back door and down the steps to coax vegetables from the earth.

Peyton glanced at the freezer. The dust hadn't been disturbed. Had he dreamt her?

*

Two mornings later Libby looked at her watch. She perched once more on the freezer. "I've been waiting for you."

Peyton shot from his knees in the soil to standing. If he turned around, would she be there? He looked to Deckard who was sounding out words printed on a seed pack.

"He can't hear me," she said. "Haven't seen you for two days, Sweetcakes."

Peyton turned. His body quivered in disbelief or terror or pleasure or he did not know what.

"Did you tell anyone about me?"

"How could I?"

Libby wondered if she should be offended. Her face turned to a pout. But she looked at Deckard and softened. "You're a better father than I would have been a mother."

Peyton swallowed hard.

"Relax, Sweetcakes," Libby said. "You won't be able to figure it out."

"Why not?"

Libby laughed. "Have you figured out life?"

"No."

"Well then, you're not likely to figure out death."

"Libby," he said. "Help me. Are you real?"

Libby leaned forward. "That's like asking if sound is real."

Peyton pondered this.

"Do you love?"

"Well, yes," said Peyton.

"Of course. It shows."

"And every day Deck hears about his mama." Seeing Libby, talking to her, stirred Peyton as he hadn't been moved in a long time, and his eyes started to tear. "Doll, I miss you so."

He'd not spent much time thinking about what kind of life he'd lived before, save for the occasional feeling of *déjà vu*, if only because the life he led in Saltine felt good as if Saltine were where he belonged. Libby had given him so much, a life and a son. Maybe his earlier existence didn't matter. It was like trying to figure out life. Or death.

Libby watched and waited for Peyton. "Wish I could nibble on your carrots."

Peyton grinned. "Me too."

The gate opened and Glory appeared with a grocery bag. "'Morning gents."

Peyton sniffed and blinked back his filling eyes.

Deckard shook two large sunflower seeds out of the pack into his palm. "Look, Papa. Two. I want to know what happened to the two."

"The two?"

"Can I have a brother?"

"Look, Glory's here."

Deck looked up. "What's in the bag, hag?"

"Deckard!" Peyton looked at Glory. "I'm telling him a story in rhyme."

"Deck," said Glory. "What else rhymes with bag?"

He said, "Will I gag on what's in the bag?"

"I hope not."

Peyton shook his head. "He's a poet. At five."

Glory had taken to spending early Monday and Thursday mornings at the Neworth household. She had, in essence, adopted the two of them, her two boys. She visited the garden and checked around the house to find if Deckard needed socks or toothpaste. She usually prepared a couple of meals, too, before heading out to open the store at 10:00 AM. She left the groceries in the kitchen then came back out to sit in a chair under the fading sun-umbrella and watch her two boys fiddle in the garden.

"The story continues." Peyton drove in a trowel to bring up a carrot. "So, Deck....

When a man goes bad,

He can turn quite mad,

And say things he may not mean...."

Deckard looked up. "I always say what I mean."

Libby's eyes widened. "Precocious, isn't he?"

"Yep." Peyton continued,

"That's because you're good, not bad

And happy, not sad, but....

Hey, just one minute, buddy. You said you didn't want to go outside this morning, but here we are."

"I didn't want to go." Deckard stared at his papa. "But I didn't want to stay, either."

"So," said Peyton, "You had to make a decision?"

"No," said Deckard. "You made the decision."

"Kid ought to be a lawyer," said Glory.

Libby looked miffed. "So now Glory gets to decide what Deck should be?"

Peyton casually looked toward the porch and shook his head, no. "Okay, Deck....

Won't do what he's told,
Thinks he's made of gold,
Complains till his teeth all turn green."

Peyton tore off a carrot top and held the fresh fronds between his teeth, letting them fall into whiskers from the corners of his mouth.

Deckard and Glory both laughed.

"When a man is good,
And works as he should,
And does what he can to be kind...."

Deckard said, "Kind of what?"

Libby chuckled.

Glory rolled her eyes.

"Kind of nice,
Kind of wise,
Kind of calm,
Never lies,
Does his best,
Gives his all to oblige...."

Peyton took a breath.

"And smiles not only,
With his strong white teeth,
But as well with his bright blue eyes."

"Humbug," said Glory. "Deck would rather have green teeth."

"Humbug is right," said Libby. "How would she know?"

Peyton hadn't foreseen Libby's attitude and it surprised him. He moved along and poked a finger two inches into the soil at ten-inch intervals.

Deckard followed, dropping two sunflower seeds into each hole then packing the soil lightly.

"You're a natural," said Peyton.

"I know," said Deckard.

"And humble too," said Glory. "How many have you planted?"

"Fourteen," Deckard said without pause.

Peyton nodded his head. "That's our boy." He glanced up and winked toward the old freezer where Libby sat.

"Certainly worth a weekly allowance of some sort," said Libby.

Libby's embodiment gave Peyton such a rush of pleasure, he blushed.

"I'm hungry," Deckard said. He dropped two seeds into a hole.

"You're always hungry," said Peyton. "That's why we plant food."

Libby said, "Don't you feed him?"

Peyton's face cramped against open laughter.

Libby said, "When's lunch?"

"One hour," said Peyton. "We'll have lunch in an hour, Deck." Peyton wished Libby would join them at the table.

"I'll put something together," said Glory. "One hour, Deck."

"I heard."

Peyton sighed toward the woman who'd become his benefactor. "Thank you. Again."

"Uh," said Libby. "You and Glory have grown rather close."

"She's a mother to me and grandmother to Deck. No one is replacing you, Doll." Then to Deckard, "So, Joe, what else do you know?"

Deckard didn't answer.

Peyton looked at Libby and raised his brows.

Deckard flattened the seed packet. "I've been meaning to tell you...."

Peyton wondered where Deckard learned such phrases. He was allowed one hour of TV per night, and Peyton monitored the shows.

"I have a friend."

Peyton put down his trowel. "It's good to have a friend. Like Glory. She's our friend."

Libby piped up, "Maybe a little too good of a friend, if you ask me."

Deckard was quiet.

"Would you introduce me to your friend?"

"I'll ask her."

Her? Peyton tried to remain neutral. "I'd like that."

Peyton had never before considered relinquishing captainship of Deckard's life raft.

"Children see things," said Libby. "Maybe he knows you have *me*."

"We live in such a small town, Deck. Where did you meet this friend?"

"You're jealous," said Libby.

I'm what? Peyton rose to his knees.

"She lives somewhere else," said Deck. "Somewhere else, but she's my friend."

Ed heard about a security guard position at the Barstow AllMart and filled out an application. Ten days later, he had an interview.

"As you can see, I was Sheriff's Deputy for eight years."

She took the pen from her mouth. "Yes, yes." The Human Resources assistant smiled then scribbled a note on Ed's application. "Just down the road a-ways, too."

"That's right ma'am. I know the territory and its people. I can handle myself to enforce the rules and do an honest day's work for the legal good. I follow rules, give the benefit of the doubt, and don't push limits. I'm a people person ... know what I mean? I know a lie from the truth– "

"Alright, then."

HR provided a binder with store rules and regulations, two uniforms, and a 10% discount on clothing and groceries. His salary was enough to cover food, rent, make below the minimum-payment on his credit cards but sufficient to keep creditors placated, and gasoline for the Cuda with something left over if he was careful. He hung his uniforms from a hook above the left rear window, jumped in, turned the ignition and grinned at himself in the rear-view mirror.

"Hey hey, Guizar, it's coming together." He patted the dog riding shotgun. "First thing: you and me need to celebrate!"

Guizar licked his chops. *I hope we're going to Maria's.*

"Then I'll tell Carole."

Buddy, don't bother. I smell trouble.

From the first time in Emergency Ed saw Carole, he'd imprinted like a baby chick, fixing his sights on her as the new One-and-Only. The woman had accepted–on behalf of the Emergency Room Staff—the bouquet he delivered, and the ones that followed, but left them with reception for the counter display. For coffee, dinner, a movie, she had rebuffed his every invitation. He'd contrived urgent physical aches and upsets requiring trips to the ER. He resorted to telling lies he thought would be seductive to a medical professional. For a thaw and a smile, he would have traded all the guacamole in Barstow.

Right after Martin Luther King Day in January, to his latest written note asking her to lunch, Carole left a voice message. "Okay, Ed. Lunch, only lunch. This Thursday. Noon."

Ed took advantage of his AllMart employee discount for a new shirt. He swung by the ER to leave at Reception a heart-shaped box of Whitman's chocolates.

*

Ed stood facing his bathroom mirror and ran a comb over his sun-bleached security guard crew cut. He'd taken a sample sachet of Stetson cologne from the cosmetics counter at work. If there ever was an occasion, he thought, this is it. Pull out all the stops. He rubbed the scented towelette over his neck and shoulders. He tore the plastic off the knit aqua polo—the blue stood out against his tanned arms, especially the left one—and tucked the hem into his jeans. He spit-polished his Ariats, donned his Stetson, and stepped out.

"You stay here, Guizar." He winked at the dog. "I have a hot date with a beautiful woman."

Beautiful, maybe. Take a sniff, Ed. Always sniff first.

Ed opened the Cuda's passenger door. I'm a respectable citizen. I have a place to live, a car, and an income. I'm a professional. I've made a life in Barstow. Carole would respect that. She isn't some small-town lifer. Carole is a worldly woman.

He gathered an armload of fast food wrappers from the floor and clutched them to the dumpster. He rubbed dog fur off the front seat onto the ground and pounded dust from the upholstery for the breeze to take. He rolled down the back windows hoping air circulation would carry out whatever dander and fuzz remained and turned on the air conditioning to help blast it all outward.

Ed walked into the ER at precisely noon to whisk Carole off to an intimate lunch. He had rehearsed this moment. "Hello, beautiful. Your carriage awaits."

"My what?" She wore a nurse's white tunic and slacks with Dansko clogs so she stood almost six feet tall.

The admittance clerk sat in her rolling chair and walked it toward Ed. "Mr. Schotz, we all love your flowers."

Carole shot her a look.

"And chocolate–"

"I have one hour, Ed."

Ed reached to hold the ER door open, but it opened automatically so he raced ahead to the Cuda for the passenger door.

Carole stopped. She looked at the seat then at Ed. "I have an idea," she said. "Let's take two cars."

"Well..." Ed mentally punched himself in the head for not vacuuming. "If that's what you want."

The Bali Hai Surf n' Turf would be dark and air conditioned. He knew what he wanted to tell her. He'd known from his initial ER visit what he wanted to say.

He arrived first. Should he wait in the parking lot? Or was that overbearing? He could help her out of her car. She might want to freshen her lipstick. Maybe at the entrance would be better. Give her breathing space, a moment to get her bearings–Carole's shiny white Datsun pulled into the lot and Ed jogged to her parking spot.

The handle and door hinges opened smooth, silent,

and solid. Inside, beyond Carole's slim thighs, the chrome sparkled and the original paint had been carefully detailed. Neither twig nor pebble had separated itself from the sole of her clog and lodged itself between the ridges in the floor mat, not a fleck of fuzz rested on the dashboard, not a smudge of wet nose disgraced any window, no Styrofoam cups and week-old newspapers lay where they had landed, and no fur of any species besmirched the upholstery.

"Wow, a 510 Coupe." Ed held out his hand to her. "Classic vehicle. You keep her fine as the day you drove her off the showroom floor."

Carole stepped out and locked the door. "It's a 1972, Ed."

"Yeah, I *know*. Did you buy her new?"

"This is 2006." She looked at Ed and didn't know what to say, so walked on.

Ed caught up. "I've heard good things about this place." He held open a door to the foyer. The Bali Hai hadn't yet taken down its Christmas Tree.

*

Carole inspected her fork. "I want you to know, Ed. I don't think of you as a bad man." She pushed the bacon to the platter under her Cobb Salad and picked at the egg. "You make jokes and don't even know it. You are polite. You try really hard."

Ed swallowed a mouthful of hamburger and picked up a fry. "I appreciate you seeing that. Few people–"

"The unfortunate fact is, Ed, we could get together every couple of weeks for coffee, but then you might think I'm encouraging you," Carole chewed on a slice of egg and stared directly at Ed. "You would be wrong. I'm sorry. And you would be sorry because you don't know me."

"I could never be sorry to know you." Ed brightened. "We could try. Like you said, I don't give up easy–"

"I was hoping.... It really isn't something I talk about.... I don't want to hurt you, or anybody... and I didn't want to tell you...." Carole looked Ed in the eye and shook her head.

"Whatever it is, Dear, we'll face it together."

Carol looked at the ceiling and gave a nervous laugh. "Somehow I don't think so."

"Dang you're even prettier when you laugh. If it's something about me, I can change."

"Oh, I'm too tall for you."

"Not really."

"Truly, I'm not your type."

Carol ate in silence. Ed finished his burger and fries.

"Thank you for lunch, Ed."

"Can we do this again?" He reached across the table for her hand and thought he felt the slightest hesitation before she pulled it away. He swore to himself, no more Maria's, no more pizza delivery. He'd join a gym, vacuum out the Cuda. He'd stop using the Lord's name in vain and Sundays he'd go to church.

"No. As I said, it wouldn't be fair." She stood.

"Carole. How do you know what I see as fair?"

"You think you know me, but...."

Ed pushed back from the table and stood, too. He left cash then followed Carole to her car. He wanted to kiss her but she slid into the Datsun's driver's seat, buckled her belt, said, "Thanks again. Bye now," and took off.

Ed drove along the streets, looking at shops and pedestrians as if, in them, he could make sense of Carole. What did she want? Why did she think he didn't know her? Ed prided himself, as a former Deputy Sheriff, in understanding human nature. He needed to find a path through her minefield of resistance and connect with Carole's heart.

Such a path appeared to him one week later. Toward the end of January, Ed awoke with a whisper in his ear that told him what he had to do. On his way to work, he detoured via the hospital to write down the contact number from a small plaque at the base of the billboard across from the ER parking lot. He stuffed the note in his chest pocket.

During his lunch break, Ed called 1-800-TAB-LOWE. He reached an answering service that transferred his call to Iowa City and a corporation that proudly covered all of America in highway advertising.

"Yes, ma'am," said Ed, "the billboard –"

"We now prefer to call them, Informational Tableaux," said the woman on the other end of the line.

"Okay," said Ed. "The Informational Tableau on the corner of Fifth and Drought Streets in Barstow, California –"

"Can you hold?"

Through the earpiece, 101 Strings rendered Black Sabbath's *Technical Ecstasy*.

"Yes." She was back. "That's a month-to-month, and available at the end of this month."

"Wow," said Ed. "That's great. What's it cost?"

"Would you like to hear about our special multi-tableaux rates?"

"Uh–"

"If you reserve the one on Drought Street, you'll pay $149.95 for the month of February."

"Jeebers, that's–"

"But for five tableaux within a one-mile radius, for the full month of February, you pay only $600, getting one tableau free, which includes design, printing, and pronto installation with no additional costs, unless you take our insurance guaranteeing upkeep throughout the term of your rental. Of course you know that repetitive viewing significantly increases customer base so you'll want to reinforce the visual message."

"Well, ma'am, thank you but I think the one billboard,

one tableau, is enough. And I don't want it up until February thirteenth. No sooner or it'll ruin the Valentine's Day surprise."

"Yes, certainly. I'll make a note. But think carefully. This is a first time offer only."

"Do you take VISA?"

"Let's get you started. Which option are you looking at?"

*

For the days of waiting, Ed's quiet moments slurred into moony anticipation of conjugal accord. She'd see it. She'd have to believe it. He enjoyed his own good mood, but had bitten down his fingernails and, despite earlier intentions, he couldn't stop eating. Guizar hit the motherload. Rib bones and chicken gristle, ice cream and cold cuts, enchiladas and whatever else was left while he sprawled and shed on the couch next to Ed, watching game shows.

For the first time since his mother died, Ed got down on his knees every night. He knew he should pray that God's will be done, but he was really looking for guidance in improving his powers of seduction. So Ed prayed for strategy, then closed his eyes. Nurse Carole turned soft in his arms.

The three weeks awaiting February 13TH had seemed an eternity, but the day arrived, finally. Workmen climbed the ladder, unfurled Ed's message, and pasted down the printed image. The tableau, illuminated 24/7 by three overhanging fluorescent spotlights, showed a single green-stemmed red rose the size of a park bench, and, from lower left to upper right, in red cursive script afloat on what should have been a paler yellow background, the message: Nurse Carole, Will You Marry Me? Love, Your Ed.

Ed crouched in the Cuda at the far end of the hospital parking lot. He wanted to see Carole's reaction.

Day staff trickled in, parked their cars, and gathered on the astroturf outside the ER to stare. Several of the women held cupped hands to their mouths, some of the men shook their heads and laughed.

They're in awe, thought Ed.

Morning sun glinted off Carol's Datsun as it turned in from the street and stopped before the crowd of physicians, technicians, and orderlies that had gathered. A nurse ran to Carole's car and opened the driver's door with one hand, while pointing to the sign with the other. Carole left the motor running. She stepped out, stared, stepped back in, maneuvered nimbly on the asphalt, moored her car crooked over two spaces, and ran to the building.

"Awwww. She's shy." Ed opened his door, then thought better. "I should wait, give her some time." He closed the door. "Well, Guizar, old bud." Ed buckled his seat belt. "They'll be ringing bells and dancing down hospital hallways this morning. Let's get breakfast." They headed for Maria's Taqueria six blocks west, but, at a green light, Ed slowed to a stop. Next to the BP station in front of him, shimmering like a sister sun, was a second Informational Tableau: bright yellow background, red rose on the left, marriage proposal arching over the expanse. "Jeebers." Ed hadn't opened his last credit card statement. He thought for a moment. "I wonder where they put the other three."

Guizar sat on the passenger seat with his head hanging out the window. He turned to look at Ed. *Your sinuses have dried up, you didn't sniff, no other explanation.*

"What the hey," said Ed. "Can't have too much of a good thing."

Six chorizo flautas and one large horchata later, Ed and Guizar strolled back to the Cuda. He opened the door for Guizar. "Come on old boy. If we hurry we can catch Regis and Kelly."

In Ed's eyes, Barstow's barren streets had become

breezy green and tree-lined, and the haze had cleared to blue, the Cuda felt like a shiny Caddie, and his dog had a full coat. He hummed "I'm getting married in the morning.... Ding dong the bells are going to chime...." and to his own ears he was the embodiment of Rex Harrison. He kept an eye out for the additional tableaux, not that he could have missed the yellow gigantus should one appear.

Sure enough, above the mini-mart half a block from his apartment, his regular stop for corn dogs and root beer, emblazoned across the western sky, his words of passion. He pulled into the parking strip, got out and gazed.

Guizar whined. *Dude, don't leave me in this hot car.*

Ed leapt back in, put the Cuda in drive, and merged onto his road for half a block, then a right and into his parking space. He flattened wrappings and empty cups from the floor and back seat into an old Maria's bag, tossed it into the trash, and hurried for the his glass door.

Taped to the slider was an envelope. It read, *Official Business: Do not Ignore*. "What the hey." Ed took out his keys. "Somebody else coming after a piece of my paycheck," he said. "But first, the Morning Show with Regis and Kathy."

He opened the slider for Guizar then slipped through and closed the glass to keep the day's early heat out. Guizar jumped onto the couch and slimed the remote with his nose.

*

Ed woke just before noon. Guizar didn't bother to look up. Ed stood and stretched, threw his head left and right to crack his neck. "Whew," he said. He picked up the Official Business envelope and sat down at the table. The seal was tight so he tore a ¼ inch strip from the end, flexed the sides and slid out the white sheet. "Robert L. German, Esquire" popped out in raised print at the header. The letter was a Cease and Desist notice with a copy of Carol's application for a restraining order.

"Naaaaaw," said Ed. "It's a joke."

He read the letter again. How could she? Ed banged his forehead on the table a couple of times, and then cried. He cried until Guizar whined. Ed blew his nose and picked up the phone to order Chinese delivery.

Ed didn't go to work the next day. He let Guizar out at dawn and went back to sleep till noon. He woke, ordered a jumbo with everything and a six pack from Pazza Pizzeria, then phoned 1-800-TAB-LOWE.

"I want a refund," he said.

The woman laughed. "Sir, I'm sorry but that's impossible."

"Then just get those dang signs down!"

"Sir, I'm sorry but that's impossible too. Most of our clients...."

Ed spoke to sales people and raised his voice to supervisors. He cried when he tried to explain his pain and humiliation. But even Mr. Tab Lowe, himself, could offer only sympathy and warn Ed not to deface private property or he'd find himself in court.

By the end of May, the tableaux–which Ed had contracted for four weeks–had graced the Barstow skyline for three and a half months and, despite no maintenance agreement, had faded almost not at all under the blistering sun. The rose remained dewy and the background was as yellow as ever. Every time Ed left his apartment, there it–they–were.

The days became hotter with summer approaching. Ed thought about moving on. Except he had to try one more time. "Carole," said Ed into her answering machine. "Don't be mad. I must apologize. Please. Agree to see me just once more."

She returned his call the next afternoon. "I'm not mad," she said.

"That's a relief."

"What is it you want, Ed?"

"Have coffee with me? Fifteen minutes. I swear. Only coffee."

After her shift, they met at Jammin' Java. He bought a cup of Earl Grey tea for Carol, and a double latte macchiato for himself. He began, "It's been more than a year and a half for us–"

"There is no us, Ed."

"Please I must know–"

"You don't want to know."

"Yes, I have to know...."

Carole looked at Ed.

Ed was bursting. "I love you more than–"

"No!" More quietly, she said, "More than what? You don't know me. You know nothing about me. You see me in uniform.... You really want me to do this?"

"With all my heart."

Carole had regarded Ed as a child, yet here he sat with adult ambition. She dreaded his reaction, but he'd begged for clarity. Carole began, "Those Tuesdays I'm never available? Where do you think I am? You have no idea, do you?"

"I figured you'd tell me when the time was right."

"The time will never be right, Ed, but I'm going to tell you anyway because even with your broken heart you want me to."

Ed wore his most sympathetic face and put his chin on his fist.

"I'm in Los Angeles."

"That's a far piece, Carole."

"I drive to San Bernardino to see a doctor."

"But you work with doctors every day."

"They're not the right kind. She's a specialist."

"What is it?"

"Oh Lord. You're going to make me do this."

"Whatever it is...." Ed looked earnest. "I'll stand by you."

"Really?" Carole fought to keep her breath even, her voice low. She'd taken her current job three years earlier and even most of her colleagues didn't know.

"So you'll stand by me during the rest of my treatments?"

"Cancer?"

"No, Ed. I've been getting hormones."

"You have female problems?"

"You could say that." Carol thought, then smiled. "See what I mean?" She shook her head. "Female problems. You made a joke."

"Explain it to me."

Carole blinked at Ed.

"Whatever it is, I'll be there by your side–"

"Wait. Wait. Wait. You'll be here after my next surgery?"

"What?" Ed jumped in his seat. "When?"

"Well, next year some time." She waited. "I had my implants four years ago."

Ed froze while the news found a synapse to connect to. Then he stared down at her chest.

Carole sat straighter. "Next step is the big one."

"The big one?"

"Yes." She took a breath. "I bid good riddance to dinky pinky and the boys."

Ed didn't understand what she'd said. Then his jaw dropped. "You're kidding, right?"

Carol shrugged.

"Are you telling me...." Ed stood.

"Don't make a scene."

He stared. Then he gasped. "You let me think... for more than a year... you never told...."

Carol eased in her chair. "I tried, Ed."

"Not *that* you didn't." Ed stumbled backward. "You didn't try hard enough." Ed turned to leave, then spun back around. He opened his mouth but no words came out. He stared at, at, he searched. He couldn't breathe.

"Now you know."

"You should have told me!" Everyone in Jammin' Java turned to stare.

"Ed...."

Ed had turned purple. "I'm sorry I ever met you." He ran through the door to his car. He slammed himself inside, banged his fists against the steering wheel, then floored the accelerator and screeched out of the parking lot. How could she. He. She. "Aw, Jeebers!" Ed felt gut-punched. He had six-thousand volt crickets in his ears. The Cuda sputtered on rusty-tank bottom-gas but Ed didn't have the will to stop. He wanted nothing but to go home and sleep.

*

Around six that evening, Ed got up to pee. He opened the fridge for a beer and pressed auto-dial to order a pizza delivery. He hung up, then took a deep breath and again called 1-800-TAB-LOWE's 24-hour hotline.

"Policy," he was told.

"Please, *please* take them down."

"It's just too expensive to remove a graphic before another client wants to rent the space. You could try to find another renter but, honestly, most clients are happy to have free–"

Ed hung up.

By July, Ed still held his job at AllMart but again had to

exchange his uniform for a size larger. Not that he cared. He'd phoned in sick as often as not and had been written up twice for poor attitude. Then, one afternoon, he picked a fight with a cashier.

"Did you let that lady pocket a Snicker's bar?"

"I didn't see anything," the young clerk said.

"She was standing right in front of you. Security can't do the job alone, you know."

"The manager gave me strict instructions to pay attention to money-handling."

Voices were raised and threats were made and the whole store stopped to watch. Ed took a swing at a customer, missed, but was fired on the spot.

In the weeks following Carol's revelation, Ed spent his waking hours ruminating on the injustice of it all. He had grown angry and gone flabby and, what's more, he'd neither shaved nor cut his hair. He spoke to no one and resented everyone. The apartment smelled bad from old food. Guizar hadn't had a bath in way too long and clumps of fur collected in every corner.

One evening, after another day of hiding indoors and feeling sorry for himself, Ed rolled off the sofa. "Come on Guizar. Let's take a drive with the windows open." He loaded Guizar into the front seat and screeched out of the lot. Ten minutes later, Ed was circling the block where Carole lived. By the fourth pass, he'd worked himself into a sweat. What happened to him would *never* happen to Magnum PI.

Ed turned off his headlights and swerved into Carole's driveway. The street was quiet and most porch lights had been turned off, not much of a moon. Ed sat for a moment, then slid from his seat to the driveway. He pulled his seat forward, grabbed what garbage he could from the back seat, and threw it across the lawn.

The porch light flickered on and the front door opened.

Ed let the engine die and got out again. "Don't bother calling the cops." He picked up the papers and cups and threw them back into the Cuda.

Carole closed her door and left the light on.

Ed turned the key and this time eased out into the street.

Back in his apartment, he spooned-up to Guizar and fell asleep.

At 5:30 AM the horizon had begun to show sunlight. Life was as full of promise as a Mojave sink hole. Ed lay there and thought about how a year and a half in Barstow had been a long enough time empty of meaningful pursuit. He showered, shaved, then carried what he could to the Cuda. Clothes, shoes, bathroom stuff. Anything edible went into a cooler or plastic grocery bags. Ed dropped his apartment key into the pinch-faced manager's mail slot with a hand-written post-it note, "Hasta la vista, baby...." thinking Magnum was too laid back and maybe The Terminator would prove more effective.

He lured Guizar with yesterday's pizza crust, gassed up, and hit the road for Laughlin. As he left, Ed cursed the brightly lit Informational Tableau near the on-ramp and resumed blaming Peyton for every disappointment, injury, and bounced check since the dinosaurs roamed Southern California.

Peyton rinsed his freshly-picked foot-long green beans then Deckard sat at the dinette table and cut them into pieces with blunt-point scissors. Peyton poured a dollop of olive oil and the beans into the wok Señor Hector senior had ordered special from his supplier.

Deckard watched steam rise.

Peyton told him, "Steam is what happens when water becomes too hot to boil."

"But there's no water in the wok."

"Oh, how right you are." Peyton was delighted by this observation. "Every plant and animal in the world, including you and me, has more water in it than anything else."

"Does sand have water?"

"Is sand a plant or an animal?

"I don't know."

"Sand is a mineral, tiny little rocks. But green beans are vegetables and when we cook them, we can watch the water escape as steam."

"Does it hurt them?"

Peyton delighted in Deckard's compassion. "No."

Deckard nodded his head in thought. "Now?"

"Watch the clock, Deck," said Peyton. "The beans need another minute to cook."

Deckard counted down exactly one minute. "Now?" He held a bowl of chopped tomatoes.

"Careful of the steam," said Peyton.

"I know."

Peyton stood aside. "Now."

He grinned down at Deckard, who was filling out and growing tall. The way he picked up information astounded Peyton, but, even more, he was knocked out by the way

Deckard turned data into understanding. The child was smarter than he himself.

"It's time," said Deckard. He poured in the bowl of chopped fresh thyme, sage, garlic, and green onion. "Can I stir?"

"*May* I," said Peyton. "Permission granted after your shoulder reaches the rim and you can see over. Won't be long."

Peyton scooped rice from the cooker onto two plates and set an empty third at the table for Deckard's friend who was maturing at the same rate as the boy. She kept Deckard company and in quite thoughtful conversation, from what Peyton could surmise. She still didn't have a name, and Peyton couldn't elicit an image, but her presence seemed a powerful salve to whatever isolation Deckard might have felt.

"Imagine the night
Filled with colorful light,"
said Peyton over dinner,
"And people surrounded with laughter.
The food tasted great,
The world stayed up late,
Life couldn't move any faster.
With cigarette smoke and
A nose full of co–"

Whoa! Peyton stopped. Where did that come from? He stared and blinked.

"Papa?" Deckard waved his fork in front of Peyton's eyes.

"Sorry," said Peyton. "Sorry." He revised in exaggerated tone.

"Smoke filled the air, but, uh,
We didn't care,
We were chasing impending disaster...."

"Ooooo," said Deckard. "I'm so scared."

"Me too," said Peyton. "Let's eat." He picked up his fork but the shock of the words that had bubbled up and nearly come from his mouth repeated in his ears. What were such images doing in his head? Moreover, why did the scene feel so exciting?

*

Peyton had cleaned the kitchen and said good night to the boy, and now stood on the back porch leaning up against the rail.

"You added chicken," said Libby, her shoulders back and her chin forward.

"Yes, Doll." Peyton smiled. He yearned to tell Libby what he'd almost blurted, and how, for a fraction of a second, only a fraction, the place and the smells and the adrenalin-packed atmosphere were so vivid. Libby was his confidante but with her own odd sense of propriety, what an unwelcome revelation she would find Peyton's nursery rhyme about a smoke-filled den populated by gambling, cackling, coke-heads. The scene felt real to Peyton–his skin prickled–and he tried to recall who else was in the room, did he recognize anyone?

Libby sat forward on the edge of the freezer. Her feet dangled over the side and she tapped her bare heels against the metal housing. "Something on your mind, Sweetcakes?"

"Nothing you haven't heard before. I'm missing you, squeezed by sadness is all."

Libby and Peyton could hear Deckard in the bedroom conversing with his own ghost.

"It's *the friend*," Peyton mouthed to Libby.

Libby sat straighter and perfectly still. "Who is it?" She strained to hear Deckard's words.

Peyton sighed, noting that he sighed more often these

days. “Doll, I’ve never had to choose, before. I’ve always been there for Deck, but now I have to abandon you to go to him. It hurts.”

“That’s touching, Sweetcakes. But he’s my priority, too.”

“I’ll go check.” He moved without a sound from the porch through the kitchen and hallway.

Deckard giggled. “Stop,” he said. “Stop it!”

Deckard’s back was to the door and he laughed so hard his breath became a wheeze. He screamed, “I’ll get you!”

Peyton backed up, out of Deckard’s bedroom doorway and into the kitchen. He opened and closed the outside door with a harder-than-usual pull. He called, “Love to hear you laughing, Deck.”

Deckard bolted upright and sober. “I didn’t know you could hear us ... me.”

“I was on the porch,” said Peyton. He walked to the bedroom door. “Folks in Niland could hear you.”

“I was imagining,” Deckard said. “I was playing a game.”

“It sounded like fun.” Peyton stood and gazed at his son. “What have you got there?”

Deckard looked to his side and his shoulders drooped. He sighed like his papa had sighed. “A book I found.”

“A book, of course.” said Peyton. He stared more intently at the open page and what looked like a photo of Libby. He knelt and placed his hand on Deckard’s shoulder. “I love you. You know that?”

Deckard looked around into his father’s eyes. “I know.”

“When you laugh it makes me happy,” said Peyton. “What’s the book?”

Deckard said, “You won’t be mad?”

“We talk about things before we get mad.”

Deckard was still looking over his shoulder, up at

Peyton, and his eyes filled as if he were about to cry. "I know."

Peyton sat down behind Deckard and embraced the boy into his biggest, skinny-man's bear hug. They rocked together for a moment, Peyton closer, now, to the open spiral-bound book and a page with a photograph of the woman he'd just left on the back porch. She was even wearing the same flowered dress. "That's your mama. And next to her is Reverend Byle and me."

Deckard squirmed and pointed to another man. "Who's that?"

"That's Stripes, your mama's papa." Peyton pointed out Stripe's age, his Stetson, the carved bone-and-turquoise-inlaid silver handle of the knife on his belt. "He's gone but he was a crazy old codger and you would have liked him."

"What's a codger?"

"Um, it means someone who's been around long enough to know all the tricks, and use them for his own benefit."

"May I have some graham crackers and milk?"

"Sure."

The corners of Deckard's mouth turned up. He amended, "In bed?"

Peyton twitched his nose. "Just this once, for my young lawyer." For the briefest instant, Peyton tickled his son, who again giggled. Peyton stood and loped into the kitchen for Deckard's snack. When he returned with a cup of milk and a paper towel folded under two graham crackers, the book lay open on the floor and Deckard lay quietly under the covers.

Peyton placed the milk on the dresser, folded the paper towel around the graham crackers and set them down next to the milk. He tiptoed to the foot of the bed and watched. It had been months since Peyton had watched

Deckard sleep. He was filling out and had even grown another couple of inches. The boy lay like a grasshopper flipped onto his wings, bony knees bent and splayed, blue cotton blanket pulled over his belly. Peyton sighed once more and tucked the book of photos next to Deck's pillow.

Six years since leaving Saltine, two since waking up in Barstow... during these years Ed had taken refuge in rest stops and campgrounds, asked everyone about Peyton and listened to gossip by of dozens of folks who all told him to come on back any time. He didn't, but his interpersonal skills did improve, somewhat. Those folks were decent people all, but Ed was tired. Tired of being broke, of bad food, of moving around, of just sitting around–even with perfectly decent folk. He was no more than fifteen miles from Laughlin where Rib said he'd worked with Peyton, but Ed was demoralized, unable to make headway into whatever new disappointment awaited him. Had he been able to think clearly, he'd have realized he'd given up.

Ed steered the Cuda down the dirt road and around the ring before choosing a vacant plot at Black Jack Green, a slab settlement southeast of Bullhead City. He let Guizar out, set up his cooler, camp chair, and sun-shower, then blended-in. Ed found squatters to be live-and-let-live kinds of people. Some might be a little rough at the edges. Most were friendly, but he had learned to be wary. Friendly did not necessarily mean a friend. And he would never want to mistake simple cordiality for a generous welcome.

Two weeks passed quietly. Kids ran wild, morning and night, but most residents of The Green disappeared during the day into air-conditioned trailers. Dinner time brought out the men to start the barbecue, and the rest followed.

On Ed's third Sunday, a huge motor home rolled up. No sooner had it parked between two well-ensconced long-termers than its door burst open and out leapt six large dogs, nine small children - none beyond adolescence, and seven adults. The three men untethered dirt bikes and dune buggies, fired up an oil-drum BBQ, tuned the boom box to KBAD, and cracked open a case of Schlitz.

Ed and Guizar each caught a nose-full of grilling steak and walked toward the smoke and steam rising off the grill. Ed called, "Smells like sweet Hickory."

Two men emerged from the plume.

"Welcome." Ed shoved out his hand. "I'm Ed. This here's my dog. Guizar."

The men looked to be in their late 30s. One bald and bare-chested, he showed no hair anywhere, just blue tattoos on his arms and hands. The other man with shoulder length brown hair jabbed a steak and left the fork upright in the meat. The two moved toward Ed and stood several feet upwind of billowing smoke.

Ed pulled back his hand.

The bald one said, "You want something?"

"Just welcoming you to the neighborhood."

The hairy man whistled and 400 pounds of canines bounded up. "Sit!" He waited, then tore fat from two of the steaks and dropped the sizzling yellow strips into the dirt. The Boxer moved. "Sit!" The man kicked at her and she yelped.

He threw down a third strip of fat. In almost a whisper, he said, "Kill Fubar! Kill! Go on, get it, go on!"

Ed's stomach turned to acid. He didn't want to show fear.

The bald man pulled out the fork and flipped the steak. He called, "Selma. Some guy to see you."

Selma, in shorts and a bikini top, appeared at the trailer door. "You a bill collector?"

"No no," said Ed. "Just passing, saying hello."

"You can come in, if you want." She smiled at him. "Twenty bucks."

Ed took a moment. "Oh. I don't have that kind of money."

The bald man held up the fork. "You think my Selma ain't good enough? That she gives it away?"

"That's not why– "

"You think she's a slut? You think she ain't pretty?" He moved nearer to Ed. "You some kind of queer?"

"No, nothing like that. I just don't have any– "

"Dark of the moon tonight, Ed," said the bald man. "Who knows what Junior's dogs get up to."

"You and Selma enjoy your steak. Come on, Guizar." Ed turned and walked away as casually as he could, wishing he could arrest them for spoiling his mood.

Ed didn't trust dogs. Guizar the exception. He'd be dead had those feral Chihuahuas weighed-in at 70 pounds apiece, like Fubar. These new neighbors–who the hell knew how long they planned to put-in for. Their dogs, their attitude, all those rug-rats.

*

The sliver of new moon had set and Ed was asleep on his air mattress but woke foggy-headed to Guizar standing above him, growling and whining, his tail stiff and still.

"Snake? What is it, boy?"

Ed reached for his flashlight and sat upright.

Fubar stood ten feet away, body tense, quivering, teeth bared.

Guizar lunged at Fubar but Fubar was fast. Guizar shrieked. Ed jumped up and aimed the beam of light to see his pal pinned to the ground at his neck by Fubar's jaws. The big dog shook his head back and forth as if Guizar were prey, and Guizar cried out in terror and pain.

Ed grabbed a frying pan ran toward them, hollering and holding out his arms to make himself big. He swung the pan at Fubar but missed. The dog dropped Guizar and licked his bloody muzzle. Rivulets of red seeped down Guizar's throat to his chest.

"Guizar! Come!"

Fubar snarled and charged toward Ed. Guizar struggled to his feet and snapped at Fubar's left ankle. Fubar turned and clamped his teeth deep into Guizar's back. The pop of bone. Guizar fell limp.

"God, Jesus! Get out!" Ed threw the pan at Fubar. "Get the hell out!" Ed ran to Guizar. "Oh baby. Oh my baby." He called, "Help! Please, somebody."

Six people stood and watched.

Ed held Guizar and rocked him. "What can I do, baby? Oh God what can I do?"

One of the long-termers said, "Man, there's not much you *can* do. You might get the same treatment if you confront those jack asses."

"A bullet to the head is the most humane," said someone from the dark.

"I can't shoot my dog." But Ed could have put a bullet in Junior's head.

Ed sat alone in the dirt and hugged Guizar. He looked into Guizar's eyes and talked about Maria's Taqueria. "Remember how we shared the taquitos? They were your favorite, boy." And watching Regis and Kathy together on the couch, about Libby and Stripes. He talked until dawn. Guizar had been dead since 4:00 AM.

Two of the long-termers walked up. "We brought a blanket." Ed let them wrap Guizar and carry him to the grave they'd dug 100 yards beyond the circle. Ed watched in tears as these two decent men lowered his best friend into the hole, bowed their heads for a moment, then shoveled sand over the corpse.

Ed whispered, "Thank you." He sucked in the contents of his sinuses. "That's the kindest anyone's ever been to me."

No telling what reckless thing he would do if he saw Junior come walking out of the motor home, so Ed threw his worldly goods into the Cuda and headed out of Black Jack Green, taking first-gear up the dusty trail and slipping onto Bullhead Parkway north to the rest stop seventeen miles outside of Laughlin. He dropped coins into the vending machines for a Baby Ruth and bag of chips, then sat at a picnic table. He felt melancholy, but mostly his mind was blank.

A breeze came up as the sun went down and Ed was on the road again. The Cuda reached its 35/MPH maximum and the horizon cast a city-glow. Ed reached to pat Guizar but his hand came up empty. Soon, pink and blue and bright white searchlights shot into the night sky from the radiant hub of Laughlin. Ten minutes later, Ed found himself cruising Casino Drive. He was both excited and flustered by flashing neon, overwhelmed by the volume of canned music and laughter on the street, and ready to leave but for the fact that every beautiful girl this side of the Mississippi was bumping-and-grinding down the sidewalk. Hundreds of half-naked young women. Belly-button-revealing short-shorts and tube-tops. Slinky sun dresses and spike heels. Showgirls in feathers!

Ed spent his first night at Laughlin's southern fringe, sleeping in his car under lights in a 7-Eleven parking lot. He wanted to grab a copy of the morning *Mojave Daily News* the minute it was delivered and start looking for a job.

He'd keep eyes and ears open, and if he stumbled onto information about Peyton, great, but he'd lost the notes he'd taken during his breakfast in Hesperia with the guy–what was his name? Rib?–who claimed to have worked with Peyton, and had plain run out of ambition. The prize was no longer worth the effort. He still dreamed about Libby, as he always had. But, hey. He was in Laughlin. A new start was right in front of him and darn if Laughlin didn't look like the kind of place a man could settle.

Ed bought the paper, two cellophane wrapped cinnamon rolls, and a 24-ounce cup of weak coffee fortified with hazelnut creamer and five packets of sugar. He sat in his car and opened to the classifieds. Three casinos were hiring security personnel. He used the 7-Eleven bathroom to wash-up, shave, and change clothes. On the way out, he dropped his pocket change into one of the slot machines by the double doors and won five dollars, took his winnings and headed downtown.

The streets were deserted. Laughlin counted 10,000 residents most of whom were out the night before, but at 9:00 AM on Thursday, downtown was abandoned. Only two cars drove the six-lane main drag. Most all the casinos lined up along the east side of the street which was the west shore of the Colorado River. Each offered special deals, slots, buffets, GIRLS GIRLS GIRLS, air conditioning, free wifi, concierge and escort services, lounges, coupons, comps, cashback, and child-sitters. The twenty-six-story Maxfield Riverfront Resort sat nestled in the middle of the strip and boasted a new multi-level pool and garden with genuine grass.

Ed took the lobby elevator one flight below ground, walked into a buzzing fluorescent hallway, and through the door labeled Personnel. He filled out paperwork, stood straight, spoke with one of the women minding the office, and was hired on the spot to start the following day. The casino would handle permits and licenses. All he needed was a white shirt and black pants, which he had. The world looked shiny new.

*

Sleeping in the Cuda ... he had no choice. The thought of setting up camp every night back at Black Jack Green gave him the creeps. And the 15-minute drive would cost him big on gas, too, though the real issue was those dogs ... and Selma. And those awful kids who, all on their own, loosed on the community the slimy family vibe. Closer-in, however, his choices were limited. Thieves made up the indigent population of any gambling town so parking and sleeping on the street, even at a rest stop, with visible police presence ... he'd be asking for trouble.

Ed dug through the pile of clothing in the back seat, locating a clean white shirt and his black trousers. He shook them out then folded them, careful to match creases left and right, and placed one on top of the other on the driver's seat. He covered them with a tee shirt, then sat down as gently as he could so as not to disturb the folding. The night was warm and while he slept, with his hot damp weight, he steam-pressed the following day's uniform. So, Ed spent a second night sitting-up in the Cuda parked under a 7-Eleven surveillance camera and spotlight.

*

Thursday morning, he walked out of the 7-Eleven restroom clean and dressed for work. He poured himself a large coffee and stopped at the counter to pay.

"One dollar," the freckled salesgirl said.

Ed paid. "Can I ask you something?"

"I'll answer if I can." She slammed shut the register drawer.

Ed reminded himself not to fidget, stand tall and still. "I'm new in town, just got here, starting a good job today and...." Ed wondered how she stayed so pale-skinned in this sun, but he liked her red hair. Maybe he'd ask her to dinner, once he got settled. Jeebers. Settled. That had a nice ring to it. "What I really want to ask is if I could I pay you something – after *I* get paid – and you agree to let me sleep in my car in your parking area? Just for the next two weeks or so."

She looked him up and down. "It's fine with me. I

won't call the cops but it's a crap-shoot before 11:00 when I get here. And I leave in the morning at 7:00."

This was a huge relief and an almost perfect solution to his tricky situation: no money, no home, no friends. Ed's life to this point had heaped one disaster on another, but, during this last day, some magic was at work, planets were realigning, and life was turning around.

"I just realized you work eleven to seven at 7-Eleven." Ed laughed.

"Uh huh."

"I'm Ed. Ed Schotz." He held out his hand.

She took it. "Cheryl. So where's this job?"

*

Ed maneuvered into the underground parking and found the employee section located near the dumpsters, farthest from the bank of elevators. The day-shift hadn't arrived, but the night shift hadn't yet left so he waited for a spot, contemplating what persona to adopt in order to make this a long-term deal. Truly, he'd had enough of the great adventure he'd envisioned during his youth. None among those he'd counted as friends had traveled, much less for a full five years, but now he had. He'd gone far from home and seen the world. Eaten foods he'd never tasted, done things in bed he'd never imagined, slept among strangers he'd never see again. And this particular morning, his clothes looked not simply pressed, but starched.

Ed's shift supervisor stood at the time-clock.

"Reporting for duty, sir."

"Good morning, Ed. I'm Javier Rodriguez Rodriguez."

"Good morning, Javier."

"Uh, right. Call me Javier. I'm head of security at Maxfield River Resort. Here is your card-key, walkie-talkie, and name badge. You'll read about how and when to use these. Your weapon will be issued in a few days, and I'll test you then."

"Great. No problem. Thank you for the opportunity–"

"And our manual detailing casino policies and procedures, your duties, access, breaks, pay, meals, and such. Spend the morning in the staff room, studying. Afternoon, I'll begin you at the low-end slots. Follow me."

The staff room was ten degrees too warm with walls painted the sleepiest of taupes, but Ed kept his coffee hot and blinked his way through eighty-three mind-numbing pages of rules and regulations. The manual covered everything from armed robbery attempts to picking cigarette butts off the carpet, inebriated gamers to rowdy diners wanting to take a swing at the chef, swimming pool rules for day-players, and privileges extended, or not, to employees. Ed read it thoroughly and hoped to recall half.

"Remember," said Javier when he returned. "You are here to work, not play."

"Yes, sir." Ed handed back the manual and followed Javier onto the floor, which, at 1:00 PM was crowded with retirees who'd arrived for the weekend by the busload from L.A.

"The old are as tempted to get something for nothing as the young," said Javier. "They're after different pleasures, of course, one's a free lunch, the other's a free party. Watch, learn, but understand it's all illusion. Nothing here is free. It's why we pay you. Your job is to make sure everyone inside these doors stays on the straight and narrow."

"Count on me." Ed nodded and stood straight. "Do I get lunch?"

Thursday was Tex-Mex Fiesta Buffet day. Ed had 30 minutes to make one pass with one plate to fill from the warming trays. This was no Maria's Taqueria, but the tortillas were hot, the chicken was savory, the flan was cold, and there was not one piece of cellophane packaging in sight.

He sat for his final five minutes, half-dozing and watching the buffet. A woman wrapped a paper napkin around two corn muffins and put them in her purse.

Ed rose from his booth. "Ma'am. Pardon me." He stood behind her.

She turned around and appeared to be about ninety years old. "You're not going to try to break into the line, are you, sonny? Because I've been standing a long time to get this far."

"No ma'am. I'd just like to check your purse."

"You'd like to what?" She clutched it under her arm. "Do you have a warrant?"

"No, but I'd wager you have a couple of illegal muffins in there."

"I have no such thing."

"It's against the rules."

The line moved and she moved with it. "What are you implying, sonny? Edith, this man is accusing me of theft."

Edith turned toward Ed. She was younger and larger than the muffin thief. "That's my mother. Why are you singling her out?"

"No, no, no," said Ed. "I'm not singling out anybody. Just–"

"We have 56 of our close friends here from the bus," said Edith.

Seniors from left and right of Edith in the buffet line turned toward Ed.

"You really want to start something with my elderly mother?"

Ed needed to consult Javier before pressing the issue. "Absolutely not. I want you to know only that I'm on duty. Enjoy the muffins."

From the restaurant, Ed heard the whoop whoop whoop of a siren along with whistles and bells from the money cages. He raced toward the mayhem to find lights flashing, people cheering, and a woman in glittering heels bouncing like a pogo stick. She'd spun, and won, the Big Deal Wheel jackpot. The mirror-ball ceiling lights vibrated for a full fifteen seconds, dropping two epileptics to the carpet and the winner hung on to the man next to her and screamed while confetti snowed from the ceiling.

Ed ran up to Javier who'd called-in the medics. "Stay calm, Ed. It happens maybe twice a year. Really pisses off the Floor Manager."

"Jeebers. How much did she win?"

"Around $1000. Here comes. Don't argue. Just nod."

"Damn it, Javier. Can't you keep this from happening?" The floor manager was red in the face. "I should take it out of your salary!"

"Yes, sir," said Javier, knowing how unlikely it was to happen.

In the two months that followed, Ed rented a one-bedroom apartment from which he could walk to work. On weekends, he watched TV. He might decide to ask around about Peyton. Next week would be soon enough.

At work, Ed's surveillance skills served him well. He busted two card-counting rings and foiled six pickpockets. He broke up a drunken fist fight, and, on BBQ night, stopped a family of four from filling a picnic basket with pork ribs and jalapeno sausage.

Javier noticed all this with increasing delight over his new hire. A raise assured every six months, Ed stayed. He took life day to day and so smooth was his personal dissipation, he didn't notice his new apartment looking a lot like his old Saltine one-bedroom on Albatross Lane. He kept the drapes closed and the AC on high. His default dinner was a family size bag of Cheetos. He was content and saw no reason to alter his habits.

His job was safe. Ed passed the next ten years pursuing an uneventful life in Laughlin.

ELEVEN YEARS LATER—2017

Paseo Central's narrow sidewalk, wavy heat rising, was whipped by winds whose persistence kept dust from settling until after the sun went down. No shadows, no plate glass reflections, the world was a haze. What remained of Saltine's greens—cacti, ice plant, flattened astroturf—dulled to disappearing. Glory's red and blue neon OPEN sign hung in the grocery window as Saltine's lone beacon, and if Glory was open, so was Señor Hector senior. Most folks had completed their chores by this time of day and stayed in their homes so not to breathe the burning air that blew east from Los Angeles over the San Bernardino mountains and then joined the reek of agricultural run-off, oil-seepage, and fish-kill concentrated and evaporating off the Salton Sea as it reached east to Saltine.

Deckard, at seventeen, stood fifty feet up the block from Glory's. His brown hair banded into a ponytail, his hands hung sweaty at his sides. He wiped his palms on his thighs and stared at the apparition born, he was certain, of his own imagination.

A young woman with the bravado of a fresh caffeine buzz stepped out of Hector's Hardware, slapped on a pair of aviator goggles and scanned the Paseo. She was exactly as Deckard always thought she would be. Perfect. Her jeans were tight. Zebra stripes in black and fuchsia covered her long-sleeved tee shirt and matched her hair which shot from her head in all directions and fell to her shoulders in thick pink and black hanks. Deckard took a step toward her. "Hey." He raised a hand in shy greeting.

She hefted her pack to her shoulder and turned to look at him.

Deckard's skin sizzled, his feet felt like slices of burning toast. The toaster shorting-out, he popped and stumbled forward.

"Hey," she said. She took her time, zigzagging toward him through the heavy air. She stopped and looked him up and down.

He looked down at himself.

"Do I know you?"

Deckard wanted to say, Yes. Instead, he opened his mouth, closed it again.

"*Do* I?"

Deckard stared. "You'll think I'm crazy."

"Maybe I already do."

"I'm not." Deckard couldn't even smile. "It's this place that's crazy."

"That's what the sign said." She dropped her pack to her elbow and lowered it to the ground. "I'm Rorie," she said, and extended her hand.

"I'm Deck." He shoved his hand out. "You're here."

"I've got to be *some*where." She lifted her goggles to her forehead. "Should I go somewhere else?"

"*Not,*" said Deckard too fast and too loud. "No," he corrected himself. "Rorie." Deckard laughed then ground his molars and panic turned his stomach. "Please stay." In his seventeen years of life, there had never been reason to panic. "What I mean.... What I want to say is...."

Rorie gazed, with neither movement nor expression, into Deckard's eyes.

Deckard thought, this must be what maturity is. The girl looked his own age but stood calm and still, two feet in front of him while his own right index finger dug at the cuticle on his thumbnail. His slim body rocked back and forth on his feet, his nostrils sensed his own fear, and his eyes teared up.

"Toxic waste getting to you?"

Deckard shook his head. "It's just that...okay I am crazy –"

"We already settled that."

"I know you."

"Yeah?" Rorie lifted her chin. "How's that?"

"You promise not to laugh."

She crossed her eyes and grinned.

Deckard stopped rocking, straightened up to his almost six-foot frame. If she laughed, he'd have to convince her.... No. If she laughed, then she wasn't the right one.

"I won't laugh. Say something not funny already. Please."

"About ten years ago...." I'm going to screw up. "No, more than ten. When I was a kid," he said. "I met you a long time ago in a dream."

Rorie leaned close. "Really?"

Deckard opened his eyes. He edged backward. "You were a little girl then, and, well, you're not going to laugh?"

"Have I yet?"

"You haven't changed all that much, black hair–well, now it's pink, too–and brown eyes and you've always been beautiful, always, only now you're grown up."

Rorie stepped closer. "Anything else?"

"Oh, you know. Lots of stuff." Deckard wasn't going to tell her she'd been sleeping with him ever since.

"How do you know it was me you saw?"

"I know. That's all."

"That's cool," she said.

"I know."

The two stood gazing at one another.

"There's a cement slab behind Glory's," said Deckard. "We can sit. I mean, out of the wind if you want, if you don't have to be somewhere."

*

Four days a week at 6:00 PM, that day no exception, Peyton opened Glory's back loading dock door, butcher case trays stacked and balanced on his hip, prepped for hose-down.

Deckard heard the click of the loading dock door-latch. He swung around on the step where he and Rorie sat. "Dad!"

Peyton stopped, surprised, letting the spring close the door behind him. He said, "Hi there."

"Do you mind?" Deckard's eyes were wide and aggressive. "This is a *private* conversation."

Peyton caught himself before his surprise turned into a stare. "And this is a private loading dock."

Rorie stood, pivoted on the step, and held out her hand. "Hi," she said. "I'm Rorie."

"Peyton." He took her hand and tried not to look at Deckard, under the heat of whose glare Peyton could have been French fried. Deckard's teenage disposition chafed. He said, "Glory missed you today, Deck."

"Dad," said Deckard, "*please?*"

Peyton had hoped they'd forego teen demons. "I've got an hour more on the clock," said Peyton. "Maybe you two should take a walk, meet me at home."

Deckard stood. "We're leaving."

Peyton looked at Rorie. "You staying for supper?"

Rorie looked at Deckard.

Deckard stood and grabbed Rorie's hand. "She's staying."

With Peyton, Glory, and Doc, Deckard had been home-birthed, home-raised, and home-schooled. He wasn't a mini-Peyton by any stretch, he had ideas and tastes quite his own, but he hadn't ever traveled far afield–beyond where the trolley could take him, at any rate–so he had no first-hand knowledge of anything outside a ten-mile radius of the pink and white double wide where, so far, he'd lived his life. Except for a spotty connection on his jalopy of a desktop computer, Saltine was his definition of normal.

He led Rorie up Sidewinder Circle, past the Polk place. Deckard could feel Marge and Scooter's stares through the blinds. He understood what his dad had told him about his mom and the town's people. He said, "Replicants. Town's full of them."

Rorie laughed. Then stopped. Then laughed again. She held tight to Deckard's hand. "Replicants," she said, finally, "From *Blade Runner*. And you're Deck, *Deckard*. How cool is that?"

"Blade runner?"

"The movie," said Rorie. "Replicants are from off-world. They look human but they're not."

"Off-world?"

"Science fiction, but there really are Eldon Tyrells, lots of them and they're evil."

"Replicants are evil?"

"Not replicants," said Rorie. "Replicants just live and die."

"I'm trying to follow," said Deckard.

"Why do you think L.A. air is orange? Who do you think poisoned the Salton Sea?"

Deckard stood next to the rebar tree, a scared little boy. "I haven't thought about it."

"My friend," said Rorie, "we have to talk."

My friend, thought Deckard. He walked up the steps to the stoop, opened the front door and held it for her. She called me her friend.

"So, Deckard," said Rorie. "What's for supper?"

*

Peyton was home as usual at 7:00. "Something smells good."

"Indian flat bread," said Deckard. He sat at the table, chopping freshly picked tomatoes. "Rorie's been cooking."

"Flat bread, rice, beans, salad," said Rorie. "Been forever since I've cooked on a stove."

Peyton regarded this domestic scene and looked at Deckard who shrugged.

"Herbs," said Rorie. "Peyton? Can you pull some from your garden?"

Peyton walked through the kitchen to the back door and leapt from the back step. He veered left, walking between his aging fence, its wood silvery, and raised growing bed full of thriving seasonal crops – the only living green in Saltine. He used scissors to snip a handful of cilantro and pinched some basil, too. He looked back at the house. Libby was waiting, seated on the freezer.

"I like her," said Libby. She gave a thumbs up.

"Yeah, Doll. I like her too," said Peyton. "She reminds me of you."

"What a nice thing to say." Libby drummed her heels against the front of the freezer. "You know, Sweetcakes, you can't keep putting off the father-son talk."

Peyton walked back to the porch. "Deck and I already... we work in the garden and talk a lot about relationships."

"Relationships." Libby nodded. "What about sex?"

"Sex?" Peyton bent backward and peeked through the screen into the kitchen. He whispered, "He's – they're so young."

"Seventeen isn't as young as it used to be." Libby took a deep breath. "Oh! Those herbs smell better than roses." She dipped her chin and looked up from under her brow.

"You can't remember your own adolescence. You'll have to trust me on this. Our boy is a long tall jug of roiling testosterone and, yes, he may know how babies are made but if he doesn't know how babies are prevented, well, let's hope Rorie does, and, actually, whether she does or doesn't, I can't have the talk with him, or them for that matter, so you need to."

"Whoa, Doll," said Peyton. "I'm –"

"Herbs!" came a duet from the kitchen. Then, "Dad! Rorie's waiting and I'm starving."

"Go on, Sweetcakes," said Libby. "Supper."

"Dad," said Deckard. "You're slowing down in your old age."

She still loves me, thought Peyton. He walked into the kitchen, stood at the sink, and rinsed nuggets of rich soil off the herbs. He shook the bunch dry and asked, "Want it chopped?" Peyton felt way too young to be a grandfather and vowed to have a serious sit-down with the boy.

"Deck's got my knife."

Deck handed Peyton the knife, butt first.

Peyton didn't take it. He hoped his shock didn't show. "You're doing great, Deck."

Deckard held the knife, a silver handle with bone and turquoise inlay. Stripes's knife.

The room swam around Peyton. He held onto the back of a chair to keep himself vertical. Stripes's knife was not something he'd expected to see ever again. Why wasn't it covered by sand? Gone with the bones? Could he lift it from her and get rid of it once and for all? Should he ask about it? He brought his breath back to normal. "I can sharpen that for you."

Rorie turned and leaned against the sink. "Did you know that Deck's a hero who crushes replicants?"

"That's what his mother said when she named him."

Peyton watched Deckard wield his grandfather's knife. If Rorie somehow knew what Peyton had done almost two decades ago and came to blackmail him, she'd have let him know by now, wouldn't she?

"We spotted two of them, behind a curtain."

"Them?" Peyton startled. He envisioned Stripes committing hari kari.

"Replicants." She spooned mounds of rice and beans on each of three plates and sprinkled herbs for color, then tossed the rest into the lettuce, tomato, and snow pea salad and placed the bowl on the table. Two rounds of flatbread on each plate.

"Deck," she said, "forks?"

Peyton watched as his insolent teenage son bolted from his seat without complaint to retrieve silverware and paper napkins from the drawer and set them in place.

Peyton stood, dazzled. "Holy Moly."

Rorie froze. "You're not, like, religious or anything, are you? I mean, I don't want to – "

"No way," said Deckard. "But, personally," puffing his bony chest and looking soberly at Rorie, "I like to think everything on earth has a spirit."

"Cool," said Rorie. "That's what I think too. The desert is full of spirits. Creepy sometimes, but creepy sometimes is okay too."

"Amen," said Peyton. He wanted the knife out of his sight, gone. "Let's eat."

They loaded beans and rice onto disks of warm, pliable Indian bread, added salad, folded one edge over like a soft taco, and bit in.

Deckard grunted. Mouth full, he said, "Perfection."

Peyton nodded to the cook. He looked at his plate and said, "Wow," but all he saw was the knife.

*

Rorie stood on the back stoop, just outside the screen door. "Don't worry about me."

"Please," said Peyton. "Take the couch." Maybe his kindness would insure hers?

"I'm used to sleeping outside."

Deckard stood just inside, in the laundry room. He said, "What about snakes?"

"I surround myself with a force-field so they stay away."

"Oh man." Deckard's eyes widened. "You gotta teach me that."

"And I'm not used to sleeping on someone's couch." Rorie turned and walked into the laundry room, Deckard following her into the kitchen.

"All I meant," said Rorie, "I'm sorry." She looked back and forth between Deckard and Peyton. "I'd probably lie awake all night, trapped inside four walls. And besides," she said, "night air is, like, my cure for the orange sludge we breathe all day. I can get up in the morning thinking it was all a dream and start the day in the cooler blue."

Deckard looked at Peyton. Peyton nodded his head.

"I'd appreciate a pillow and blanket, if you can spare them."

"No problem," said Peyton. "The door is never locked. And, Deckard, uh, *Deck*.... Mind the hour?"

Deckard swallowed a groan behind clenched jaws. "Dad. *You* mind the hour?"

Peyton mocked a *mea culpa*, eyes wide, arms spread, kowtowing backward into his bedroom.

"Sometimes I wish he'd just go away," said Deckard.

"Really?"

"No, not really but sometimes I feel like that." Deckard walked out the back door into the dark and jumped off the stoop. "I'll show you around." He held the garden gate for Rorie and led her around the side of the double wide.

"There used to be goats, then chickens. Mom and Dad ate them before I was born."

"If I lived here, I'd have chickens." Rorie put her fingers through a piece of bent fence wire and pulled upward to straighten it. "You have enough here to build a small coop under the tree."

"Mom's buried under the tree on the other side. She died when I was born."

"Sorry," said Rorie. "Mine kicked me out when I turned fourteen." She looked at the small hillock of shrubs. "Been a long two years. I'd bet Peyton would let you keep chickens."

"I figured out which came first," said Deckard.

"What do you mean?"

"It was the egg."

They stood facing one another across the small café table under the rebar tree, no longer heavy with flotsam which had blown away or been taken down and used elsewhere. The wrought iron chairs had oxidized and rusted but remained on Libby's mosaic pavement. Deckard took off the button-up over his tee shirt and laid it on Rorie's seat. He said, "Do you really like to sleep outside?"

She sat. "Do you really like to sleep closed-in?"

"I never thought about it."

"Yeah." She watched him pick at his cuticle. "Nervous?"

He sat still. "I've slept in that room my whole life."

"I can't remember all the places I've slept. I'm not acting too weird, am I?" Rorie took a deep breath. "I usually don't get this involved."

"A lot of folks are like that."

She looked at Deckard, stared into his eyes. "I can trust you. I mean, I want to."

"Oh, you can," said Deckard. "You really can."

She took a small glass pipe out of her pocket, lit the nug of weed, and inhaled. She handed the pipe to Deckard.

He stared. "No. Thanks."

"Replicants might be friendlier if we all inhaled. No one who smokes wants to fight." Rorie ran her fingers through her hair. "How do you know it was the egg?"

"What? Oh because," said Deckard. "The very first *real* chicken had to evolve from some earlier *almost* chicken, and the new mutation–our current real chicken–had to hatch from an egg."

Rorie smiled at Deckard for a long moment. She nodded. "You figure that out yourself?"

"You're the first person I've told."

"Three years ago, my mom and I had a huge fight. It was about nothing, you know how it happens."

Deckard didn't know. He and Peyton had never fought like that. But he nodded.

"Mom told me to get out, not exactly in those words, and not come back. So I did."

"That sucks."

"It did at first. Guess it still does."

"Where'd you go?"

"Nowhere. Around. Mostly in the Mojave, camps near Jesus Rock–nice people, some nutcase fanatics, too. I've walked every foot of this area and hitched rides along the tracks." Rorie shook her head. "I haven't taken anything from anyone who wanted something in return."

"I won't ask for anything," said Deckard.

"Everybody wants something."

"I won't ask you for a thing. Where did you sleep? How did you eat?"

"Lots of men will buy a girl dinner. I've got the old five-finger discount down cold."

"The what?"

Rorie reached into her jeans pocket and pulled out Deck's red bandanna.

"Where'd you get–" He laughed. "Oh."

"Mom kicked me out but also taught me how to get by."

Deckard was ready to reach over the table, lift the girl out of her seat, hold her to him and zoom upward, inseparable for eternity in a caress of clouds. "What about your dad?"

Rorie's forehead crimped. "Never met him."

"Rorie," said Deckard.

"Deckard," said Rorie.

"You can ask me for anything," said Deckard.

"No one has ever told me that."

Deckard imagined taking her hand, but that would be asking for something. He wanted to kiss her cheek, her lips, to sit with her all night and listen to her stories or, even better, lie down on the ground with her and count stars in the sky, learn to make a force field. Oh, just her name, the sound of her voice. "I've waited my whole life for this."

A light went on and Peyton coughed in the kitchen.

Rorie pushed her hair back off her face. "Subtle."

"It's his MO."

"What do you say, Deck. My backpack?"

"And a blanket?"

"And a pillow."

*

Peyton woke the next morning putting the knife out of his thoughts and missing Libby something awful. He wished she could meet this girl who'd walked into their lives, made dinner, then posted a flashing Exit-Up-Ahead sign on the freeway of Deckard's childhood. Her presence signaled the end of an imaginary friend and a start to the acquisition of stinky male grooming products. Through the living room window the night before, Peyton had watched his adolescent Romeo's knee bounce frantically as he took a swing at manly charm. He'd hit home, too, if Rorie's demeanor was any indication: elbows on the table, leaning-in, and the smile ... more tender than she'd ever admit. It reminded Peyton of the smile Libby wore the morning they married.

Peyton peed and washed up. He pulled on his jeans and boots and walked through the kitchen to the back porch. He looked to the freezer and stretched wide. "Morning, Doll."

Libby's flowered dress and good mood were intact. "Morning, husband."

"There was a wild lass from Mecca," said Peyton "whose arrival caused Deckard's young pecka, to rise and stay risen, while Peyton's lay wizened.... Crap. I'm old."

"Aw, Sweetcakes," said Libby. "To me you're still the handsomest bohunk on the block."

"I'm an old fart. I should be down at Hector's drinking coffee with the other geezers."

"Mid-life crisis?"

Peyton looked at his garden. The asparagus were finally coming in.

"Deck needs you," said Libby.

"Try telling him."

"Now you have a daughter, too."

"Do you think she'll stay?"

"Do you think Deck would let her leave? Remember to have that talk, Sweetcakes."

Peyton heard the toaster pop, and the smell of coffee reached his nostrils. He bent backwards and glanced through the screen. Rorie was filling the sink with soapy water.

Without looking, she said, "Beautiful day, Peyton. You talking to your vegetables?"

Libby was gone. Had Rorie heard his thoughts? "Yep ... want herbs?"

"Sage. For the eggs."

"Coming up." Peyton hopped down and combed the patch of silver leaves, then snipped a handful of chives, too. "Got a couple of ripe tomatoes here."

"Cool. And we have lift off."

Lift off. Peyton grinned. Almost fifteen years. He'd thought about Libby every day of those years but hadn't realized how much he'd missed banter from the kitchen. It wasn't an art he'd cultivated with Deckard who was so serious, not the type for banter. So he had simply let it go, along with sex. Not since Libby stood at that sink had Peyton had such verbal exchanges. Not even with Glory, who was no slouch, conversationally. Peyton walked into the kitchen.

"Wash," said Rorie, "then sit and chop." She stood at the counter, shredding potatoes for hash browns. "Carbs. Staff of life."

Peyton grinned again. "You're pretty smart."

"I have an answer for everything," said Rorie. "Have to. And nobody's telling me otherwise. I don't know, though, if what I know is right." She stopped short. "Deck still asleep?"

"Till noon if left alone."

"I've never in my entire life slept till noon."

"And he's a grouch the first hour, too. Hey," said Peyton. "If it was your lovely face he saw first thing, instead of my grizzled old one, maybe he'd wake sweet as marmalade."

"Marmalade. That stuff's nasty." She scooped the bacon onto a paper towel and dumped the potatoes into the grease. "After I flip the taters."

Peyton liked the way Rorie kept her own counsel but made herself right at home. She really did remind him of Libby, and whether Deckard had somehow conjured this flesh and blood from years of pretending, or whether he simply had the brains to recognize someone special when he saw her, more power to him. He'd done well. Which meant Peyton had done well, and Libby could be proud. Peyton took a breath.

"Done." He stood and placed the chopping block on the counter.

"Okay. Watch the potatoes. Don't do anything to them. Just watch."

Rorie could hear Deckard's light snore. She stepped over clothing and looked around the small room, waiting for her eyes to adjust. An Albert Einstein poster hung over the bed, two shelves of empty beer cans, each one different, a desk with a computer. Rorie deepened her voice to sound like Peyton. "Deck. Breakfast." It worked well enough, too.

"Leave me alone."

"Oh, Deck," she sang sweetly, "Time to get up."

Deckard bolted to sitting. He coughed and caught his breath. "What. Jeez. I'm asleep."

"I can see that. Breakfast is ready."

"Give me a minute."

"One minute."

"Do I have to dress?"

Rorie raced from the room to slide the hash browns out of the pan before they burned. "He'll be out." She mixed the cheddar and tomatoes, sage and chives with the eggs and used the same pan to fry up a scramble. "I love to cook," said Rorie. "Been forever since I had a kitchen. Cooking's like making art, edible art. Not always pretty, but creative."

Deckard stumbled in, pre-verbal, barefoot and wearing pajama bottoms. He plopped onto a seat and drank his orange juice in one breath. He blinked half a dozen times and looked at Rorie, then Peyton. "I can't help it," he said. "I'm hard-wired for sleep." He stared at his plate. "Breakfast looks good."

"Surprised?" Rorie pulled the band out of her hair and shook her head.

"What," said Deckard. "Did you make this yourself?"

"Sage in an omelet...." Peyton looked at the egg on his fork. "Brilliant."

If either of the men had been watching Rorie instead of their plates, they'd have noticed a rosy hue brighten her golden-brown face.

"*Really* good," said Peyton. "A fellow could get used to this."

Deckard winced. Peyton was asking Rorie for something; to do it again tomorrow.

"Mmmm... *mmm*! I'll pick up another dozen eggs."

"Dad. *Enough*."

"It's okay, Deck." Rorie stood and took her plate to the sink. "And Peyton, don't worry about the eggs."

"Really? Why not?"

"I have a source," said Rorie. "Deckard'll do the dishes. You are good people. I'm going to take a walk."

Deckard gasped. He stared at Peyton. "See what you've done?"

Peyton was baffled.

Rorie reached into her pack and pulled out her goggles.

Deckard jumped up. He hadn't dressed. "I mean, I'm not asking, you're not leaving –"

Rorie swung her pack over her shoulder. "I'm used to roaming, Deck. Don't sweat it. I need space. I told you."

"Will you come back?"

Rorie smiled and kissed Deckard on the cheek. She said, "Enjoy your omelet."

Deckard followed her to the front door, the fingers of his right hand on his cheek where he'd been kissed, the left hand curling into a fist. He watched Rorie walk down the steps and around the side of the double wide toward the tracks and out of sight. He'd said he'd never ask her for anything. If he pushed, well, he didn't want to know. Yes, he did. No, he didn't.... He walked to his room and slammed the door.

Peyton sat for several minutes. He finished his plate, trying to focus on what he put into his mouth, then cleared the table and stepped out onto the back porch. "What just happened?"

"High drama," said Libby. "Smelly grooming products and high drama."

"Did I do something wrong?

"You breathed. Drama is native to the age."

Peyton shook his head. "So this is normal?"

"Nothing is normal. We have a teenager inventing love for the first time in human history. No adult could possibly ever understand."

"How do you know this?"

"Peyton," said Libby. "She'll be back."

"And Deck?" Peyton's eyes filled. "He's declared war on me."

"The boy is aching."

"I've been aching for years," said Peyton.

"His will pass, Sweetcakes. Not every calamity will always be your fault." Libby blew Peyton a kiss. "Tend your garden."

Peyton descended the steps and surveyed his crop of leafy greens, a portent of healthy carrots and potatoes and beets. He turned on the soaker hose and recalled a decade earlier, Deckard dropping seeds into thumb-holes, Glory making lunch in the kitchen. Life then was so much simpler. He felt now as if he'd been punted into the end zone of a Greek tragedy: wailers, mourners, a cataclysm of divine intervention and retribution, lightning bolts and all. At least he'd had a great breakfast.

Deckard lay on his stomach, sideways across his bed, certain he should not *ever* again get up before noon because look what happens. He'd never love again, either. Everything was ruined. Life was over. Why had his dad gotten so weird? And, he was still hungry. If Peyton were in the kitchen, Deckard would lie on his bed and starve to death. He'd teach his dad to stick his nose where it wasn't welcome. He'd lock himself in, write a suicide note. And a love letter. They'll find him cold and dead. He imagined Peyton and Rorie, crying at his grave, fresh next to his mother's. Deckard rose to compose a lover's lament, but his stomach squawked and he cracked open his bedroom door. Nothing. No sound. And the house still smelled of bacon.

Deckard eased into the kitchen. His plate sat on the sink. What food was left had cooled and congealed, but he inhaled every crumb, then finished what Rorie hadn't. Hers, he relished more intently, savoring each morsel, for her fork and maybe her actual lips had touched what he was consuming, he'd been kissed, a union to carry him through this crappy excuse for a life.

In the sixteen-plus years Peyton had worked for Glory, he'd never found the loading dock door locked. He knocked. He called her name. He mounted the wood staircase up the back of the building to her apartment and knocked. No response.

Peyton walked along the narrow space between her building and Hector's to Paseo Centro and read the "Closed" sign on the glass door.

He peered through the plate glass storefront, the sinking sun reflecting back on him, and eased along the length of the window to check the aisles. Maybe Hector Senior knew something.

"Hmm," said Hector Senior, bagging a half-dozen rubber washers for a customer. He took a ring of keys from under the cash register. "We can let ourselves in. We traded."

He slid the key into the dead bolt and turned it. The two walked into the store. Ceiling lights were on. Hector called, "Glory?"

"Oh thank goodness."

Peyton and Hector Senior ran to the sound of her voice. Glory was on the floor next to the clock. She hadn't felt well, but dressed for the day, made her way inside but not much farther. "I'm such a mess. If I try to move, oh it hurts."

"Lie still," said Peyton. "How long have you been here?"

"My stomach, my abdomen. I can't straighten up."

"Hector, stay. I'll get Doc."

Peyton raced across Paseo Centro, around the corner to Doc's and into the front office.

"Doc?" Peyton peeked into the examination room. He called more loudly, "Doc!"

Doc appeared from the living room. "Oh, Peyton. So glad you're here. Tea?"

"No, no. Get your bag."

Doc slipped his feet into his loafers, grabbed his bag, and followed Peyton across the street.

"She's on the floor, all balled up."

Doc knelt down. "Good evening, Glory. Are you hurt?"

"I want to puke. It's my gut."

"Left or right?"

"I don't know, dammit. I've been lying here all day. It hurts too much to stand."

"I'm going to touch your abdomen," said Doc.

Glory let out a ragged scream and balled-up even tighter.

"We need to get you to the clinic in Mecca."

She tried to take a deep breath. "And how are we supposed to make that happen?"

The three men looked at one another.

"Right," said Peyton. "We need some kind of stretcher."

"Hold on," said Doc. "Let me call Life Flight. Stay with her."

Libby's sepsis, almost sixteen years earlier, was the last time Doc had tried this. He hobbled down Paseo Centro to Mayor Nuckle's office. "I need to use the telephone," he said. "Glory's in trouble."

"Possible acute appendicitis," he told them. In any case, the gut was not something to play around with.

"Such a fuss. I'm so sorry," said Glory.

"Damn that broken bridge," said Doc. "Twenty years and not the town, not the county–"

"Doc?" Peyton understood.

"Let's pray it doesn't burst. She'll be out of surgery in no time, if all goes well. They'll want to monitor her for a couple of days."

"Should I go to Mecca with her?"

"No, Peyton. You can pick her up afterward. At the moment, there's nothing else."

"Why'd this happen?"

"The body wears out."

"Jeeez." Peyton let out a heavy sigh. "Maybe Deck and I will open for her tomorrow. Give folks a chance to buy a few things. Close down early, restock. We need that woman." He turned to Glory. "Can you hold on to a stretcher or should we tie you down?"

"I'm not an invalid, Peyton."

"Yes you are."

"You've got my purse and identification? Medicare card?"

He heard the effort in her voice. "You be nice to me," said Peyton, "or I'll make sure they drop you."

"Don't make me laugh. Oh, Lordy, that hurts. This nausea...."

Life Flight landed 90 minutes later in the rough behind the shop and kept the rotor moving. Dust and grit flew into a cloud. Two EMTs entered through the back door and lifted Glory onto the stretcher. One completed paperwork with Doc. The other strapped Glory to the gurney.

"I'll see you in a few days," said Peyton.

They rolled her as far as they could, then carried the gurney, with Glory on it, to the helicopter. They packed up their equipment and rose into the sky, heading north. The entire procedure took no more than fifteen minutes.

Peyton walked home. Sepsis. Appendicitis. Viruses. Was there any sense to life? He could understand the need people had for faith. It explained–or at least balmed–so many of life's problems. But understanding the need for faith was different from having it. Deck would have to fill any spiritual needs somehow else, perhaps through Rorie.

Young love provided structure for him and, despite Rorie's eccentricities, security. The two had already developed a foundation that appeared to strengthen daily. Yet, to Peyton, love remained as mysterious an impulse as a seed rooting and opening into a plant.

He entered through the garden gate.

"You are still my hero," said Libby.

"I'm plum worn out, Doll."

"You saved Glory's life."

"Hector had a key. Doc made a diagnosis. I made wisecracks. My stomach's a mess."

"Get some sleep, Sweetcakes."

*

Three mornings later, Peyton arrived in Mecca to retrieve Glory and escort her home. The trolley had taken two and a half hours, straight north to where the LED on Bank of America said 9:15 AM. He asked directions to Cabazon Valley Clinic and walked the ten blocks west.

"Oh, yes," said the receptionist. "Everyone here has met Glory. Yesterday she started haunting the halls, amusing the nurses, greeting patients."

"Ha! I knew it," said Peyton. "I'm here for her checkout."

He took care of the administrative paperwork, phoned for a cab, and waited by the business office. The elevator opened and three nurses–two from the ward, one from post-op–wheeled Glory out into the lobby.

"Peyton," laughed Glory. "Meet my new best friends. Wonderful, kind, generous, women who fed and healed me, made me cough to clear my lungs and get up and walk. And they gave me lip at every opportunity...."

All three balked. "We're the sweetest girls in the world."

Peyton shook the hand of each.... Leigh, Josie, Carole.

They'd clearly formed friendships, and put everyone in high spirits.

Glory stood from the wheelchair, a nurse at each arm until she straightened. "She'll be tender for about a week, but don't let her sit around lazy," Josie said to Peyton.

"And," said Carole, "no lifting more than five pounds at a time. If she runs a fever or is in any way compromised, call us immediately. We want to keep this one alive!" She winked at her patient.

Peyton held his arm for Glory to hang on to, they waved goodbye with their free arms and half a dozen people had collected to wave back. Peyton instructed the cab driver to a café near the spur.

They sat and ordered coffee and pie. The next trolley would leave in about 90 minutes.

"Peyton," she said. "You would not believe the energy and intelligence of these women. They work so hard and remain so upbeat, I stand in awe." She tasted her coffee and poured in two teaspoons of sugar.

"Sounds like a vacation. You didn't have such a bad time of it."

"Surgery is no fun, and I'm really sore, but in a healing way. If I'd been a nurse... well, I love those people and only hope after someone comes into my store, they feel as appreciated as I do coming out of that clinic. I must write and thank them again."

"I hope you do." Peyton was relieved. He hadn't known in what shape he'd find her, post-appendectomy–which Deckard called her 'apocalyptomy'–but Glory was back and lively. Everyone in town would be happy. "Deck and I opened the store during the afternoons to give folks a chance to buy groceries."

"Oh Peyton. That's the nicest thing anyone's ever done for me."

"Nicer than saving your life?"

"You *had* to do that. But you and Hector.... I can never thank you enough."

"All you've done for Deck and me.... I can never thank *you* enough."

"Okay," she said. "This just got embarrassing."

"We want you back."

The trolley had them in Saltine about 3:00 PM and Glory was able to walk slowly from the spur and even mount the steps to her apartment. Peyton offered to stay, but she wished to sleep, saying if she felt hungry, downstairs she had two dozen cans of Spaghetti Os.

"What's going on?"

Deckard didn't answer.

Peyton caught himself heating up and took a cooling breath. "Deck. I asked politely."

"You'll just ruin it." Deckard was dragging his mattress out of the bedroom.

"Just the opposite, son." Peyton hated tension. "If I know, I can be more useful."

"I'm moving."

"And taking with you your most valued possession?"

"I'm suffering infinite despair and what do you do?" Deckard couldn't bend the mattress around the corner into the kitchen. "You can make fun of me and let me die a thousand deaths, or you can help like you said."

"Oh, well then. I'll help. Where we going?"

Together they carried the mattress through the kitchen and living room, down the front steps into the dusk to the rebar tree.

"Right here," said Deckard. "I'm going to sleep outside."

"Like Rorie."

"This has nothing to do with Rorie."

"Wait," said Peyton.

"Why?"

"I'll grab a tarp." Peyton ducked around the double wide to the storage bin and came back with a piece of plastic for a ground cloth. He snapped it open and let it float to the ground, overlapping onto Libby's old mosaic. "There."

"And I think we should raise chickens."

"Okay." Peyton looked at Deckard's new digs. "Want company?"

Deckard squinted at his father, searching for traces of sarcasm and found none. "Maybe later."

*

The next morning, Deckard woke but didn't move. If he lay still, maybe sleep would come again and he would not see the light through his lids or sense the already warm air or – dousing his dreams – feel the pressure from his bladder. He sniffed at his own night breath, sighed and rolled halfway off the mattress to face the rebar tree. Libby's old mosaic felt cool against his hip but a raised shard dug into his ribs.

"It's later than you think," said Rorie.

Deckard's eyes sprung wide. He grabbed the sheet that half covered him and bunched it around his waist. He stared and blinked. "I thought you – "

Rorie sat in the chair she'd occupied three evenings earlier. "You thought what?"

"I thought you were gone."

"Well, I was."

"No," he said. "Really gone." Deckard would have sworn he could feel her breath dimpling his naked torso. "And that – "

"Maybe someday. But why such low expectations?" Rorie grinned.

Deckard adjusted the sheet, wishing he could stand up and think straight. She sat there so sure of herself. He wobbled on the ground, off-balance, and out-numbered. "I've always considered my expectations to be rather high."

Rorie stared into Deckard's still wide eyes and raised her brows. "You are *so* much like your father."

"I am *nothing* like my father."

"You were talking in your sleep."

"I was solving problems."

"What problems?"

"I watched the sky last night. Planets are made of rock and dust so how can they reflect so much light? They should absorb it. Not reflect it."

"You spent time on this? You really are evolved. Me, I'm more practical." Rorie moved her foot against the lumpy burlap sack she'd dropped earlier. The sack jumped.

Deckard froze. "Snakes?"

Rorie laughed. "Expectations, Deck." She watched him for a moment, then her gaze softened. "I'm sorry." She upended the sack and shook the contents to the ground. Out dropped two chickens and one rooster. They flapped and squawked and lost a few feathers before righting themselves, able to go nowhere, bound together at the ankles with twine.

"Wow," said Deckard. He pulled the sheet up to his neck. "Where'd you get those?"

"Really?"

"No. I guess not." Deckard marveled at the animals, the only parts of them moving were their eyes, and they all seemed to be looking at him.

"Leave them where they stand." Rorie stood.

Lie down with me, he wanted to say. I looked at you all night long and haven't stopped thinking about you. I thought I'd never see you again and you were lost forever. I didn't know what to do or where to look. You turned and walked away from me. I hated you.

"What about girls?" said Rorie. "Any girls our age in town?"

"Sure we have a dozen or so, but they're all replicants."

"How do you know?"

"Talk to one and you'll hear it right away."

"What do you mean?"

"I listen to their blah blah blah. I try to find meaning. But there's no information or thought or interest. I can't imagine day after day with so few signs of life ... with nothing to talk about."

"Maybe I'm a replicant."

Deckard shook his head. "No way." He saw a faint twitch of a smile.

"Maybe you're a snob."

"You think so?"

Rorie shrugged. "Maybe."

"I hope not."

"I bet I've come face to face with a lot of them. They're not only in Saltine you know. I agree with you, basically." Rorie stretched and turned her face to the sun. "Where's Peyton?"

"Probably in the garden."

"I'll make breakfast. Then we repair the fence? Build a coop?"

She's magical, She's perfect. Deckard pushed himself off the ground, keeping the sheet loose around him, and followed her up the front steps and into the house. He passed behind her in the kitchen and went straight to the bathroom to pee and pull on his jeans. Bathroom water-pressure fell when she filled the kitchen sink.

"Peyton! We need herbs!"

Deckard imagined his father smiling. "Crap," he said to himself. "If you think my dad is so great, marry him." I am nothing like my father. Deckard walked out of the bathroom and sat at the table, bare-chested.

"Put on a shirt, son."

Deckard lifted his chin. Make me.

Peyton looked hard at the boy. "What's wrong with you?"

It took more time than it would have only a week earlier,

but Deckard finally stood. He'd grown taller than Peyton. He walked to his room.

"I don't know." Peyton looked at Rorie. "Maybe you can figure him out."

Rorie lay slices of bacon in the hot pan and jumped back from the spatter. She cracked six eggs into a bowl and handed it to Peyton with a whisk. "Before Mom put her boot to my butt, she told me our fighting had permanently fouled her formerly pleasant nest. Fouled her nest. Like I was a chicken stinking up the house. She said I did it because what I really wanted was to leave, so what was I waiting for? Get out."

Rorie pulled Stripes's knife out of her pocket. She sawed across the chives and worked to chop the dill.

Peyton tried to sound casual. "Should we add them to the eggs?"

"Uh-huh." She picked up a fork and poked at the frying bacon. "Maybe Deck's doing the same thing. Fouling your nest. I mean not so you can throw him out, but so he can...."

"So he can grow up a little."

"Something like that, maybe. Bet he'll stick around, though." Rorie lifted the last strip of pork off the cast iron.

Peyton poured the eggs into the grease. The eggs bubbled and Rorie turned off the heat. She put slices of Swiss cheese down the middle and half a cup of salsa. With the spatula she folded one edge, then the other, up and over the filling to melt inside the log, sliced it into three portions and dropped a lid on.

"Oh Deckard," she called. "Vittles."

Deckard's bad attitude preceded him into the kitchen but Rorie had arranged the chairs so the two of them sat shoulders almost touching, across from Peyton, and the mood lightened.

He wasn't conscious of doing so, but Peyton always waited for the cook to lift her fork before he picked up his. Deckard didn't analyze it, but he waited until Peyton dug in before he did the same.

"Jeez," said Deckard. "This is so good. Everything you cook. How...."

In his seventeen years, Deckard had never endured the vertigo he suffered now, high as a cirrus cloud with confidence just as thin. Somewhere in that box of random books-to-borrow the Niland library sent weekly to Glory's, Deckard had read that girls mature faster than boys but he didn't remember reading about when it was boys are supposed to catch up.

Peyton put down his fork and patted his flat belly. "You're staying, then?"

Deckard stared at his plate. His body seized. Do not ask her for anything.

Rorie cleaned her plate. She said, "Chickens," and bumped her shoulder against Deckard's tense arm. "Ready?"

"Almost." Deckard's eyes met Peyton's.

*

What was left of the goat pen, lengths of wire not raided to line the planting beds, was enough to work with. "We'll have to reduce the circumference," said Deckard.

Rorie was eyeing the low grassy mound.

"Encircle that small rise," said Deckard. "And use the tree so the chickens have shade."

"They'll have a coop."

"We can shade the coop, then, and be under the tree ourselves when we collect eggs." Deckard felt very adult.

"I'm convinced," said Rorie. "Got wood?"

At the far end of the property, just outside Peyton's aged-to-silver artisan garden wall, lay a precariously stacked pile of irregular planks and poles. Odds and ends of cedar, oak, bamboo, cholla, and Joshua tree had lain for more than a decade awaiting utility.

"Careful," said Deckard. "Spiders."

Deckard lifted a length from the top and poked until the pile broke apart. Pieces tumbled and lizards scrambled. Spiders fled into burrows or jumped and ran for cover.

Rorie kicked at sections of wood with her boot. "Out, scorpions. Back off, black widows." She laughed. "Your lease is up!"

Deckard backed away. "What now?"

"Now we build."

Beyond dropping seeds into holes to grow sunflowers as a child, Deckard had never taken much interest in physical activity. Peyton gardened. Deckard read. Long before he cared about girls, he'd read that girls liked muscles on guys, and now he wished he'd taken more interest in the outdoors. Although, he had to say, gardening hadn't made much improvement in his dad's physique.

Deckard and Rorie each carried an armload of wood.

"That's probably enough," she said. "What about a hammer? And nails?"

"Okay." Deckard headed toward the house. "Dad?" Deckard considered that she hadn't laughed when he was shirtless before breakfast so maybe she wouldn't make fun if he bared his pale torso for the heavy construction. "Do we have any tools?"

By 10:00 AM, the mercury had already climbed to hot, and Deckard had stripped down without comment. He used a pick-axe to hack at hard ground, making holes for posts. He started on his fifth hole a foot from the tree. Six inches down he struck aluminum.

"Hey Rorie." He bent to look more closely and used the claw hammer to scratch at the surrounding dirt.

"What is it?" Rorie stood next to Deckard.

Deckard excavated down and pried an old aluminum can from the cement-like ground. Some of the fruit cocktail label remained, the top was pushed in and its side dented. He blew dirt from its surface, shook it, and heard a thunking sound.

He looked at Rorie then smiled and took off in a slow run. "You're it." He skipped past Peyton's fence, the wood pile, and toward the scrub, then turned and called back, "Want to know what's inside? You have to catch me."

She ran after him. "You have to run slower."

Deckard turned and ran backward until Rorie tackled him. Rorie hung onto to his right ankle. She spit sand. "Blech! Tastes like coyote piss."

Deckard drew-in his feet and sat on the ground cross-legged. Rorie mirrored him. She wore no makeup except for lipstick that matched the magenta in her hair. She was perfect and this was the perfect moment. Her face not two feet from his. All he had to do was lean forward....

"So are we going to open the can?"

Deckard looked at the can in his left hand. "Yes."

Rorie handed him her knife. He used the point to lever the lid outward. He held it out to her, she put her fingers in and pulled out a decaying piece of daisy-print cloth wrapped loosely around a roll of bills.

"Whoa," said Rorie.

"How much did we find?"

Rorie looked closely at what was left of the thick rubber band. "What does it say?"

Deckard took the roll. He spit on a finger and rubbed it across the print. "It looks like, WOW."

"No, silly. You have it upside-down. It says MOM, no. MGM. And look." Rorie pointed to the rest. "Resort Casino."

"Well, obviously that explains it." Deckard opened his arms.

"Explains what?"

Deckard couldn't wait any longer. He leaned forward and brushed his lips across Rorie's.

Her face turned pink and she looked down, but Deckard could see a smile on her lips. Maybe she liked him. Maybe he would do it again.

She tilted her head and asked, "How much did we find?"

He'd done it and he was glad. No apologies. There was a grown-up lesson here, something about listening to one's innards and going for it. He handed the roll to Rorie. "You count."

She bent the bills back and forth to separate them and shuffled them like a deck of cards. "Throw the dice?" She counted out $300.00 in twenties. "Where did this come from?"

"I can't even guess but it must have been here forever. I need to think."

*

By 1:00 PM, with only one purpled thumbnail, Deckard had relaxed enough to gracefully take direction from Rorie and he wielded the hammer with ease, pounding stakes into the ground. He'd climbed the tree to suspend the chicken-wire via rope, circus-tent style so the roof wouldn't slump, and was feeling accomplished and manly.

At early afternoon, Rorie stepped back. She said, "Deck, you're a natural."

"You think so?" His muscles ached. He wiped sweat from his upper lip.

Rorie looked at him for a moment. "I'm going in to start lunch."

"Wait." Deckard was quiet. "Maybe we should keep the cash a secret."

"Why?"

"It's not about the money so much as Dad knowing everything about me, what I do, where I go." He rocked on his feet and looked at the ground. "I want something private, something he doesn't know."

"Strange, isn't it? Everything about me is private," she said, "the opposite of you, and maybe I'd *like* someone to know something about me." Rorie walked toward the double wide.

Deckard let the hammer swing by his side, then walked through the gate into the garden. "Lunch in fifteen, Dad." She said I'm a natural. "Bring lettuce."

Peyton saluted.

Deckard hopped up the steps to the back porch. He stepped into the laundry room, returned the tools to their shuttered shelf, and slipped into the bathroom to wash and put on a fresh tee.

Rorie made tuna salad with more celery, green onion, and pickle than tuna, put it into sandwiches with lettuce, mayo, and mustard, and cut them in half on a serving plate along with three napkins and three glasses of milk. She sat and looked at Deckard.

Deckard glanced at Rorie. She nodded. "Dad, Rorie and I have something to tell you."

Peyton's jaw dropped but then he laughed. "Well, you two haven't known one another long enough to announce grandchildren."

"Dad!"

Libby from the back porch gasped and said, "Oh my God!"

"Well, what usually follows when a young couple says, 'We have something to tell you.'?"

Rorie chuckled and nudged Deckard. "He's got a point."

"Okay, okay, okay," said Peyton. He took a gulp of milk. "What do you have to tell me."

"When I was digging a hole near the tree, we hit an aluminum can."

"Yeah," said Rorie. "It was corroded and dinged and the top was pushed-in but Deck got it open and we found old cloth wrapped around a roll of money."

Peyton stopped smiling. He sat there, but in his head he was running down a wide street with what must have been 10,000 people laughing and talking, all going somewhere but in no hurry. He'd been drinking or had snorted something because the neon lights were bright and moving but not well-defined. He pushed his way through the bodies. Someone was chasing him. He had to run.

"Dad?"

"A roll of money. From where? How much?"

"That's just it," said Rorie. "The rubber band said MGM and was wrapped around $300."

Peyton looked from Rorie to Deckard. He said, "In a roll of twenties."

"Yes," said Deckard. "How did you know?"

"I don't know."

Peyton was riding shotgun in a yellow Ford. He didn't recognize the man behind the wheel, but looked past him through the window into the rising morning sun. They stopped in a desert town called Glamis, where Peyton got out of the car.

Peyton looked at Deckard. "I started with $400. Gave $100 to the man driving the Fairlane."

"What man?"

"Deck, I'm telling you I don't know. This is a lost memory coming back." He wanted to tell Libby about it.

"The rubber band also said 'Resort Casino'," said Rorie.

Peyton felt completely off-balance. Clearly these were memories, but detached not only from current reality, but from one another.

"I really need to eat," said Deckard.

"Do," said Rorie. She reached for a half-sandwich so Peyton and Deckard did, too. After lunch, Deckard cleared the table and washed the dishes without being asked. He used the soapy water Rorie had run earlier and stacked every piece neatly to drain. He asked, "Should I dry them?"

Deck offering to help. Peyton held himself back from a show of wild disbelief.

"That's what air is for," said Rorie. "We have something to do. Come on."

"Me too?" Peyton wanted to watch.

"Sure," said Rorie.

Deckard scowled.

The layout for the pen stretched about ten feet in diameter, its perimeter broken once by the tree, and once by the coop they'd built. The coop looked like Peyton's fence–unique and pleasingly full of bent wood but with air holes.

"Chickens need ventilation," Rorie had said.

The coop's back-end was a liftable hatch for egg-collecting with a latch for keeping it closed. The strips of chicken wire fit perfectly over the pen to keep out predators, and it was all held together with twist-ties saved from bread bags–from among the last of Libby's collections.

Peyton, hands on hips, shook his head. "You and Rorie built this?" Deckard looked up from under his eyebrows. "So?"

"It's a chicken-wire circus tent. You are an amazing team."

"Rorie brought chickens, too," Deck said. "And a rooster."

Peyton started pecking his head forward in a chicken

dance outside the coop. Before long, he was on the far side, singing *Dancin' With My Se-elf,* jumping and flapping like a Rhode Island Red on acid. He'd done this dance before. He felt the liberation in his body. Why couldn't his head remember where? *Dancin' With My Se-elf....*

Deckard wanted to crawl into a hole and cover himself with dirt.

Rorie started pecking and squawking, so Deckard had no choice but to join in and when he did, Rorie took his hands in hers. She squawked at Deckard. Deckard squawked back. Peyton came around and all three danced.

"Nice, very nice," said Peyton, breathless. "Where are those critters?"

Rorie left to retrieve the birds.

Peyton and Deckard broke-up twigs, mulching the pieces with hay and dry leaves for nesting. "Son, your mother wants–rather, I know your mother would want me to talk to you about sex."

"Dad!"

"No, no. We have a couple of minutes and might as well begin."

"I know about sex."

"How?"

"Everything is on the internet."

"Everything?"

"Absolutely *everything.*"

Peyton had never once looked at the internet. "What about how *not* to get pregnant?"

"Dad. *Everything.* Can we talk about something else?"

Peyton wondered if there was anything in this new world that wouldn't baffle him. "Señor Hector senior carries feed. I'll pick some up." Then Peyton thought better of it. "Unless you and Rorie want to." He reached into his pocket and handed Deckard five dollars.

"Thanks."

Rorie swung around the corner of the house, carrying the animals upside down by the twine binding their feet. Deckard knelt and opened the hatch on the coop. One-by-one Rorie freed the foul and pushed them through the hatch. They clucked and stumbled out the other end into the pen, righted themselves and began pecking at the sandy dirt.

"Let's get some feed," said Deckard. He took her hand, she waved to Peyton with the other, and they walked toward Paseo Centro and Hector's Hardware.

*

By mid-afternoon, Peyton, alone in his garden, couldn't get the song out of his head. He was having flashbacks. He kept seeing a sign, "Area 52"–what the hell was Area 52? Area 51, sure, everyone knew about that: aliens and spaceships in the middle of the south Nevada desert. But Area 52? Uniformed men–he among them–dancing to Billy Idol in a fenced, flat dry field? *Dancin' With My Se-elf.* Descending into bunkers for sleep. And goats. Dozens of goats, opening their mouths with no sound coming out. He hadn't dreamt it. He'd had a goat tied to his wrist when Libby found him. So long ago. Still a mystery. The hour was late. Time to get to Glory's.

*

Senor Hector senior charged 69¢ per pound for feed. Deckard bought three pounds of high-protein chicken pellets and introduced Rorie as his friend from out of town. With $2.93 remaining, they stopped in at Glory's Groceries.

"Hey, young man! I've missed you."

"I'd like to introduce Rorie. She's from–well she's kind of from all over, but originally from the teeming megalopolis of Frink."

Rorie extended her hand. "Pleased. Rorie Boreanaz."

Peyton had let himself in at the loading dock door and heard their voices. His heart hung on his sleeve. Rorie was indeed terrific and Deckard was smitten. If this is whom Deckard had imagined for the past ten-or-so years, Peyton was confident his son knew more about the world than he himself did. Peyton was grateful for the girl and happy for them but their attraction left him alone, and lonely.

Rorie shopped for almonds, an apple, and a banana.

Deckard handed money to Glory. "Thanks, Grandma."

"Come here, young man." She wrapped her arms around his stick of a body in a bosomy hug that lasted too long but he indulged her.

Back at home, Deckard threw a handful of pellets, several almonds, and a piece of banana into the pen. He bit into the apple, twice, and spit both chunks in as well. He and Rorie together gazed like new parents while Sophie, Martha, and Greedy-Bastard pecked and squabbled over the food.

"We should give them broccoli, too," said Rorie. "Greedy-Bastard will have his way with the ladies and before long, more chicks and more eggs that we can eat, we can sell the excess."

Did that mean she planned to stay? Deckard shook his head. He said, "Don't you find it remarkable? They take that stuff and turn it into egg."

"Indeed. Now," said Rorie. "To the garden. Do you think Peyton would mind if I copped a couple of square feet?"

"Can't imagine he would." Deckard used his thumb to make four shallow holes, about 18″ apart in a square of damp soil at the far left corner. "What are we planting?"

*

Peyton arrived home jittery, Glory's birthday closing-in and he having no idea what to do to celebrate it. There would never be a way to repay all she'd done for him and Deckard, but he hoped the satisfaction she'd felt from watching Deck grow up smart and strong was a start. Sixty-five was a milestone. Maybe Rorie would have an idea.

"A surprise party," she said, without even thinking. "Has that ever happened around here?"

"I can't remember one," said Peyton. "Deck, you?"

"Not that I was invited to."

"Okay," said Rorie.

A party is what Libby would have done. Peyton said, "Tell me how I can help."

"This is probably a good time to tell you," she said. "I borrowed a square foot of garden."

"What for?"

"I traded my cow for a handful of magic beans. They needed planting."

"She wouldn't tell me either," said Deckard.

Rorie was all smiles.

Peyton left Deckard and Rorie in the kitchen. He stepped out onto the back porch in the quiet dusk and surveilled his planting boxes. The potato greens were lush and his cabbages solid. Never having felt great ambition that he could recall, Peyton was content in the life fate had dealt. Growing food out of the ground gave him joy and he saw Rorie introducing Deckard to related pleasures, and maybe more. The biggest piece amiss, aside of course from Libby, was the whole-of-a-life his scraps of memory should come together to make, but didn't.

"You're serene this evening," said Libby.

Peyton turned toward the freezer. "A thin veneer, Doll. So much going on."

"About Rorie?"

"Rorie, Deck, teen angst, Glory's party." Every time

Libby appeared, Peyton wondered if she had run into Stripes yet, somewhere in the either.

"Aw, Sweetcakes. You've lived through worse."

"Also," Peyton hesitated. "Doll, I might be remembering things."

She sat straight. "What kinds of things?"

"Just... *things*. Random images. A yellow placard on a chain link fence that says, 'Area 52–Keep Out'. What is that from?"

Libby's swinging feet stopped. Why now, for heaven's sake after all these years, did that man have to start remembering? What good could come of it? It was so long ago and, heck, she was dead. Why should she have to explain?

"The kids dug up $300 in a can while building a chicken pen. Did I bury it there? I swear I know something about that money. I just can't remember what."

Libby sat icy still. If she kept the lie going, would he forgive her when he found out? And he would, eventually, find out. If she fessed-up in tears, would he let it go? She hadn't really done anything wrong. She'd saved his life. So what if she'd made up a history for him, picked his pocket? She was going to take him on an anniversary trip with the money. It's not like she could have put a stamp on his forehead, after all, and returned the package to sender.

She let go of a deep sigh. "Daddy was keen on Area 52, aliens and all. He even took out abduction insurance one year. You probably got an earful from him. It's an old rumor most people have forgotten about."

Peyton didn't want to upset Libby. He'd always backed off–not asking, not knowing, but he was entitled to a past, wasn't he? Especially now that it was coming back. "Doll. Please?"

Libby watched him for a moment. "They used to say

it was a top-secret military base where the government did experiments on animals and people and it started with Ronald Reagan and Nancy and their psychic stuff and the Russians. Anyway, if Area 52 actually existed, it was mostly hidden underground southeast of here." She paused and watched Peyton for signs of recognition. "Psychedelic drugs and mind research and experiments on Communists and goats–oh my gosh. Nanny." She spoke more slowly. "Peyton! Were you and Nanny at Area 52?"

"I don't know. Wherever I was, I was dancing. And staring at goats."

"I've seen you dance. Naked." She desperately wanted to change the subject. "You know, Sweetcakes, I do like this girl. Is she the Rorie who's been Deck's secret friend all these years? I thought I'd be jealous. But I'm not. She understands replicants. Unbelievable."

It was Peyton who felt jealous. Whether Deckard and Rorie had been doing the horizontal two-step or were still simply holding hands, Peyton didn't know, but he couldn't do even *that* with Libby. He sunk into self-pity only after talking to her, but he didn't want *not* to talk to her. "Doll, I need help. What am I supposed to do?"

*

"Two weeks should be just enough time," Rorie had said when Peyton asked further about the celebration for Glory. "Maybe Deck can find a suitably festive spot."

That night, at dinner, Deckard announced, "I found it."

The apparition of Stripes's knife never left Peyton. He wasn't sure he wanted anything else found. "What did you find?"

"A place for the party."

Rorie lit up. "Already? Where?"

"Well," said Deckard. "Glory's birthday falls on a

Sunday so I thought maybe Reverend Byle would let us use the church yard after services."

"Perfect," said Peyton. "Glory attends Sunday morning sermon."

"Not only that, but Mrs. Byle offered to make a fruit punch, and walk Glory out the back door where we can be waiting."

Rorie looked at Deckard as if he'd worked a miracle. "You are good."

"Indeed he is." Peyton felt pride, but also something else he couldn't name.

From feeding and bathing to story-telling when Deckard was small, to shopping and cleaning as the boy grew, Peyton had always taken care of everything. He'd done the planning, fixing, repairing, gluing, painting, cooking, comfort-giving, band-aid applying, and deciding. He'd done it all and had felt useful doing it. Deckard needed him. Until now–that was the wave washing over him. Without anything to compare it to, Peyton didn't know if it was healthy or not.

Deckard looked like he'd won a million bucks. "What should I do next?"

"Well, I was thinking." Rorie looked to Peyton. "Rather than ask everyone for a card, cards Glory will put in a shoebox somewhere and never see, I think we should buy a large piece of white board and ask everyone who wants to, to sign it with a birthday wish. We'll frame it and she can hang it."

From the back porch, Libby said, "I approve."

Peyton said, "You're breaking me into little sentimental pieces."

"Maybe you and Deck can take the trolley to Niland Stationary to buy board and a frame? I'll stay here with the chickens."

Peyton and Deckard looked at one another and nodded.

"And as long as you're going to the city, I'll give you a shopping list. I love this."

*

Deckard slept in his jeans and tee shirt and woke as the eastern sky turned from cobalt to hazy peach. He rolled off the mattress to the mosaic and pulled on his boots. Rorie had moved with her blanket and pillow from wherever it was she'd been spending the night, to the edge of Deckard's bed. He didn't know when. He lay down again. "Rorie?"

She rolled onto her back. "Mmm."

"You wake up beautiful."

"Mmm."

Deckard leaned close. This seemed a good time. "When I was about five, I met an imaginary friend. Someone who grew up with me."

"Uh huh. You said."

"Did I tell you her name was Rorie? I've known you since I was five?"

Rorie turned toward Deckard and opened her eyes. "That's spooky."

"Yeah. Do you believe me?"

"I guess I do." She smiled at him. "Must have been you keeping me safe."

"We ate at the table every night. You slept in my bed–"

"Indoors?"

"With me." Deckard shifted closer. "That's the only weird part. Yeah, indoors." He put his arm over Rorie's waist and she snuggled closer. "Will you let me kiss you? I mean, you're lying here. It's a dumb question." Deckard closed his eyes and put his lips against Rorie's for the briefest moment, then pulled away dizzy.

He rose to his feet in a cloud of fantasy and tiptoed up the front steps, opened the door to Peyton's room and touched his dad's shoulder. "Wake up, old man."

"Abe?"

"Who?"

"Abe leave me alone. Oh, it's you. Deck." Peyton sat up and rubbed his eyes. "What time is it? Everything okay?"

"We're going to Niland, remember?"

"Right. Right. I've been dreaming." Peyton dressed quickly, made sure he had his wallet. "Let's eat in Niland. Take some of the cash."

In his imagination, Deckard had re-kissed Rorie twenty times that morning before he and Peyton caught the trolley. He hoped he'd done it right and wished he could talk about it but it seemed plain wrong to talk with his dad. The thought made him queasy. He understood why guys in town hung out together. They needed to share their ignorance and spread their anxiety.

Peyton and Deckard used flashlights and stomped the desert floor to scare away night creatures, and made their way to the spur for the 6:00 AM ride.

"You called me Abe," said Deckard. "Who's Abe?"

"I don't know. When I search for a face.... Do you remember a long time ago when I used to tell you stories in rhyme?"

"You told me all kinds of whack stuff. You thought it had geeky charm."

"Geeky charms. Sounds like a breakfast cereal."

"Good one." Deckard couldn't help but smile. "You told me about brothers growing up together, escaping danger, bright lights, dancing, guy-fairy-tales. You made me laugh but I don't remember the point."

"They were pictures that came to me from nowhere I could name. When you and Rorie found that $300, the rhymes in my head started again. I get disconnected images. I make them rhyme but don't know where they come from. Am I nuts?"

He hoped Deckard would be satisfied with that. Peyton himself, of course, was not. He was frustrated. Nothing connected. The more pointed his gaze, the more blurred his vision.

On the trolley to Niland, sitting beside Deckard, Peyton began to recite.

"*From Laughlin to Amboy to Yucca on south,*
Area 52 banished all doubt.
51 is well-known though a secret no less,
52 is less-sought but more chilling I'd guess.
The New Earth Battalion was where I would thrive,
Went underground so long though, the sun hurt my eyes.
A sea where naught floats, a shed full of goats,
A battalion and bunker, in which to hunker,
We smoked plenty weed, and lived by a creed,
Warrior monks, we danced to good deeds.
But one day I killed by the look in my eyes,
The goat keeled over, and I agonized,
I grabbed its sister before she, too, died,
Took off overland, alone, compromised.
They chased me to Mecca where I hopped the spur,
I took the first trolley, an easy detour,
But must have blacked-out, then learned I'd a wife,
Woke up in Saltine for the rest of my life."

Deckard stared at Peyton "Yeah, Dad. You are nuts. And you make bad poems."

*

At 3:00 PM, after a long morning of shopping Peyton and Deckard climbed the back steps of the pink and white double wide. From Niland, Peyton carried a plastic

Thrifty Foods shopping bag in each hand. Deckard managed a flat three-by-four-foot package wrapped in brown craft paper.

Rorie sat at the dining table, snapping the ends off beans and pulling away the long fiber that gets caught in teeth. "What kept ya?"

"We were kidnapped by aliens." Deckard leaned the package against the table.

Rorie laughed and kept working.

"I sure like to hear you laugh," said Peyton.

"Well," she said. "Say something funny."

"I have to get ready for work. Here are your groceries." Peyton left the sacks on the Formica counter and walked into his bedroom.

Deckard waited for his dad to close the door. "He was acting so strange." Deckard turned to Rorie. "We found everything on your list."

"Cool." Rorie was quiet for a moment. "I swept the house, prepped dinner, checked on my seedlings–oh they're so pretty, and fed the chickens."

"How are they?"

"No eggs yet, but the kids are good. All I've thought about all day, though..."

Deckard's sunburnt face turned redder. "Me too." Deckard had read that boys were always more interested in sex than girls, but he wondered where that information came from.

"Okay you." Peyton had changed his clothes. He walked through the house, let the front door screen close behind him and leapt from the porch down to the ground. He called back, "See you at seven. Be good."

"I've been good all my life," said Deckard. He looked at Rorie. "I want to try bad. Although not in any deep sense."

She pushed a hank of thick black hair behind her ear. "People assume because I've been on the road that I've done all kinds of nasty stuff." Rorie laughed. "Well, I've done maybe more than you." She glanced up.

She wasn't ready to admit it, but this was new for Rorie, as well. True, she wasn't a virgin. A month after she left home, she hadn't eaten for almost three days so sat for dinner with a slab city occupant who later in the evening wouldn't let her go, no matter how she fought or how she tried to scream with his hand over her mouth. She ran as soon as he'd passed out and pushed the ordeal into deepest memory along with other childhood hurts. She didn't want to feel pain. And she certainly wasn't quite ready to give herself over to deep feelings, even if Deckard would never intentionally hurt her.

"Maybe more, but not by much. I don't accept anything from anyone because it's never free. Even from my mom. Even her. You and Peyton seem different."

"Your mom wanted you to pay her?"

"She called it a return on her investment. Like if she fed me and kept me alive, I should turn into money she could spend. It's why I steal instead. I'd rather steal than be beholden."

Deckard nodded, trying to understand what he'd never experienced. He thought for a moment. "Do you ever wonder if learning a lesson is less important than figuring out what stops you from learning it? Not *you* necessarily, but all of us, me."

"You're deep," said Rorie.

"I want it now, that's all."

Rorie laughed. "Keep looking, Deck."

"You are so, so perfect."

"Ha!"

"Don't laugh." Deckard was hurt. "Are you laughing at me?"

"I'm sorry. But I'm not perfect. Trust me." She laughed again.

"Jeez, Rorie." Was paying her a compliment the same as asking for something? He changed the subject. "Let's go outside. Under the tree. Count our chickens."

Deckard grabbed a blanket from the laundry. Libby watched them walk out of the house, down the back steps, and out of the gate. Deckard shook the blanket and let it float to the ground under the tree. "You and me, let's make a scene and scandalize the replicants."

Rorie looked around and behind her. "Nobody's watching. Unless Mrs. Polk's got binoculars."

"She does. Let's make a scene."

"A small, quiet one."

They sat on the blanket, side by side, then lay back and turned toward one another. Rorie put her head on Deckard's right arm, cool next to her ear and without padding.

Deckard put his left arm around Rorie's waist, his hand on her back, and pulled her close enough that their chests pressed together and their legs entangled. Her feet hit just below his knees. Chaste dry kisses, to start. Deckard wanted to hold her tightly, as powerfully as his boney body could, but was restrained by a fear of not knowing what was right–if what he did would please her or if she'd feel trapped and want to escape.

Rorie didn't defend herself against Deckard's tenderness–a new sensation, tenderness. Her own fantasies were less explicit than what she'd heard guys always wanted, but she responded to Deckard's hesitation as if he were being sweet, intentionally gentle, and, because of it, she didn't need to protect herself, she could let herself go just a little bit.

Their mouths opened against one another's. No clothes came off, but their bodies were learning to move together. Through her tee shirt, Deckard's left hand moved to hold Rorie's breast. Deckard pulled his head back, wide-eyed, gulping air. She recognized his body language. Deckard's body quivered and spasmed, then relaxed. His brain relaxed, too. His eyes closed.

"So," said Rorie to herself because no one else was awake. "This is how it's gonna be."

Deckard woke after an hour. His right arm was asleep. He gazed at the most beautiful woman he'd ever seen, couldn't believe what was happening, dream becoming reality, this creature he'd always known and still had yet to know. His first orgasm with a woman. Kind of. His arm was dead. "Rorie," he said, as quietly as he could. "Rorie."

She opened her eyes and blinked several times.

"I have to move my arm or it's going to turn black and fall off."

"Ewww." Rorie lifted her head and rolled onto her back. She yawned. "We kiss well together."

"I'd say so." Deckard bent his arm at the elbow and tried to flex his muscles. He whispered in Rorie's ear, "I'm sorry. I know I was supposed to wait."

"You'll pay." Rorie patted the dust from her clothes into the air. "You ticklish?"

Arm dead or not, Deckard jumped to his feet and stepped back, bumping the coop. "No."

Greedy-Bastard crowed.

Peyton arrived home at 7:00 PM with a flank steak and in a great mood. "What have you two been up to?"

Deckard looked up from the kitchen sink. "Nothing."

"Uh huh. What do you say we take those cobs of corn and the steak, and grill them?"

Rorie unwrapped the steak. "What are we celebrating?"

"Life. Good fortune. Glory's party. We have a grill, somewhere," said Peyton. "And all that old, dry, left-over wood. We'll make a fire pit and char this hunky piece of meat."

Peyton watched Deckard turn red. Yep. A changed energy.

By 7:30, the breeze had died down and Rorie had built a rock-ring near the back steps but with enough clear space to avoid burning down the house or singeing the greenery. From the garden, Peyton watched her go back inside, then he arranged kindling and larger branches.

"You're right, Sweetcakes." Libby sat on the freezer. "It's as you thought."

"Did you actually watch?"

"I'm stuck here on this box, so no, but I could hear the Mmmms and Ahhhhs of lift-off. His, anyway."

"Remember our first time?" Peyton poked at the new fire and added another branch.

"We waited for what seemed like forever – "

"It was two weeks, Doll."

"A year and two weeks." Libby thought maybe she shouldn't have said that. "I was the first to reach the moon. You were such a gentleman. But then I fortified you with breakfast, and, well!"

"You're killing me, Doll."

In the kitchen, Deckard slathered butter, salt and pepper on the corn, then pulled the husks back up for grilling. "These should go on first," he said as Rorie walked in.

She stood behind him and wrapped her arms around him. Deckard's body stiffened.

She pulled away. "What? Did I do something wrong?"

"Dad's right outside."

"You think he hasn't guessed?"

"But he's right outside and I'd rather keep us, to ourselves."

"Us?" Rorie gathered up the cobs of corn and let the spring slam the screen door behind her as she walked outside.

Peyton balanced the metal grate over the fire. "We should start the corn."

Rorie sat on the steps and said nothing.

Peyton sensed the drop in voltage. He minded the coals and wasn't going to ask.

"Asbestos fingers, huh," she asked.

"Calluses from garden work."

Rorie spoke down to her feet. "Why is he so weird?"

"I take it you're referring to the infant in the kitchen?"

Rorie chuckled and looked up.

"It's the species. It's men."

"All of you?"

Peyton wanted to laugh, but didn't. "Women are such a mystery. It's a rare man who isn't scared to death of humiliation. We screw things up, hurt you, and end up looking stupid."

"Even the smart ones?"

"Hell, Rorie. The smart ones are the worst. Before they move, they've thought of ten things that can go wrong, and they've thought about each at least ten times, so it seems like a hundred things can go wrong with no possible way they can go right."

"So? I'm new at this."

If Peyton was right about Rorie, she might pick up and leave before working out a reason to stay. Her bravado hid fear, and how deep her fear ran, he didn't know. He hoped she wouldn't run, though if she were going to, she'd wait until after Glory's party.

"Give the boy time to catch up with the man I know he'll be." He rotated the corn. "With your help, maybe." He called, "Deck! We should put the steak on."

Deckard slunk out of the house with the slab of flank steak seasoned on a flat of wood. "I found a piece of cedar. It's supposed to add flavor."

"Well, put it right in the middle, son, and we'll see."

Deckard lowered the planked steak onto the grill, then backed away. "I don't know. Will there be enough heat? And what about grill marks? Maybe cedar planks are for barbecues that close on top. Or the wood should be on top to trap the heat, not underneath–"

"Deck," said Peyton. "Relax."

Deckard backed up farther and sat on the step next to Rorie. He smiled at her but she didn't look at him. He put his arm around her shoulders and moved closer. Rorie glanced at Peyton and the corners of her mouth trembled.

"Let's start the way you prepped it," said Peyton. "If cedar turns to cinder, we can always get those grill marks."

*

The moon had set and the air was clear enough to see spots of twinkling wildfire beaming through a million punctures in the indigo dome. Deckard lay under the stars on his mattress and remembered when he and his dad invented answers each time a question came up that neither knew the real answer to—they devised half a dozen answers to each question. Rorie presented him with unspoken questions to which he couldn't even imagine answers. Deckard watched the stars and pondered what made one answer better than another.

Rorie appeared at the front door and turned off the porch light. She let her eyes adjust before taking the steps one at a time, and joining Deckard lying down and looking up.

"I forget how beautiful it is," said Deckard. "I used to try to count the stars. Dad and I did it when I couldn't sleep. We'd come out here."

"You're lucky." Rorie stayed on top of the blanket but turned on her side to face Deckard. "I don't think my mother ever cared about such things.... I mean, I never really figured out why she even bothered to have me."

Deckard didn't know what to say.

"She put me in school because it was free baby-sitting."

He pushed the blanket off and rolled close to Rorie. "Would you let me hug you?"

"Yes."

Deckard worked one arm under her and wrapped the other arm over her. "I'm sorry about before. I won't do that again, push you away."

"I worry sometimes if I let myself cry, will I ever be able to stop."

"You will stop. I promise."

Rorie's eyes were already closed and her breathing slowed.

Deckard wanted to take her clothes off, but she was asleep so instead shifted onto his back, drawing Rorie's arm over his chest and her body into his side. He pulled the blanket over them and looked at the sky.

*

Before dawn Deckard woke ready to leap because some critter had crawled under his shirt and up his belly. What he actually felt was Rorie's arm moving on his chest. She had spooned-up behind him. He tried to turn to face her, but she tightened so he lay still.

Rorie spread her fingers and with their tips explored his chest, his throat, his face. He stretched to kiss her palm but she pulled her hand. She kneaded at the front of Deckard's shoulders and he moved his head to give more room to her hand.

"Ah, Rorie. This is a dream."

She pulled at his shirt and slid her hand underneath, she brushed his stomach. "Yes, this is a dream," she said. She kissed his neck and he turned liquid. Without seeming to move, he rolled to face her. Her hand now on his back, his hand on her back under her camisole. He wanted more of her. He slipped his hand up past her neck into her hair, he caught it and pulled back her head. He looked into her eyes and grinned.

She grinned back. "Am I funny?"

"I had to stop," said Deckard. "Just for a minute. I've been so ready.... My body...." He calmed, then drew Rorie's camisole over her head and nudged her onto her back. "You are so beautiful," he said. "Do you know how beautiful you are?"

She shook her head.

He kissed her stomach and up between her breasts to her throat and neck, her ears. He paused to watch. Her eyes closed, head back, shoulders raised. He covered a breast with his hand and took a nipple between his lips, a nipple that hardened under his tongue. She gave in. She tossed her head side to side. A quick breath between words, she said, "Ah, Deck."

Her eyes closed, back arched, mouth open to make

sound out of pleasure, so wild. He wondered, was that real?

Rorie's body eased. "That was sweet."

She hadn't played games before. He understood what he'd done for her, and he marveled at the mystery.

Rorie unhooked the prong and pulled the belt from its loops then tugged at Deckard's 501s. Pop, pop, pop, pop, pop. Deckard's eyes jumped from Rorie's face to her breasts which, even in the dark, bounced along with the pop of each button just enough for him to see. She drew her fingertips over his belly and reached into his boxers.

Deckard responded as a man bursting from jail, breathing air for the first time in freedom. His body demanded he push her hand down and keep it there, but his mind maintained enough control to let her do as she pleased.

Rorie stood and slipped her own jeans to her ankles. Deckard sat-up. She balanced with a hand on his head and lifted her left foot. Deckard pulled off the jean. She lifted the other foot. He removed the other leg.

Deckard couldn't look up at her. She was naked, but it was he who felt too exposed. He pulled her back down and turned his 501s inside out, twisting them with his boxers to get them past his feet and off. He grabbed the blanket to cover Rorie and himself, together.

He'd imagined sex with Rorie hundreds of times. In his bedroom they'd screwed just about every night for at least five years, but it had never been anything like this. He'd watched porn, seen a thousand bodies, masturbated and compared himself to the men, then got bored with the emotional flatness of it all. He couldn't relate to those people, some of whom looked diseased.

For the emotion, he tried poetry and liked Robert Browning and Dylan Thomas, but the closest he found to his own predilections were bawdy troubadour lyrics of

16th century France. Try explaining that to a replicant. He always returned to Rorie.

"Deck," she said. "Wait."

"What?"

She climbed over him and reached for her jeans. From her back pocket she held up the condom she'd been carrying since the day she stole the chickens.

"I've never actually used one," said Deckard.

"Me neither."

Deckard took the square. "How do you want to do this?"

"If you figure out how to get the thing open...."

Deck laughed and tore at the packet.... "You'll feel your way in the dark?"

Rorie took the ring of latex and Deckard lay back.

She ran her hand from Deckard's knee up the inside of his thigh and light-as-moonbeams over his balls.

"Are you still in the dream?"

"Uh huh."

Rorie had to think...no. Don't unroll it first. She released the ring slowly down over him.

Deckard moaned. "Everything you do to me...your touch is so...."

He had managed to stay under control but wasn't sure he could much longer. He wanted to be a little bad. He squirmed toward her, their bodies connecting skin to skin from legs to shoulders, face to face, arms at their sides, holding hands with fingers locked.

His hips pushed toward her and she could feel between them that thing a man once used against her like a weapon. Let that go. Let that go. She pressed back and opened her legs around his thighs. He rolled over, on top of her.

"Rorie." Deck looked down into her eyes.

Rorie breathed hard. “Deck.”

He pushed into her as slowly as he could and held still. If he moved, he’d come. So he pushed and held his breath.

“Perfect,” said Rorie. “Perfect.” Her breath grew louder.

Deckard kissed her neck, and pushed. Rorie made a sound more animal than human and Deckard, holding as still as he could, felt pulsing from her that he no longer could resist. He moved only slightly, but that was enough and he followed Rorie into a new grown-up dream.

Ed finished his fish and chips and sucked the straw to gurgle the last of his root beer. Lunch was on-the-house from this day hence as part of his ten-year-employee bonus package at the Maxfield. He watched, as he had from day-one, the buffet line for pocket-stuffing of food items, but not since that first day with the senior citizens had he confronted anyone for such a minor offense. Javier, Ed's boss, had convinced him his time cost the casino more than a couple of muffins and that the principle of the thing–like so many in Laughlin–was a non-starter.

Ten years. In fact, he'd worked at the Maxfield Riverfront Resort twelve years but the first two had been contract so they weren't counted. Twelve years since he drove into Laughlin, with its neon and gamblers and tour buses. He'd occupied the same apartment. Early-on he'd had to declare bankruptcy but he located a lawyer who got the interest forgiven and worked out an easy payment plan which Ed honored faithfully and would continue to until he died, with a balloon payment at the end. A normal economic life, by most measures.

The town had grown. Business had moved-in. He'd put down roots, suffered through several relationships, gotten to know most of Laughlin's Social Compliance professionals–no longer called "Security"–who formed a bowling league named *The Pinheads*. They planned to enter next year's Southern California All-county Tournament.

A year earlier the bowling league took on a new member. He and Ed were about the same height and would have been close to the same weight too, if, after Milly stopped returning his calls, Ed hadn't bought a 47″ flat screen, paying it off with his gym membership fees.

Something about this new guy, Abe.... Ed couldn't name it, but he found Abe odious.

Abe also worked in Social Compliance, but at the Seventh Day Spa next to the outlet mall on the west side of Casino Drive, away from the river and overlooking nothing. The man dressed well enough, seemed responsible and sociable, yet Ed was repelled by some sort of a force-field.

"Give the guy a break," said Ed's buddy Jesus. "He's nervous 'cause he can tell you don't like him."

"I haven't said anything to anyone, except you."

"You're my friend and I love ya, man," said Jesus. "But you know how you're so *not* good at poker?"

"Yeah. And that makes a difference how?"

"Eddie," said Jesus, "Even a blind man could read your face at fifty yards."

Over the next month, Abe turned into a bowler the Pinheads were happy to include. Spares and strikes became his norm and he kept accurate team stats. Ed eventually softened, even if there was something about this new guy that irked the piss out of him. Perseverance, however, had given Ed seniority among fellow Pinheads, and his position at the Maxfield gave him professional status over the new guy. Ed used this in finally befriending the fellow, taking him under his wing.

Valentine's Day weekend, every room in Laughlin was occupied and the town bulged at its borders. Neither Ed nor his new best bud, Abe, had a date for the evening and buzzing among the social swarm held no attraction for either man. Ed kept a case of Dos Equis in the fridge and had just subscribed to Crime TV so he suggested Abe pick up a load of Mexican take-out and come over for the evening.

"You weren't in Laughlin last year," said Ed, "but I ended up rescuing a drunken couple making-it in the river. If they'd just been quieter about it–"

"Screwing in the river under fireworks?" Abe laughed. "Sounds like fun. Were they bothering anyone?"

"I carried a dripping nude woman to dry land, then dragged a screaming naked guy with a stiffy to shore, who chased me back into the river." Ed took a swig of beer. "So I asked for the day off this year."

"Does that sort of thing happen often?"

"Until last year, only on July 4th and New Year's Eve. What's gotten into people?"

Abe made a mental note. "All the hearts and flowers stuff. I've never been in a relationship long enough for when the time came for that."

"I have," said Ed. "And never again. Take it from me, it makes no difference. They eat your chocolate and take your jewelry, then dump you for the next sucker. You can court them with kindness and all the while they're lying and scheming...how can I get more from him?" Ed drank from his Dos Equis. "Abe, I'm a good man. I'd never hurt a woman. But I tell you from experience. They don't want a good man. They want, well, frankly, I've never figured that out. Women are capable of crimes against humanity you wouldn't believe. I could tell you stories – "

"I bet you could," said Abe. He cracked-open a beer. "Have some chips and guacamole, Ed, and tell me, what's good on Crime TV."

Ed dropped cheese crumbs on his chest, loaded an entire taquito into his mouth, and flipped through the TV Guide. He swallowed. "You have two choices: *The Dark Side of Santa Barbara* or *Brother vs. Brother*."

"Brother vs. Brother," said Abe. "Sounds like Mad Magazine. I already have a brother. Let's watch Santa Barbara."

Ed tuned-in for opening credits with a backdrop of East Beach full of tanned, bikini-clad college-girls playing volleyball. In contrast, a voice-over and a bloody font across the foamy ocean waves proclaimed, "Every party town has a dark side".

"I'm an only child," said Ed. "I sure wish I had a brother."

"It's a ride," said Abe. "We parted on not the best of terms. At the time, I felt like he stole from me and ran off to spend it while I got caught. We were kids. Oh was I livid." Abe laughed at himself. "I swore I'd get revenge. I wanted to beat the shit out of him and leave him totally broken."

"Oh, check this out," said Ed. "They're going to bust some street kids for stealing."

"That was me, as a twenty-something."

"No kidding?" Ed was interested. "I've never done anything like that. Why'd he run off, your brother?"

"We were in Las Vegas. You really want to hear this?"

"Yeah. Crime TV, without the TV."

"I pickpocketed a man who'd cashed in his chips."

"How much did you get?"

"Four hundred dollars, and because I was sure the cops saw me do it, I gave the money to Peyton to hold."

Ed froze. If hair on a body could actually stand up, his would have. "You gave it to who?"

"Peyton. No idea what happened to him, or the money, but I went to jail. Since then I've been on the right side of the–"

"Your brother's name is Peyton?"

"Yep."

"That's not a common name."

"Peyton's a family name."

"But your last name is Sterling?"

"Right."

"I know a Peyton–thin, sandy hair, kind of scruffy. But his last name isn't Sterling."

"Where is this Peyton?" Abe sat straight, interested.

Ed didn't know how to react. His heartbeat quickened and his breathing went choppy, his eyes widened, he wanted to hold Abe to the floor and pound him for information. After almost two decades against the current, underwater, forgetting even to swim, Ed had reached the surface. He wasn't going to disclose his long-time quest or the situation that provoked it, nor would he make a scene, but it had to be the same Peyton.

Whatever family resemblance Abe and Peyton bore, however subtle, this must have been what he'd disliked in Abe, meeting him for the first time. It made sense. He'd known it all along Peyton had been up to no damn good. Ed contained himself and said, "I can take you to see him."

Abe laughed again. "You kidding me?"

"Honest. You can finally beat him up." Everyone in Saltine would have to admit Ed had been right. They'd all have to apologize. "Can you get a week off?"

"Ed, my job is so insignificant, nobody's gonna miss me. When do we leave?"

"I have a two-week vacation due. I'll let you know."

Rorie was on her knees, checking the coop and hoping for eggs when Glory walked up with a tray of freshly-baked cinnamon rolls.

"Good morning, young woman," she said. She checked her watch. "Everyone still asleep?"

Rorie stood. She held out her right hand, but seeing it covered in chicken crud, pulled it back. "Sorry. I think so. I'm the first up. We were all so worried about you."

"Let's make coffee." Glory walked up the steps. "I brought goodies."

Glory had gifted baked goods every couple of weeks for the past several years. No reason or excuse was needed. But today, she wanted to get to know the newcomer.

"Your cinnamon smells heavenly, like a bakery." Rorie didn't know if she had the right to invite someone into the Neworth home but since the old woman and Deckard had seemed so close...she followed Glory inside, glad Deck had washed dishes the night before and she'd stored the board, frame, cake mixes, tinfoil, balloons, and crepe paper in Deckard's room.

"I used to cook a lot for these two men," said Glory, "so I know where most everything is. I'll do the brewing if you'll cut the buns apart."

Rorie washed her hands and took Stripe's knife out of the drawer.

Glory gulped air and stared.

"Coffee's in the cupboard, Glory."

"Yes." Glory turned to the sink. She measured cold water into the carafe. Did Peyton know? Had he seen the knife?

Rorie rinsed the blade and left it in the rack. "These buns are gorgeous. And still warm."

How'd this young woman get Stripes's knife? "Uh, Rorie," said Glory, fumbling with the coffee maker. "I need to ask...." No. The words didn't come. "...uh, cream and sugar?"

Peyton stood, dressed, in the doorway. "Is there enough for me?"

"It's your house." Rorie laughed. "The question should be, is there enough for *me*?"

"Good morning, Peyton." Glory gave Peyton a look of panic. "Thought I'd drop by." She poured a third cup of coffee and mindlessly added cream and sugar to all three. "Peyton," she said. "I need a word."

"You're here to fire me finally?"

Glory didn't respond.

Peyton looked concerned. "Glory?"

"Oh, yes. Absolutely. I really need garden veggies. Peyton? Show me your broccoli."

Glory and Peyton walked out and into the garden. Peyton looked back and winked at Libby.

"Now, Peyton," said Glory. "You are well aware I don't like to rock the boat, and Lord knows I've kept more secrets than anyone else in this town.... I don't know how to say it otherwise, so I'm just going to come right out–"

"Glory, Glory. What is it?"

Glory cleared her throat and wiped her hands on her apron. "Have you seen Rorie's...well.... Stripes's knife? She's got Stripes's knife!"

"What!?" screamed Libby.

"Okay. Calm down," said Peyton.

"Don't tell me to calm down!" Libby was breathless.

"I've seen the knife," said Peyton, "but I'm confused

about how she got it." Peyton lifted his eyebrows. "She seems to know nothing. How it ended up with her is a mystery."

"Yes," said Glory.

"I've been waiting for the right time to ask," said Peyton.

"There is no right time," screamed Libby. "And why did you not tell me she has it?"

"Deck has never been so happy," said Peyton.

"Maybe this, right now, is the right time," said Glory.

"Yes, yes, yes," Libby huffed.

"I'll pick a cantaloupe," said Peyton. "You ask her to cut it open. You ask."

Peyton walked along the right side of the garden to one of the larger boxes. He'd built a grid in the ground to keep the melons from lying in the soil and developing rot. He lifted a vine and pulled off a very ripe cantaloupe.

The two walked past Libby back into the kitchen. Peyton didn't dare look at her. He held up the fragrant melon, warmed by the morning sun. "If we don't eat this today, it'll be no good."

"Here, let me." Rorie once again picked up the knife and sliced the melon in half.

Glory took a deep breath and held onto the table. "That's an unusual knife, Rorie."

"Isn't it?"

"Um ... did you buy it locally?"

"I got it from a guy who...." she paused and turned. "Why?"

Glory looked at Peyton. She said, "You were the last person to see Stripes, weren't you?"

Rorie said, "Who?"

"Yes, to my everlasting shame. Nuckle and Ed–remember Ed Schotz?

"Of course," said Glory.

Peyton looked toward Rorie. "Ed was a deputy sheriff, here in Saltine." He turned back to Glory. He said, "The three of us went over everything, must have been a hundred times. Stripes was drunk, I mean falling down drunk after you, Ed, and Nuckle took Libby home. He let Guizar attack me and then tried to knife me. I married his daughter, took her away from him and he was so angry. I wanted to get home to Libby and he wouldn't come. I couldn't just leave him so I stayed till he and his dog stomped off. What could I do? I didn't follow."

Oh Oh Oh, thought Peyton, may the universe forgive me for the lie I just told. I will see Stripes again in Hell for that lie.

"Then you came home to our wedding bed," called Libby from the porch.

"Figuring Stripes would sleep it off, I came home to our wedding bed. He never returned."

Peyton and Glory stopped abruptly and looked over at Rorie who was staring. Nobody moved and nobody even breathed.

Rorie spoke first. "So, okay then. I've carried this knife for almost two years."

Peyton said, "Two years?"

"Well, 18 months. Actually, I stole it after a really hard time from a man who'd taken advantage, well, who raped me. Wanted to kill him with the knife, but didn't."

Peyton and Glory remained silent and continued to look at Rorie.

"I'd been hanging around Salvation Mountain hoping for healing and insight. In vain, as it turned out. Anyway, like I said, I stole it from some young creep and used it for everything from protection to cooking."

Libby, still listening from the freezer, relaxed a bit.

Rorie's tale was not out of line with whatever had done-in her daddy.

"I oiled the hinge, sanded and sharpened the blade. Probably saved my life a couple of times and sure has made it easier." She scooped out the cantaloupe seeds with a spoon then used the knife to slice the fruit and peel-off the skin. "I've never seen turquoise inlay so gorgeous. And voilà." She placed a bowl of melon chunks on the table.

Peyton looked to Glory. Glory said, "It's very much like a knife Deck's grandpa had. And we don't know what happened to him. He just disappeared. Near Salvation Mountain. So naturally we're curious."

"I'm using a dead man's knife? Peyton why haven't you said?"

"I wasn't sure. I knew the man only two weeks. Glory knew him 20 years."

"It's so pretty, I mean, as implements-of-death go. It belonged to Deck's grandfather? Does he know?"

Peyton's bowels were a mess. He excused himself to the bathroom. He'd left the knife, in Stripes, in the desert, on that blessed awful dawn so many years ago. Rorie's attacker must have found it. What other explanation could there be?

Deckard walked in the front door and into the kitchen. "I smell cinnamon rolls." He smiled at Rorie. "You feeling better, Glory?"

"I'm fine, Deck. They took out my appendix and now I'm good forever."

"I need to learn how to make these," said Rorie.

"What were you talking about?" Deckard took a plate from the dish rack and served himself. He smiled at Glory, "Thanks." He arched his brows at Rorie. "You too. Thanks."

She was happy. He was transformed. He felt so good, so manly, he stood straight. "Do I get seconds?" He looked first at Glory, who nodded, then at Rorie, who turned red.

Peyton understood the subtext. His son was no longer innocent, and parenting was about to change, radically. Peyton had to accept that fact and tell Libby so they could–what? Not exactly commiserate, not celebrate, either. He'd known for years that a boy has to abandon his father in order to grow up. He wasn't consciously competitive or envious of his son's other interests. Or, maybe he was. Peyton remembered carrying Deckard on his shoulders, naming plants on the way home from work, making up stories together, begging the boy to join him in the garden. He gazed at his now 6′ boy with straight white teeth and wild sun-streaked hair, happy to know he was smart and kind. He'd treasure those early days, but everyday life wasn't about their relationship anymore. No fault of anyone. He'd raised a child to become an adult. Deckard was the fruit of his labor. Growing up was normal. Peyton had great respect for a normal life. He himself had lived one for the previous seventeen years.

Deckard and Rorie woke around 7:30, before the heat of the day set in. They drank coffee under the rebar tree and reviewed the canvassing map Rorie had laid out. They planned to begin at the far side of town, leaving stragglers near Paseo Centro until after Glory closed the Grocery and went home.

The spoken invitation was quick. "Good morning, Mrs. Filbert." Most residents knew Deckard, so he was the one to make the introductions. "We are throwing a birthday bash for Glory's 67TH. Would you like to sign the community card and join us for cake after church service this Sunday?"

Deckard said the phrase close to 100 times that day, trying to sound like the first time, every time. Between houses, the words became nonsense. We're throwing hot birthday hash farther than we can see it…join us for a cake-fight… blow off Byle's sermon and BYOB….

Almost everyone responded with an enthusiastic, "Yes. Of course!" and "My wife wants to sign, too." So Rorie handed over a pen and held the board stable for a signature. "Thank you," she said. And Deckard added, "Remember. Say nothing. It's a surprise. See you Sunday in the churchyard." Wait, my 18 cats want to add their paw prints…. Remember, it's top secret and you *will* be detained if….

They walked Paseo Centro and caught Doc, Nuckle, the Byles, and the Hectors Senior and Junior.

The board ended up crowded and full to its edges. Everyone loved Glory. Probably a hundred and fifty people signed, including a half dozen x's, and more than that would attend the event.

Rorie was glad she'd instructed Peyton and Deckard to buy six boxes of cake mix and six cans of frosting, two hundred and fifty paper napkins and punch cups. They'd need it all.

"That is so cool," Peyton said when he saw the board. He examined it closely. No dirt or grease stains. No smears. It appeared every adult in Saltine had taken a moment to wish Glory everything from a great day to a prosperous future to a thanks for all you do. He wanted to read them and sign his own name before framing. "You had a classy idea, Rorie, and you two did a super job. Glory will treasure this." Peyton thought for a moment. "The cooking. The chicken coop. Now the gift. So capable.... I shouldn't worry about you, should I?"

Deckard answered. "No, Dad. You shouldn't."

"I'll bake all day Saturday," said Rorie. "Mrs. Byle offered tables, chairs, and her boom box so we'll play music and dance. A lot of people said they'll have a gift and Mr. Henriquez will hang two candy-filled piñatas for the kids. Sunday morning while the pious pray, we'll decorate the yard. The Hectors will help. They'll bring ladders. So, Peyton, no worries. It's all written down and on the fridge."

*

Rorie awoke Saturday early, and went to the garden to harvest buds from the seeds she'd planted. She snipped-off the ripe ones, brought them inside and lay them in the sun on the windowsill.

She sat at the kitchen table and tweaked the birthday party lists she'd been making all week long: who was responsible for what, and by what time. She taped the lists to the refrigerator door again and turned on the oven to preheat. She'd get the baking done in the morning. One aluminum sheet pan at a time fit into the oven, but two boxes of mix fit into each pan.

"Peyton," said Rorie. "One more thing."

"Name it."

"You and Deck are having breakfast at Hector Senior's lunch counter, right?"

"Yep."

"Good. That's all."

"Rorie. Relax."

*

Deckard dragged his feet the entire way downtown. "Do I have to? Really? Like I'm your performing seal." He put his bags of crêpe paper on the ground, held his arms out straight, clapped and barked like a seal. "What am I gonna say to all those old farts?"

"Look," said Peyton. "You're doing this for Rorie as much as for anyone. She needs us out of the way, and this crazy celebration you planned requires this tiny sacrifice of your precious time, so put-on a happy face, take credit for a fabulous idea, and pretend to enjoy yourself just this once." He pulled open the door to Hector's Hardware.

The geezer squad sat at the counter drinking coffee. "Two stools empty down here," Doc called to Peyton. Then, more quietly, "Glory received a big shipment of dry goods. She'll be restocking all day and Hector Senior will keep an eye out, just in case."

"Great!" said Deckard. "See you tomorrow, then."

"*Por supuesto!*" said Doc in a whisper. "I'm learning Spanish. That means, of course!"

Doc was getting-on, thought Peyton. But who wasn't?

Doc sat with Mayor Nuckle who was still in charge since no one else wanted to be, Scooter Polk who still lived with Marge, the owner of the Magic Lantern Cinema whose name–even after all these years–Peyton could never remember, and a couple other older men. Peyton called down the line, "We'll see all of you tomorrow?"

They answered in unison. "Wouldn't miss it. *Por supuesto.*"

"So, Deck," said Nuckle. "You'll be joining us for breakfast from now on?"

Deckard laughed. He said, "Will you arrest me if I don't?"

"We could use some young blood."

"Maybe once in a while, Mayor."

Hector Junior was the short-order cook and server, about Deckard's age but that's all they had in common. When Peyton and Deckard got up to leave, Hector Junior left too, to join the Neworths at the church.

At Reverend Byle's church, Mrs. Byle showed the men the long tables and stackable chairs in the basement, which they carried up the stairs and out into the yard. They swept and de-bugged and arranged three tables along the close-in side of the yard making it easier to refill the punch bowl from the kitchen. Chairs lined the three free-standing stucco walls of the yard, beyond which was more slough and scrub desert. There wasn't really that much more to do. Rorie had made crepe paper flowers for above the chairs–wall flowers–for those who won't dance. She'd hang them Sunday morning. Everything then would have to be wiped down again for dust, but more people would be helping.

They'd picked up what had blown-in and cleared the concrete pathways around the small center garden which was fenced in pickets and grew plastic bouquets. Around 2:00 PM, Peyton and Deckard walked home. They approached Glory's Groceries and peeked in to say hello and buy a couple of sodas. Waved to Hector Senior as they passed. They had a laugh making up bogus names for plants. Mice-plant. Hacked-us. You-forbia....

*

"I harvested a cauliflower and two zucchini–hope you don't mind." Rorie smiled at Peyton. "Made us a veggie and cheese lasagna for lunch. Wash up. Have a seat. I am in manic mode. After lunch, I need the two of you to frame the big card, beautify the craft paper the frame came in, and re-wrap the whole thing."

"Beautify." Deckard was puzzled.

"Paint hearts or something. Find ribbon for a bow. You know. Beautify."

Rorie served Peyton and Deckard each a mound of lasagna, herself as well. "Either of you know anything about the punch?"

"Rorie," said Peyton. "Rorie, take a breath. You'll give yourself indigestion."

"No I won't and so what if I do?"

"It's me you'll barf on."

Deckard laughed. "Mrs. Byle raided the church pantry. She found party-size packs of powdered Hawaiian Punch. They don't ever expire. She's been making ice for the past week."

Deckard put his plate in the sink and sniffed the cooling cakes. "They smell really chocolatey. Who're these minis for?"

"I think it's creepy when someone blows out a candle." said Rorie. "Especially old people. Sorry Peyton."

"No offense taken."

"So one's for Glory. I bet she spits when she blows, then we're supposed to eat it? So I made a cupcake for the candle."

Deckard widened his eyes and nodded. "Good thinking."

"The other?" said Peyton.

"You leave it alone for now. It's for us."

"I want chocolate cake," said Deckard.

"Hands off," said Rorie.

After lunch, laid low by exertion and carbohydrates, everyone took a siesta. Peyton snoozed on his bed. Deckard and Rorie lay in one another's arms on his mattress under the rebar tree.

Deck said quietly, "You did a great thing bringing this off."

"Group effort."

"Maybe," he said. "But we know who organized it." He didn't let her answer, but kissed her and she kissed back and held him tightly before falling asleep.

*

Peyton unwrapped the frame, careful to pull off the tape without tearing the paper. He flattened it on the dining table and hoped the young'uns had some facility with decoration because he had none. He walked to the door and called, "Deck. Wake up. I need your help."

Rorie was already back at work. She popped open two cans of Milk Chocolate frosting and used a rubber spatula to remove every bit onto one of the cakes, then took a heaping spoonful from the cake and globbed it onto a mini. She used the spatula to spread the soft fudgy topping over the surface.

Peyton brewed a cup of extra-strong coffee and found a pastry brush. He said, "I can make a checkerboard pattern on the wrapping paper."

"That'll work," said Rorie. She opened two more cans of frosting, this time strawberry.

Deckard leaned against the door frame. "What time is it?"

Peyton took a pencil and drew a four-inch grid, then painted every other square. Deckard watched his dad for about five minutes then went to a drawer and dug around. He found a Q-tip and old red food coloring to follow Peyton and make hearts flowers in the empty squares.

Rorie finished the second cake and opened the last two cans of French Vanilla frosting. She washed the spatula and covered the third cake in thick sticky white icing. If she cut each party cake into two-by-three-inch pieces, she'd feed 216 guests, plus Glory's cupcake.

*

Late that afternoon–the cakes iced, the card framed and wrapped–the three of them sitting under the rebar tree, Rorie said, "You two want to try something?"

"Sure," said Peyton.

"What," said Deckard.

"The strawberry-frosted cupcake," said Rorie.

"Yes," said Deckard.

"It's a magic cupcake."

"Rorie," said Deckard, "everything you do is magic."

"Glad we understand one another. I'm telling you, though, the cupcake has magic powers."

Peyton showed a slow enlightenment. "I thought it might."

Peyton had taken note of Rorie's agricultural endeavor in the far corner of his garden. He didn't mind but he hadn't asked about it, either. Visually it was anonymous enough and could have been a tomato of some variety, but the smell–he recognized the smell. From where, he hadn't a clue, yet inhaling the unmistakable skunky fragrance elicited images of more goats and the elation of unrestrained dancing under a night sky.

"What?" said Deckard. "What are you talking about?"

"I can't remember the last time," said Peyton, "but I'm sure I have."

"Have *what!*" Deckard was angry. "Is it a secret between you? Should I leave? What the hell are you two talking about?"

Peyton said, "You tell him."

Rorie moved her chair to sit closer to Deckard. "Deck," said Rorie. "You remember my magic beans?"

"Yeah."

"They've done well."

"So?"

"Well, they weren't really beans. They were seeds."

"So?"

"Magic seeds."

Deckard was miffed. "So Jack's not going to climb a beanstalk after all?"

"I wouldn't say that, exactly. They are Mother Nature's way of, yes, lifting you to the clouds, freeing your imagination, salving what ails you in one little organically-grown flower."

Deckard nodded. "Weed. You're growing weed in Dad's vegetable garden."

"Yes. And the buds I cut this morning, I dried in the oven and put into the pink-frosted cupcake." She couldn't tell if Deckard was still angry. "For us three, for tonight."

Deckard hated the guessing games in which he was the only ignoramus. On the other hand, Rorie had risked both his and Peyton's reaction to provide some unexpected fun. Deckard didn't know about his dad, but he himself had never actually tried marijuana. Who better to experiment with? And sex? Having sex while high? With Rorie? He said, "Don't you have to smoke it?"

"Baking activates it. If you eat it, it might take a little longer but, then, it will last longer, too. From what I hear." She paused. "And it's healthier for the lungs. It may taste a little grassy, not terribly fruity, but I made an intense iced tea to wash it down."

Deckard acted cool. Inside, the prospect excited him.

This girl, this woman, every day she expanded his world in some way. She knew things he didn't. She challenged him. She aroused him. He wasn't even going to ask whether weed was safe.

"Is it Indica or Sativa?" Deckard had read about the different strains on the internet and tried to sound knowledgeable.

Peyton and Rorie stared. Then Peyton laughed.

Rorie said, "I don't know."

"Never mind."

"Well," said Rorie, "since I don't know what the seeds were, let's experiment on ourselves and assess later." She rose and said, "I'll be right back."

Rorie climbed the three steps. She took Stripes's knife from the drying rack and sliced the cupcake right through the paper into thirds. She held three stacking cups between her arm and chest, folded paper napkins in the top cup, took the pitcher of tea from the fridge in her left hand and picked up the cupcake in her right.

She called from the front door, "Deck. Help. Please?"

He leapt to the landing and opened the screen. Peyton watched Rorie give Deckard an affectionate nudge and he melted into her. How easily youth makes everything right again.

Deckard leaned toward the cupcake on the table. "I'm not sure I like the smell."

"No," said Rorie. "It's bitter. If you can relax, though, you'll like the effect. Everything is softer. And you'll sleep great."

Peyton's mind drifted off to somewhere else and he watched himself pull a bent joint out of his chest pocket while sitting along a rail. He was alone, just outside of Mecca with nothing to do and nowhere to go. He lit-up and exhaled. Nanny came close, curious, so after the next draw, he blew smoke in her nostrils figuring she'd enjoy the high as much as he. They finished it off. The last thing Peyton remembered was having to lift Nanny onto the trolley for the ride south.

"Three equal pieces," said Rorie. "Dig in." She looked from Peyton to Deckard and back. "No?" She put a whole piece in her mouth and tried to chew but almost choked, then washed it down with iced tea. "The frosting helps it slide. And masks the taste."

"Okay," said Peyton. "Down the hatch." He followed Rorie's lead and swallowed it whole. "Blech!"

"I was looking forward to chocolate." Deckard picked up the last third and examined it. He took a nibble and swished it around. "Blech is the right word, Dad. People pay money for this?"

"Big money," said Peyton.

Deckard popped the rest into his mouth, put his hands around his throat, made strangling noises, then drank his tea. "How long do we wait?"

"Hard to say, but it'll happen slowly. You'll look at something, and realize you're stoned. We'll be hungry and nobody will want to cook so the green bean casserole goes in the oven now.

Deckard watched her leave. "Isn't she something?"

Peyton almost opened his mouth to compare her to Libby, then thought, Why? This was Deck's moment, it had no comparison. He said, simply, "Yes."

*

An hour later, the timer sounded its nasal beep which Peyton imitated and Deckard started to laugh. Rorie went in to stop the oven. When she got back, both Deckard and Peyton were laughing so hard they could barely breathe.

Peyton was slumped in his chair and Deckard had slid off of his onto the ground and rolled back and forth. He was trying to say something but he couldn't get it out.

Rorie sat, then started to rise, slowly, up above the earth into the universe, not touching the ground at all–

"Hey, hey Rorie." Deckard had crawled toward Rorie's feet and started to pull on her boots.

"Is that you, Deck? You wouldn't believe the view from here."

"I want your feet naked." Deckard pulled off her boots, and then her socks. "That's better."

"My toes are in the clouds."

"Go on and wiggle them. Make waves in the clouds." After a moment, Deckard flung his torso onto her lap and wrapped his arms around her waist. "You are so wonderful."

Peyton pushed himself off the chair and walked into the back yard. He closed the gate behind him. "Hi Doll."

"Sweetcakes."

Peyton stripped off his shirt, then his jeans. Then his boxers.

"Peyton!"

"I want to feel the earth."

"With mud in your nether regions?"

"In all my regions."

"Do I know you?"

"We ate marijuana."

The sun had set and the moon was just at the downside of full, lighting the early night.

Peyton, naked among the vegetables, danced up the aisles between planting boxes. He bent to pick a small cuke and ate it while standing. Nothing had ever tasted so good. Teeth breaking the skin with its tender give, the initial crunch, the juice, the pure sweetness of bounty. Could there be a better place, anywhere along the Milky Way?

He heard Rorie sing. "*Out in Arizona where the bad men are, and the only friend to guide you is an evening star....*" Then both Rorie and Deckard laughed.

Libby sighed. "I was never that young."

"You are still that young, Doll, and beautiful, and desirable, and clever, and–"

"Oh stop. You're being silly."

"I'm being stoned." Peyton kicked off his shoes and pulled off his socks and stepped between heads of lettuce into a box. "It's cool and squishy." He moved with great care so not to damage the plants, then sat on the soil, lay down in a furrow, and fell asleep.

Deckard sang, "*This sweet and merry month of May, While nature wantons in her prime, Birds do sing, and beasts do play, For pleasure of the joyful time....* Owie! You punched me."

"It was a love punch."

"Love punch. Is that what Mrs. Byle is serving tomorrow?"

"She ain't serving what I'm serving."

"What are you serving?"

"Come closer, Deck, and I'll show you."

"If I come closer I'll be on top of you. I love you, Rorie."

With his eyes open, he kissed her. She kissed back. Tender, then wild and deep, and again open-eyed, together moving very slowly, rising up above the earth.

The sun wasn't yet above the horizon but the sky was pink. Peyton awoke, his lips against an eggplant. He rolled onto his back and looked up from his furrow as a bird flew over. "How perfectly lovely," he said. He took a deep breath, relaxed and smiled. Maybe he would lie there all day and enjoy the cool, damp soil, the fragrance of living greenery, the slack-muscled after-effects of last evening's weed. His stomach squealed a complaint. They, at least *he,* hadn't eaten last night.

Peyton reckoned the time to be around 7:00 AM. He got to his feet and brushed garden soil off his dimpled side but couldn't reach his back. Being naked in the garden was divine, closer to nature than he'd dreamed possible and the experience was one he promised himself to repeat. Maybe he'd make a sign for the gate:

"EDEN"

Peyton found his shoes and clothes and entered the house through the back door. He left everything in the laundry room, grabbed a fresh towel, and jumped into the shower. Earth Goddesses and Water Nymphs swirled around and through him.

"Dad. Hurry up."

"Out in a minute."

First Peyton, then Deckard, then Rorie showered. Peyton and Deck each put on clean jeans and tee shirt. Rorie grabbed a layered, orange gauze shirt out of her backpack, shook it out, and pulled it over her head.

One followed another into the kitchen to shovel spoonsful of green bean casserole from the baking dish into their mouths. Nobody spoke much before it was time to leave. Rorie had stretched plastic wrap over the cakes. She went through the checklist: decorations and paper goods were already at the church; Peyton will carry Glory's big card; Rorie will carry one cake, a candle, and a lighter; Deckard will take two cakes and the cupcake on a board and music CD's in his pocket. Chickens are fed. Reverend Byle's sermons always begin at 10:30 and let-out 60 minutes later. They had two and a half hours.

Rorie looked at the men and smiled. "I'll get the door." She lay her cake on the landing and held the door for both Peyton and Deckard, to whom she blew a kiss as he passed. She closed the door, picked up her cake, and followed Peyton and Deckard through the shortcut across the field.

"Deck," said Peyton. "Do you remember the bottomless trash can tied to a pole we used to use for basketball? Somebody'd set it up in this field. I wonder what happened to it."

"I remember it the way you remember things, Dad. I can see it in my mind, but I don't really remember it."

"My ancestors' language has no past or future," said Rorie. "I can't figure how they explain memories."

"Isn't it strange?" Peyton thought Rorie was right. He wondered how to explain memory if there is no past, no concept of it. Had he ever known Libby or was she as fugitive as his other memories? No, of course he'd known her. Deckard was physical evidence of a past, wasn't he? What about when he couldn't see Deck? Didn't have him as evidence? Peyton started to laugh. "I think I'm still stoned."

"Yeah," said Rorie. "We're going to have an even better time at this party than most. These cakes need refrigeration. I hope Mrs. Byle has space cleared."

They walked in a straight line diagonally across town to the church and its yard, avoiding Paseo Centro and any glimpse of Glory.

Mrs. Byle, in a starched blue cotton shirtwaist dress, was at the back door between the yard and the big church kitchen. "Welcome, welcome, I did so wonder what time you'd be here there's so much left to do and you know the Reverend can't assist and I've gotten so old I'm of no use I was beginning to worry–"

Rorie entered the kitchen and put her cake on a counter. She wrapped her arm around Mrs. Byle's shoulder and glanced at Deckard, then the industrial refrigerator. She urged Mrs. Byle toward the chapel. "You and the good Reverend have been so very generous, so gracious."

Mrs. Byle looked pleased. "Do you really think so?"

"But for you, and the church, this would not be happening." But for last night's weed, Rorie could never be so benign and affable. "You and the Reverend have contributed more than your share and your only job, now, is to walk Glory to the yard after service."

"I can do that, child. Bless you."

"And you, Mrs. Byle. I'm going out back now to blow up balloons."

Mrs. Byle headed toward the Reverend's quarters. Rorie walked fast toward the yard.

Peyton was loading the third cake into the fridge and caught Rorie in the kitchen. "I don't really know what you just did, but it was good. There are six, five-gallon bottles of punch in the fridge and, like, a cubic yard of ice in the freezer."

"Great. I'm going to work on balloons and crepe paper flowers. Would you organize whoever is out there to wipe everything down, find a couple of clean rocks to keep stacks of paper napkins from blowing away. Maybe Deck can set up a table for gifts and such? Everyone has to be quiet enough not to be heard inside, okay? Keep an ear out. When the cakes are colder, I'll slice them while you and Deck hang decorations. How's that sound?"

"I'm in awe."

Rorie whispered, "And if Mrs. Byle can find her way to the yard at 11:30, and actually remembers to bring Glory, we'll be able to exhale."

Peyton walked out laughing. "Okay everyone," he said in low voice, "listen up...."

The crew consisted of Deck, Hector Junior and his girlfriend, and another young couple, friends of Hector Junior. Together they coordinated the tasks so that everything got done and nothing was done twice. The yard was larger than a tennis court. Its concrete walls, while needing paint, were nonetheless now clean of cobwebs and the corners free of critters. With two large piñatas hung from a tree whose untrimmed branches spread over a far corner of the courtyard, garlands and flowers of crepe paper along with balloons hung from them draped along the walls, the entire yard showed a peculiar Old World border charm. Chairs lined the perimeter, the boom box sat on the gift table, and the checkerboard-wrapped community Happy Birthday card leaned against it.

"*Hola amigos!*" Hector called. He stood at the garden gate and waved.

"Shhhhh," the chorus of workers responded.

He looked around. "Oops. Sorry."

A week earlier, Peyton had used Sheriff Nuckle's phone to make the arrangements, and Hector Senior did the footwork. He'd been to the spur to await the trolley and now walked in with three nurses, Glory's buddies, from Mecca, A dozen Saltine citizens followed.

"Everyone introduce yourselves," said Hector Senior, "and don't be shy about it."

Rorie closed the kitchen door behind her and waved her arms in the air. "Hey, people!" she said, more air than voice. "When Glory walks in, we'll sing Happy Birthday. After that, make all noise you want." She looked around the yard and thought, screw it.

Rorie beckoned Deck toward her, then disappeared into the kitchen.

He followed and bumped up behind her. "Oops. Inertia."

"Right." She smiled over her shoulder. "Help me with the punch?"

"Let's stay in here and take turns lying on our backs on the cool tile."

"Take turns?"

"That way, we can take turns lying on each other."

"I love the way you see the world," said Rorie.

She filled the large bowl half with ice and carried it out to the table, which also held the boom box loaded with three discs programmed to random. Deckard poured punch over the ice from a five-gallon plastic bottle then broke up the cubes and returned the unused portion to the fridge. He'd keep the bowl full.

The air was calm–no dust devils, no flying grit–and the temperature couldn't have been more than 75° which meant the frosting wouldn't melt nor would the ice disappear too fast, and the guests wouldn't have heatstroke in the early afternoon sun. Rorie took a loose count of around 75 guests so far.

Hector laughed loudly, but Rorie wasn't going to stop him. Rorie looked around the yard for any job left undone and finally sat just inside to await Glory.

Hector Senior played a fabulous host, introducing the nurses–out of uniform and looking like neighbors–and everyone else, even the locals who might have known one another by sight but had never spoken. He set a great party mood. Indeed, this would be an occasion for the memory books.

Rorie heard voices and the heels of women's Sunday shoes on the hard hallway floor, then the click of the door leading from the church into the far end of the kitchen. She leapt to the yard, pulling the outside door closed behind her, and yelled, "Quiet! QUIET!!"

The crowd silenced, even those just arriving stopped their chatter. Everyone froze and looked toward the door.

Mrs. Byle appeared first, then Glory. Glory looked up. "Oh my goodness!" Her jaw dropped and she became teary-eyed. "What did you...."

Rorie raised her hands as the conductor, she began to sing and a hundred and fifty voices–each in its own key–belted out, "Happy Birthday to you, Happy birthday to you...." She looked out at this gathering of replicants. Maybe they're not so evil after all.

Hector was hidden in the crowd, but he jumped and waved wildly. Glory waved back.

"Come on, Sweetheart," said Peyton. "This is to celebrate *you,* Saltine's own Miss Congeniality."

"Oh no, oh no, I can't–"

Deckard laughed. "We won't make you give a speech." He guided Glory down the steps and to a chair. Friends and customers surrounded her with hugs and best wishes, and sang again.

Peyton poured a cup of punch and lit the candle on the cupcake. "Everyone," he hollered above the din, "just for a minute. Quiet, please! Glory," he made his way to her. "Blow out your candle and make a wish."

She thought for a moment and blew out the single flame. "Done," she said. Everyone cheered. She looked at Peyton like a son. "Thank you."

Deckard flipped the switch to start the music, a selection of Country Classics, Mexican Favorites, and Talking Heads. Folks lined up for cake, others for punch, and newcomers walked over to greet the star of the day. Young people danced. Old people sat and visited, bottles and flasks appeared from pockets. Laughter, conversation in English and Spanish mixed with Quechua.

Deckard made his way to Glory. He asked, "What did you wish for?"

"I can't tell you that."

Reverend Byle had taken off his vestments and joined the crowd. Hector Senior herded the nurses over to greet their recent patient. Glory stood and put her hands to her cheeks, shocked, then almost fainted back into her chair. "Oh," she said. "This is too much to take in. How did you know?"

Cake service went smoothly. Deckard filled the punch bowl three times before demand slowed. Cards and small gifts piled up next to the boom box. Glory never stopped smiling.

Peyton moseyed up to the birthday girl. He did an awkward dance step and said, "Got to free your feet, Glory, before you can free your mind. What say you and me tear-up the floor?"

"Free my mind? I'll bust my stitches."

Doc stood behind her. "No excuses. I removed your stitches."

She looked over her shoulder. "Okay. Then I'm too old."

"We'll dance slow." Peyton held out his hand. "Glory?"

She finally pushed herself off the seat and allowed Peyton to lead her into the crush. While Bob Wills and his Texas Playboys yodeled-forth *Rose of San Antone,* she and Peyton heard the *Old Tennessee Waltz*. The floor cleared for them. Halfway through, Hector cut-in, spun Glory around a couple of times then showed her back to her chair. Cameras and cell phones flashed for snapshots. Glory said, "I haven't done that in thirty years." Deckard lead the applause.

Glory grinned at Peyton and said, "My mind feels so free."

Rorie leaned in to Deckard. "Our job is done here. Want to go make out?"

"Is that all you think about?"

"Most days." She took his hand and they walked out the gate. Two hundred people crowded the churchyard. The town had emptied. "Feels eerie, doesn't it?"

"I know exactly where to go," said Deckard.

*

Several years earlier, Hector Senior had built a modest *palapa* on the roof of his hardware shop and sat there some evenings to drink a beer at sundown. Deckard had seen him from a distance. A set of narrow steps like those to Glory's apartment provided access from the rear of the hardware building. It was the perfect look-out.

"What a cool thing," said Rorie. She stood on Hector's roof and waited for Deckard. "I can see the spur from here."

"All I can see is you."

"You pay me a lot of compliments."

"They're real." Deckard sat down on a piece of carpet under the *palapa*.

"I know." She reminded herself to take the compliment at face value. She didn't have to overthink or wonder if she was being buttered-up. Not with Deckard. Rorie watched the horizon then sat. "It's really nice up here. I mean really. Like sleeping here would be excellent."

Deckard lay back and looked at the palm fronds

overhead. The sun had dried them to a crisp but they still offered shade. If he wanted something from Rorie, he had to let her come to him. He wasn't sure how he felt about that. For him, it was a game and he didn't like games. For her, though, it was no game. Rather, it seemed a matter of safety.

Rorie eased down and turned toward Deckard. She put her head on his shoulder, reached up and kissed his chin.

Who was it being manipulated if he got what he wanted without asking for it? He lowered his chin and rolled to face Rorie, lips on lips. Deckard's hands wandered but mostly they kissed and dozed for almost an hour.

At 1:00 PM they roused themselves and looked out over the town. The only movement was from two men, far in the distance, walking south along the spur toward Saltine.

Rorie said, "Latecomers?"

"Can't tell."

Deckard descended the steps first, then Rorie. They held hands and walked to the church. The music was loud, but voices were louder and the gathering was more crowded than when they left. Glory held court from her chair, surrounded by well-wishers. Mayor Nuckle and Doc had parked themselves near what was left of the final cake. Peyton danced with himself in the middle of the throng. Someone had kept the punch bowl full.

"Good juju here. Want to dance?"

Deckard pretended to be a chicken and kept moving. He and Rorie squawked at one another and performed do-si-dos, they stood together and swayed, then joined in a wild Mexican *Jarabe* until more than a hundred dancers were laughing loudly and sweat dampened everyone's back.

At the gate stood the men who had been walking along the spur. Both were just under six foot and looked about fifty years old, one larger than the other. They wore cowboy boots, jeans, plaid shirts, and Stetson hats. They scanned the crowd, then entered the yard.

Deckard had never seen either. He said to Rorie, "You recognize them?"

"Nope."

"Dad," called Deckard. He and Peyton walked toward one another. "A couple of men just arrived. Over by the table."

"Hmm."

Deckard didn't want trouble. He had no experience in confrontation. He followed his dad who walked up behind the men. Peyton smiled his friendliest, and said, "Howdy, gentlemen. Have we met?"

They turned.

To Deckard, it looked as if his dad had been locked in place by a bolt of electric current.

Peyton stood, transfixed and stiff but starting to vibrate, facing these two men. His eyes switched from one to the other and back again.

Deckard put a hand on Peyton's shoulder. "Dad?"

None of the three men moved.

"Dad!" Deckard was alarmed. He looked at the two strangers. "Do you know each other?"

Peyton took a breath. "Hello, Ed."

Ed nodded. "Asshole."

"What?" said Deckard. "Who the hell do you–"

"Simmer down, Deck. He's a prehistoric adversary."

Peyton extended his hand. The gesture was not reciprocated. The other man watched.

"A skunk doesn't change its stripe. I'll be damned," said Peyton. "Deck," Peyton turned to his son. "Ed was your mother's friend. He left town about the time you were born."

"Tell him the real story," said Ed. "The whole story. You knocked up my girl."

"Fully chaste, we were, until married, Ed."

"Where is she?"

Deckard stood baffled. Were they talking about his mother?

It hadn't occurred to Peyton that Ed wouldn't know Libby was gone. Peyton had to think, yes, Ed left before Libby died. "I talk to her daily, but I don't think she'll talk to you."

"I said, Asshole, where is she?" Ed raised his voice. "You won't keep me from her."

Rorie stood beside Deckard. Partiers had begun to form a circle to watch.

"She's at home, Ed, and she's at peace."

This took a moment to register. "Stripes wasn't enough?" He was outraged. "You killed Libby, too?"

Peyton was frightened. He'd kept so many secrets over the years.

Mayor Nuckle made his way through the onlookers. "Oh good grief, we can't even have a party.... Who killed who here?" He stared at the two strangers. "Ed? Is that you?"

"Stripes first, then Libby? Asshole killed Libby, too?"

"No, Ed. Neither." Mayor Nuckle couldn't believe his eyes. "Why are you here?"

"Shut up, Nuckle," hollered Ed. "Shut up!"

"Who are you to tell me–"

"I took your dumb orders and listened to your lame excuses for too many years and I'm not going to hear them again."

"Are you looking to get arrested? I can arrest you if you keep it up."

Ed's nostrils flared. He started to shake, then turned,

pulled back his right fist, swung, and connected at Peyton's abdomen. Peyton flew backward a couple of feet and hit the ground.

Rorie reflexively jumped on Ed's back and wrapped her arms around his neck. She choked and kicked and screamed so the rest of the crowd screamed, too, rooting for Rorie, who by her actions, found her niche in the hearts of the replicants. They rooted for her against this bully whom most remembered and whose meanness many still hadn't forgiven.

The other man, who until now had remained silent, was looking increasingly perturbed and took a swing at Ed, the two more evenly matched. Ed slugged back, Rorie clinging like a knapsack, and a fight was on.

Ed hollered, "Stop hitting me, Abe." He tried to shield himself. "Stop!"

Abe backed off.

Ed wrestled Rorie's arms and she dropped to her feet. He turned to look, ready to strike but froze. This young woman with her golden skin and black hair.... "Jeebers." Ed staggered back. "Luna?"

Rorie took a defensive stance. "No."

"You look like Luna."

"How do you know my mother, jerk?"

"Your mother?" Ed blinked.

"Doesn't mean I'm anything like her."

The pink envelope.... Nine months after our ronday-voo.... "Who are you?"

"I'm Rorie."

"You were born under northern lights. You're Aurora. Arora Boreanaz."

"My name is Rorie."

All the fight left Ed. "Jeebers." He stared.

"What kind of stupid word is that?"

This would never happen to Thomas Magnum. "You're my daughter."

"You're full of shit."

"No. Seriously–"

"Seriously full of shit." He looked like an older, fatter version of the man in the Polaroid Luna had kept in a drawer. "If you think because some single-celled swimmer knocked-up Luna, you have the right to call yourself my father, you can haul your pathetic nuts back to the tree they dropped from. You and your Jeebers. That trolley left the platform years ago. You're nothing." She backed away. "Nothing. Peyton's more of a father...."

Abe shook his head. He stared at Schotz. "You and me were friends, man. You abandoned your own daughter?" He took another swing at Ed. "I don't know you."

Ed defended himself but Abe swung hard. Ed hollered, "Abe, stop! Stop!"

Deck heard, "Abe." It's what Peyton had called him.

Abe took another slug at Ed.

"Stop, you idiot! Why are you mad at me? It's not me you want to beat the crap out of."

"I don't want to beat the crap out of anybody."

"Back in Laughlin you were hoppin' mad, talking about what you wanted to do to, beat the crap out of Peyton if you ever saw him again."

"Just talk, man. You think I'd do those things? To my own brother?"

"Those things are precisely what I want to see you do to the asshole."

Abe had kept his guard up. "You're sick, man."

"I'm not sick," gasped Ed. "I should have known. You're a treacherous asshole, too." He swung hard but Abe backed away.

"You think I'd take your side?"

Glory and the nurses peeked from the back of the crowd, and with each breathless thud, all of them cringed. "I'm sorry about this," said Glory. "We almost made it through the day."

Peyton came-to and groaned. "What happened?"

"Stay down, Dad. These hyenas will shred you."

Hector Senior waded into the mix and pulled Ed and Abe apart. The disappointed crowd complained and hurled insults at Hector who said, "This is a birthday celebration, people. What in God's name– Ed? Ed Schotz? What the–"

Ed smiled a bloody smile, wobbled on his feet, and crumbled to the ground.

Deckard looked at Rorie. "Another day in paradise."

Doc had drunk a fifth of tequila, so Glory asked her friends to have a look. Josie took Ed's pulse and used a wad of paper napkins to mop his bloody nose and mouth. Leigh found ice in the kitchen. Carole killed the blaring boom box. In less than a minute, Ed regained consciousness but not his breath. He stayed down.

"Dad," said Deckard, his mouth hanging open. "You have a brother?"

Peyton stared at Deckard for a long moment. "Abe. I have a brother, Abe."

"Well," said Deckard. "Uncle Abe has come to visit."

"What?"

"All I know," said Deckard, "is he's here. The other guy brought him to beat you up."

"What? The other guy? Oh, Ed. How does Ed know Abe? Abe?"

Abe stood behind Deckard. "Peyton?"

Peyton got to his feet. "Oh, my ribs."

"Blame Ed," said Rorie.

"Okay, folks," called Mayor Nuckle. "Fight's over. Have

another cup of punch–pardon the expression." He turned the boom box on again and lowered the volume.

Leigh and Carole helped Ed to his feet. "Thanks," he said, "Abe used to be...." He looked at the nurses for the first time. "I know you."

"Yes," said the tall, slim brunette. "You do." She smiled and stood taller.

Ed stumbled back. "No!"

"How've you been, Ed?"

"No bloody way!" Ed stared and swallowed, trying to find his voice. "How ... what...."

"I'm a friend of Glory's."

Ed looked around. "Does anyone know this, this freak? What it put me through?"

Nurse Carole laughed. "It?"

"Shut up, Ed," said Glory. "Shut your face. Whatever you're going to say, we don't care."

"But–"

"It's my party, my birthday, these are my friends, and you are *not*, so get the hell out!"

"You go, girl," screamed Rorie, jumping up and down. She looked at Deckard and shrugged. "Jeebers."

Ed stood unable to move his feet, hyperventilating, veins popping from his neck.

Deck supported his dad's weight. "Did he break your ribs?"

"No, no." Peyton straightened. "Ed stormed out of Saltine almost two decades ago. Today of all days, he chooses to show up. And he's still the gummed-up dim bulb he was when he left."

Rorie whispered, "He thinks he's my Daddy."

"And, Dad," said Deckard, "He brings your brother, my uncle, to beat you up?"

Peyton's grey matter was circling the drain. "Oh jeez," said Peyton. "I need to think."

Glory stood facing Ed, diminutive but with her chin up in defiance, her arm outstretched, her finger pointing to the gate. "Get out and don't come back."

Ed tucked-in his shirt and pulled himself to his full height. "I should–"

"You should what?" Hector Senior cut in.

"Damn it, Hector," said Glory. "Are you really going to deny me this pleasure?" She stretched her arm out of her sleeve two inches longer and pointed again at the gate.

Ed turned and stumbled away, shaking his head, not looking back. Carole watched him cross Paseo Centro then weave through the field toward the spur.

*

"Hey, old man," said Abe. He threw his arm around Peyton's shoulder' and walked him to a couple of empty chairs. "Been a long time."

"I can't believe this." Peyton sat. He stared at his brother. "I don't remember ever being punched in the gut. I didn't remember *you* until just now. But I can't remember most things–amnesia. Son of a bitch, that hurts. How on earth?"

Abe filled in some of the bigger blanks. He and Peyton laughed about their youthful scam, how it worked for a couple of years, and they lived high and well before getting caught. Abe described jail, and the jobs he'd held afterward, and twenty years-worth of wondering what became of his brother.

"That was the worst," said Abe. "Not knowing what happened to you. Hoping you got away, that you knew I didn't blame you for running."

"I showed up here," said Peyton, "with no memory of who I was or what I'd done or where I came from. I don't even remember our childhood."

"No memory of me?"

"Nothing. I showed up here, unconscious, with nothing but a goat."

"Well I can fill you in on the early years. You landed here, and stayed."

"Where was I going to go? I woke at Doc's and Libby sat there claiming we were to be married. I didn't know different. I did fall in love. She's gone, but I have a son. A couple of years are still missing. I think I was a member of something called the New Earth Battalion at a government –"

"New Earth?" Abe thought a moment. "Is that why you took the name Neworth?"

"That never occurred to me." Peyton stopped. "Neworth isn't our name?"

"I'm Sterling."

"Life is strange," said Peyton. He looked at his brother and grinned. "Well, you're coming home with me. I want you to meet Deck. And his girlfriend. You'll like them. I'm trying to take all this in. I'm happy you're here."

Hector escorted the nurses back to the Mecca-bound trolley, then returned to take Glory home, carrying all the cards, gifts, and pieces of leftover cake. The last guest walked out the gate at 4:00, about the time the afternoon wind started to blow. Deckard, Rorie, and the other two young couples stayed to tear-down crepe paper, fold the tables, and clean the yard of trash. Rorie left the thank you note she'd written the day before for Reverend and Mrs. Byle, and everyone was gone by six o'clock.

"What a great day," said Deckard. "It was totally perfect." He and Rorie walked down Paseo Centro, holding hands.

Rorie startled. "Where are Peyton and Abe?"

"Probably at home."

“Can we do the meet and greet tomorrow? Right now, the only thing I want is to shower, lay my head on a pillow, snuggle up to you, and pass out. On Hector Senior’s roof would be my first choice.”

“Great minds thinking alike.”

The two ambled up Sidewinder Circle toward the pink and white double wide. Rorie took a quick shower. Deckard crept inside for a glass of water which he took out front. He set it on Libby’s mosaic next to the mattress then lay down. Rorie joined Deckard under the rebar tree and snuggled-up.

Abe lay fast asleep in Peyton’s bed, and Peyton had dozed-off on the couch.

Deckard, Rorie, Peyton, and Abe were finishing their first cup of coffee the morning after the party.

"I was thinking," said Deckard.

"Uh oh," said Peyton with a grin, his elbows on the table, chin in hands.

"I was thinking I hope Uncle Abe sticks around." He looked at Abe. "That you stay in Saltine. But the house might feel tight."

Peyton nodded. "And?"

"So, Dad, you and Abe share the house, and together we build a palapa for Rorie and me. Nothing fancy, just a palapa." Deckard turned to Rorie. "Like we talked about yesterday. Make it match Dad's garden fence." Deckard was excited.

Rorie stiffened.

Peyton looked at Abe. "What's a palapa?"

"I don't know, but I can swing a hammer."

"The thing is, Dad, Abe, it's your money"

Peyton nodded.

Abe said, "It was never our money."

Peyton looked at Rorie.

She smiled then stretched and said, "Good coffee. I'm taking a walk."

*

Rorie grabbed her backpack and went out the back door. It should have been easy to put her life in the hands of these men. They'd be good to her, and Uncle Abe would be another plus, but–whether it was appropriating chickens or baking weed cakes or learning about sex–she'd begun to see how she, herself, could make things happen rather than just have things happen to her, and she wanted to try it out. She hadn't ever decided anything for herself. First it was Luna, then, like a virus, she had depended on chance for opportunities.

She snipped the top buds from one of her plants and headed east toward the spur.

In the distance, through the mid-day haze, Rorie saw the silhouette of a car parked half a mile away in the sand. By the time she reached the rail, her walk had become a run and she kept going. A man leaned into the steering wheel, asleep or passed-out. Maybe she could help push the car out of the sand. Maybe she could catch a ride to Mecca.

She walked up from behind to the passenger side, slapped the fender to announce herself, and bent over to look through the rolled-down window.

The man in the driver's seat startled. He sat straight up and, with his mouth agape and his eyes open wide, stared at Rorie.

Rorie stared too, then backed up. She opened the rear door, threw her pack onto the seat, pulled open the front door, climbed in. She said, "You want me to call you, *Daddy*?"

*

That night, Abe fell deeply asleep in Peyton's bed. A day of coffee and talk left him jittery but exhausted. Deckard lay awake and alone under the Rebar tree with a headache the size of all Frink. He reminded himself that this wasn't the first time Rorie had left, but she had come back. Where was she? She said she was taking a walk. Peyton couldn't sleep. He sat on the back-porch steps.

"Doll," he said. "You would not believe the revelations of the past two days."

"I watched from the church roof."

"You what?" Peyton turned toward Libby. "I didn't think you could do that. You saw Ed?"

"The leopard might wear seersucker in summer, but underneath he's still got spots."

Peyton looked out at his garden. "Something I want to know."

"What's that?"

"How my $300 got buried in a can."

"Ah, yes. Well," Libby figured this had to come up someday. "I found it on you when I found you, and didn't want Daddy or Nuckle, or especially Ed seeing it. Thought maybe we'd use it for an anniversary trip."

"We would have had fun."

"We had our fun anyway." If Libby were ever to tell Peyton, this would be the time. "I imagine you guessed I wasn't exactly truthful all those years ago when explaining we were engaged...."

"No hard feeling on this end, Doll."

She added, "There's something *I* want to know."

Peyton held his hand out to Libby. "Just ask."

"Stripes?"

"Oh, Doll." He let his hand drop.

Peyton had thought a hundred times about what to say if he ever had to relate the facts. Most of those times he concluded what he'd say would come from his heart. At this point, how could he keep up the ruse? And, moreover, why? Of course, her theft wasn't on par with his murder, although coerced matrimony might be.

"I tried to get him home safely," Peyton finally said. "I really did. He'd drunk too much and was shooting snakes, then he tried to shoot me. I wrestled the gun from him, so he told Guizar to kill get me, then honest-to-God, he stabbed himself. I wanted to run and get Doc, get you. I swear it's the truth. Ed would have made a case and–"

"Peyton, stop."

"But I swear that's the–"

"I believe you."

"Really?" Peyton sighed.

"I'm sorry you had to keep it secret all these years." Libby smiled at Peyton. Everything as it should be. "Thank you for coming into my life and staying."

"And you mine, Doll."

"Sweetcakes. I've got to go."

Peyton searched for the tease but found none. His forehead creased and tears ran down his cheeks. "Why?"

"Time's up."

Peyton gazed at his garden. He'd thought about this earlier, comparing love to the impulse of a seed to split open and make a plant. He'd eat the plant and transform it into energy. Libby would advise him to see love the same way. Take the energy of love and use it to make more. He said, "You've been a gift, Doll. The best gift." Peyton blinked and Libby was no longer on the porch. Whether Libby on the freezer had been the product of his imagination or a tangible being did not matter.

The world was moving. She was floating above it.

Peyton stood. He stripped naked and danced a waltz between the boxes as far as the green beans. He wondered if Abe liked vegetables, then stepped into the moist soil, lay down in a cool furrow, looked up, and counted stars.

END

ACKNOWLEDGEMENTS

With high regard for the talents and perspectives of each: thank you Tom Spanbauer – always, Karen Karbo, Kim Barnes, Chris Abani, Kathleen Concannon, Jonathan Eaton, Patsy Kuhlberg, Deborah Reed, Linda Sladek, Paul Buchman, Debi O'Donnell, Phyllis Lindsley, Barbara Roth, Michael Adelsheim, Joshua Waldman, Lily Ningsih, Larry Hopkins, Rodger Larson, Deborah Shapiro, André Shapiro, Stephen B. Samerjan III, Susan Sweeting, Dawn Carol, Zoe Primrose, Alice Primrose, Ava Hiller, and Jay Gucker. Also Dr. R Prince Davis for my left eye, George Clooney and David Byrne for alternate realities.

Special thanks to Ieva Balode and Andris Akmenis, the staff and residents of the International Writers and Translators House in Ventspils, Latvia, and Fulbright-Latvia. My time there liberated me from a memoir and hatched *Saltine,* the two volumes offering little in common but the absurdity of life.

Finally, to Professor Guy Bennett of Otis Books for his kindness, humor, and smarts, and to Julia Zellie, talented editor and liaison, I offer my humble and sincere gratitude for bringing *Saltine* to publication.

Other Titles from Otis Books

Erik Anderson, *The Poetics of Trespass*
J. Reuben Appelman, *Make Loneliness*
Renée Ashley, *Ruined Traveler*
Guy Bennett, *Self-Evident Poems*
Guy Bennett and Béatrice Mousli, Editors, *Seeing Los Angeles: A Different Look at a Different City*
Chris Campanioni, *A and B and Also Nothing*
Steve Castro, *Blue Whale Phenomena*
Geneva Chao, *one of us is wave one of us is shore*
Robert Crosson, *Signs / & Signals: The Daybooks of Robert Crosson*
———, *Daybook (1983–86)*
Neeli Cherkovski and Bill Mohr, Editors, *Cross-Strokes: Poetry between Los Angeles and San Francisco*
Mohammed Dib, *Tlemcen or Places of Writing*
Ray DiPalma, *The Ancient Use of Stone: Journals and Daybooks, 1998–2008*
———, *Obedient Laughter*
François Dominique, *Solène*
Tim Erickson, *Egopolis*
Jean-Michel Espitallier, *Espitallier's Theorem*
Forrest Gander, Editor, *Panic Cure: Poems from Spain for the 21st Century*
Van G. Garrett, *Water Bodies*
Leland Hickman, *Tiresias: The Collected Poems of Leland Hickman*
Michael Joyce, *Twentieth Century Man*
Lew S. Klatt, *The Wilderness After Which*
Norman M. Klein, *Freud in Coney Island and Other Tales*
Christopher Linsforth, *Directory*
Alan Loney, *Beginnings*
Luxorius, *Opera Omnia or, a Duet for Sitar and Trombone*
Sara Marchant, *Proof of Loss*
Ken McCullough, *Left Hand*
Gary McDowell, *Cæsura: Essays*
Béatrice Mousli, Editor, *Review of Two Worlds: French and American Poetry in Translation*
Laura Mullen, *Enduring Freedom*
Ryan Murphy, *Down with the Ship*
Mostafa Nissabouri, *For an Ineffable Metrics of the Desert*

Aldo Palazzeschi, *The Arsonist*
Dennis Phillips, *Navigation: Selected Poems, 1985–2010*
Antonio Porta, *Piercing the Page: Selected Poems 1958–1989*
Eric Priestley, *For Keeps*
Sophie Rachmuhl, *A Higher Form of Politics: The Rise of a Poetry Scene, Los Angeles, 1950–1990*
Dorothy Rice, *Gray Is the New Black*
Norberto Luis Romero, *The Obscure Side of the Night*
Olivia Rosenthal, *We're Not Here to Disappear*
Noah Ross, *Swell*
Amelia Rosselli, *Hospital Series*
———, *War Variations*
Ari Samsky, *The Capricious Critic*
Giovanna Sandri, *only fragments found: selected poems, 1969–1998*
Hélène Sanguinetti, *Hence This Cradle*
Janet Sarbanes, *Army of One*
Severo Sarduy, *Beach Birds*
Adriano Spatola, *The Porthole*
———, *Toward Total Poetry*
Billie R. Tadros, *The Tree We Planted and Buried You In*
Carol Treadwell, *Spots and Trouble Spots*
Paul Vangelisti, *Wholly Falsetto with People Dancing*
Paul Vangelisti & Dennis Phillips, *Mapping Stone*
Cassondra Windwalker, *tide tables and tea with god*
Allyssa Wolf, *Vaudeville*

All of our titles are available from Small Press Distribution.
Order them at www.spdbooks.org